COURTNEY COTY

All I Never Wanted

Christine,
Find your Happy!
♡ Courtney

First edition

This book was professionally typeset on Reedsy.
Find out more at reedsy.com

For Ruth

who inspires me, makes me laugh,

and always saves the pinwheels for me.

Acknowledgement

For my first readers, thank you for taking the time to read, give notes, and push me to actually go ahead with this. I appreciate you all.

For my family, thank you for your patience and understanding while I was glued to my laptop. Love you guys.

xo

PROLOGUE

Glancing at my rearview mirror, I watched their silhouettes slowly shrinking as I sped away. Shrouded in a cloud of smoke and dust, they stood stock-still like wax figures fixed in time. They were lucky I hadn't run them both down. A morbid vision of their bodies bouncing off my bumper like ragdolls gave me a momentary thrill.

My train was due to depart in an hour, so I had plenty of time to get to the station but pressed my foot down harder on the gas pedal anyway. Zooming past the stately homes on Main Street, I left downtown behind me in a blur. The more I thought about it, the faster I drove, racing away from the memory.

Scoffing in disgust, I couldn't believe I'd ever considered turning down Mr. Anderson's offer for someone who clearly wasn't thinking about me. I'd make him eat his words. I was going to be the best dancer Rockland had ever seen. Then maybe he'd realize that my talent was worth something, too. He was going to regret ever making me his fool. With a self-satisfied smile, I rounded the corner headed toward bigger and better things.

CHAPTER ONE

Entering Steiger's, I felt a rush of excitement. The expansive department store felt so glamorous with its marble columns and stained-glass windows. New lingerie was the perfect parting gift for Charlie. I couldn't remember the last time I'd shopped for any.

Browsing the latest fashions and sampling perfumes along the way, I took my time getting to the undergarments section. Perusing the racks, I looked at the various bra and panty sets, garters, flowing sheer chemises, and satin slips. Accents of lace, ruffles, and bows in every color of the rainbow were laid out before me. A nude set embellished with Swiss Lace in lilac and pale blue caught my eye. The push-up bra and garter were just racy enough for my taste, with floral detailing that softened the look. It was the perfect balance of alluring and innocent.

"Good morning," a friendly voice spoke from beside me. "May I help you with anything?"

I turned to see a smartly dressed saleswoman awaiting my reply. "Thank you, I'd like to try this on please," I answered.

"Wonderful choice," she said. "This bra provides a nice lift and the detailing on this set is exquisite. I'll take you to the fitting rooms. Right this way please."

Following her, I glanced at the other pieces as we passed, but none matched the beauty of the set I'd chosen. Feeling pleased with my selection, I was anxious to try it on to check the fit.

"Here we are," she said, opening the door to a small changing room with a full-length mirror. I'll check back with you in a few moments. My name is

Lucy if you need anything."

"Thank you, Lucy."

Closing the door to the fitting room, I undressed, changing into the delicate set. Standing tall, I examined myself in the mirror. The pastel lace highlighted my attributes nicely. Not bad at all, I thought. This will do the trick.

Securing the dainty pieces back on their hangers, I heard footfalls and the creaking of a door closing as someone else entered the fitting rooms. Changing back into my clothing, I had my hand on the door handle when an all-too-familiar voice stopped me in my tracks and sent my eyes rolling back in their sockets.

"What do you think, Lucy? Is it too much?" the voice demurely asked.

Curiosity getting the best of me, I quietly cracked the door open a hair, stealthily peeking through the crevice. Dressed in a lacy fire engine red teddy that left very little to the imagination was, as I had suspected, none other than Alice Baker. The sight of the proprietress of our local coffee shop feigning innocence, while clearly impressed with herself, had me fighting the urge to gag. I couldn't stand that woman. She was so full of herself. The last thing I felt like doing was making small talk with Alice Baker. Thankfully she was so busy admiring herself in the communal 3-way mirror, she was oblivious to my presence. I mouthed a thank goodness to myself, silently closing the door to figure out my next move.

"Ma'am? Is everything alright? Can I help with anything?" Lucy's voice called from right outside my door.

I replied quietly, "Be right out. It was perfect. I'm going to take it."

"Wonderful, I'll meet you at the counter."

Slowly opening the door a few moments later, I surveyed the dressing area. Seeing no sign of Alice, I tiptoed out of the dressing room, making a beeline for Lucy who was waiting at the counter as promised.

"All set?" she asked.

"Yes, thank you," I replied, desperate to move things along.

"I'll just wrap this in tissue paper for you," Lucy declared, carefully removing the delicate lace pieces from the hanger as my eyes darted back toward the fitting rooms.

"Oh, that's not necessary," I replied, hastily pulling out my wallet and placing the proper bills on the counter.

"It's not a problem at all," she answered, selecting a few sheets of lilac tissue that matched the set. Deftly folding the sheets, she painstakingly packaged my purchase as I eyed the fitting rooms. Placing the tissue-wrapped lingerie neatly in a black gift box, she fitted it with a matching lid emblazoned with the store's gold "S" logo and gently put the package into a shopping bag before finally handing it over to me. "Thank you for shopping with us and enjoy your afternoon."

"You as well, Lucy," I called over my shoulder after practically snatching the bag from her and hightailing it out of the store. Once I reached the exit, I burst onto the sidewalk, victorious. It was a successful shopping trip, and I'd escaped before Alice had the chance to put a damper on my mood. A win in my book.

Walking to the car, my mind wandered back to her racy red getup. From the looks of it, there was most certainly a man in Alice's life. Either that or she planned on snagging one. Good luck to him, I thought. He was going to need it.

CHAPTER TWO

Tapping my fingers to the beat on the steering wheel as Frank Sinatra crooned, I cruised down Main Street. Turning the volume dial up, I belted out the lyrics, thoroughly enjoying myself. I had just enough time to stop by my husband's autobody shop before my train to Rockland departed.

Nosing the car into an open spot in front of the coffee shop, I straightened my hat, checking my reflection in the rearview mirror before stepping out. Opening the door to Baker's Brew, the scent of freshly brewed coffee and just-baked confections swirled around me. As much as I disliked Alice, there was no denying the fact that her shop sold the best coffee and baked goods in town. Stepping up to the counter, I was relieved to see that she was nowhere in sight. I'd managed to avoid her a second time. It was my lucky day.

I inspected the sweets in the glass case before me. Several variations of donuts, muffins, and pastry filled the shelves. I spotted one plain old-fashioned donut, Charlie's favorite.

"What can I get you, Mrs. Abbott?" Jenny, the young girl behind the counter, asked.

"I'd like that old-fashioned and a cup of coffee to go, light and sweetened, please."

"Coming right up."

I watched as Jenny grabbed the donut with a sheet of waxed paper, placing it in a paper bag. She poured a cup of freshly brewed coffee into a paper cup, swirling in just the right amount of cream and sugar before affixing the lid.

"Is that all, Mrs. Abbott?" she asked.

"Yes, Jenny, that will be all for today," I replied.

"Any plans for the holidays?" she asked.

"You know," I leaned forward excitedly, "I do. It's been a bit of a whirlwind, but I'm leaving on the noon train for upstate New York. I've been cast as a dancer in the Rockland Holiday Show."

"Oh! Mrs. Abbott, that's wonderful news! Congratulations!"

"Thank you, Jenny. It's a dream come true. I've dreamt of being in the show since I was a little girl. I can hardly believe it's happening," I gushed. "And please, call me Lottie."

"Wow! That's so exciting! Okay," she agreed. "Lottie it is. It's just that Mrs. Baker instructs us to 'always address our customers as Mr. and Mrs., no exceptions,'" Jenny mimicked.

"No need for formalities with me," I said with a wink.

"I like that. I'm so happy for you. Enjoy every second of your trip, *Lottie,*" she exaggerated. "Of course, if *she's* here, I'll be forced to call you Mrs. Abbott."

"Understood," I laughed, handing Jenny a crisp five-dollar bill. She gave me my change, the bag, and the to-go coffee and I was on my way.

"Merry Christmas!" she hollered after me, bells on the door jingling.

"Merry Christmas!" I called back.

Smiling to myself as the door jangled shut, I walked over to the crosswalk. Apparently, I wasn't the only one who found Alice off-putting. Pressing the button, I waited for the light to change, anxious with anticipation. Hopefully, Charlie was already in his office, otherwise I'd have to concoct a reason to get him in there without tipping off the other guys. The closed blinds would be a dead giveaway, but better than the alternative.

Crossing the street, I headed toward the garage humming to myself. Today was the day everything was going to change. This was 1956, after all. I could have a family and a career. If Lucille Ball could do it, why couldn't I?

A gust of wind blew, leaves swirling around my feet. I felt the draft through my overcoat and visibly shuddered.

"Chilly day," a passing man on the sidewalk said, nodding in my direction.

"Sure is," I replied, hiding a smirk. Under my wool coat I wore my new lingerie set and nothing else. I had never done anything like this before and my secret gave me a little thrill. It felt a little like when Charlie and I had first met, all excitement and anticipation. It had been some time since I'd made any effort to spice things up.

Approaching the garage, I gave myself a little pep talk. I could do this. I could be sexy. Reaching out to grab the door handle, I took a deep breath steeling myself to enter with confidence. As I pulled on the handle, my gaze landed on Charlie, and I stopped dead in my tracks. I couldn't make sense of what I was seeing. I felt stuck, like I was sinking in quicksand.

My husband and Alice Baker tangled in an embrace. I watched, wide-eyed, as Charlie brought his hands up toward Alice's face. It was like time had slowed and every movement lasted an eternity. I didn't want to look but couldn't manage to turn away. I couldn't believe what I was seeing. What was Alice doing at the garage? A vision of her flaunting herself in the red teddy flashed before my eyes as I felt bile rise from my stomach. Was I hallucinating? I shook my head hoping it was all a bad dream.

I watched in shock as Charlie, his eyes locked on Alice's, hesitated for a moment, then pulled her hands apart, removing her arms from where they'd been resting on his shoulders. Holding her hands in his he opened his mouth to speak when a car pulled into the service bay, the driver jauntily honking the horn to announce his arrival.

The blast of the horn startling me out of my frozen state, I dropped the coffee cup I'd been clutching to the ground. The lid flew off as it bounced off the pavement, hot coffee scalding my bare legs. Crying out as the hot liquid burned my ankles, Charlie turned, making eye contact with me, and hastily dropping Alice's hands. Registering that I'd just witnessed their intimate moment, his face instantly fell, his expression a mixture of shock and shame. That look told me everything I needed to know.

Blood boiling in my veins, I felt like I would combust at any moment, my cheeks burning even more than my scalded legs. Rage consuming me, I chucked the bag containing the single donut at the shop window. It connected with the glass with a resounding thud before dropping dead to the ground. Turning on my heel, I marched straight to my car without a second thought about oncoming traffic or the sound of my husband's voice calling my name.

I had never been so angry in all my life. Slamming the car door shut, I cranked the key in the ignition. Zooming out of my parking spot, I was met with a red light. Perfect timing, I thought. Waiting for the light to turn, I watched in disgust as Charlie sprinted from the garage toward the crosswalk, Alice nipping at his heels as he called my name. Just before the light turned, he reached my car, placing a hand on the hood. Doubled over, he attempted to catch his breath.

Pulling my sunglasses down to the bridge of my nose, I glared at them both, my eyes slanted into slits. Stomping my left foot down on the brake, I jammed the right one down hard onto the gas pedal. The Cadillac roared to life, the engine revving. I watched in satisfaction as Charlie leapt back from the car, nearly knocking Alice to the ground as he scrambled to move out of my path. Regaining her balance, Alice trembled in shock, visibly frightened. As she should be. Placing my sunglasses squarely back on, I gave a little wave of my fingers before placing extra emphasis on the middle one. With their jaws almost reaching the pavement, I slammed my foot down hard on the gas pedal sending up a cloud of dirt and exhaust leaving them to literally eat my dust.

CHAPTER THREE

Easing the car into the farthest spot in the lot, I put it in park and slumped back in my seat. My mind was a jumbled mess. Snapshots of Charlie and Alice invaded my brain and made my stomach turn. I sat still, almost in a trance, watching the people coming and going. Finally leaning over to open my case, I grabbed a skirt and blouse. First looking around to be sure no one was nearby, I quickly shrugged off my overcoat. Feeling exposed wearing next to nothing, I wasted no time slipping on my clothing.

A wave of embarrassment washed over me. Forced to get dressed for my trip in the car. How humiliating. So many questions ran through my mind, and I wasn't sure I wanted the answers. It would be a few weeks before I even saw Charlie. I never said goodbye, unless you counted flipping the bird as a farewell. Pulling my coat back up over my shoulders, I fastened it closed and grabbed my things. Shuffling through the crowd to my platform, I wished it had all been a bad dream that I'd wake from at any minute. I'd roll over, angry at my innocently sleeping husband for an imagined tryst.

Settling into a seat after checking my bag with the porter, I gazed out the window. I replayed the day's events over and over in my mind as if on a loop. Had Alice been wearing the teddy when I'd shown up? Did she buy it with Charlie in mind? The fury I'd felt earlier threatened to return, my stomach turning at the thought of the two of them together.

I was certain something more had happened between them. The look on his face had said it all.

Was Alice frequenting the garage? I vaguely remembered Charlie mentioning something about afternoon coffee breaks. Were they seeing each other while I was home caring for our girls or folding endless loads of laundry? Was I preparing his meals while he treated himself to a snack on the side? What if we'd both been shopping with Charlie in mind? What a sickening coincidence. That thought created another wave of nausea. Shuddering, I grabbed the armrest to steady myself, taking a deep breath hoping to keep the contents of my stomach contained.

Letting out a few quick blasts, the train whistle sounded, letting the passengers know we were departing. The car lurched forward slowly. Carefully folding my driving gloves, I placed them safely inside my handbag. As I closed the bag, the sunlight streaming through the window caught my wedding ring, throwing glistening refractions of light around me. What I would've once viewed as beautiful, I now regarded as an offensive stain on a new blouse.

"Mind if I sit here?" a deep voice asked, breaking me from my thoughts.

I looked up to see a fine-looking man in dress slacks and a matching suit jacket waiting for my reply. He looked like he belonged in Hollywood with his chiseled features and fit physique. My cheeks immediately flushed, betraying my thoughts, as I stammered, "Oh! I mean, yes, sure. Seat's open."

"Name's Walt," he said extending his hand.

"Hello, Walt. I'm Charlotte," I replied, accepting it, "but my friends call me Lottie."

His hand felt strong and rough. I'd assumed he was a businessman, but his calloused hands and firm grip hinted that he did more physical work.

"Okay then, Lottie," he said with a smile, sitting down beside me.

"I never said we were friends," I quipped, eyebrow raised.

"Give me time," he winked good-naturedly. "By the end of this trip, I bet we'll be great friends."

Smiling, I shifted my gaze back to the window. As the train rolled past the station, I looked out at the parking lot, half-expecting, hoping, to see Charlie. But there was no sign of him. I let out an exasperated sigh, forgetting about Walt for a moment.

"Tough day?" he asked.

"I'm sorry, I didn't mean for that to come out so loudly," I replied, slightly embarrassed. "Yes. Somehow the best and the worst all wrapped into one."

"Oh boy," Walt said considering my response. "In that case, I'd say you're entitled to a drink. On me, of course."

My face must have conveyed my thoughts, something along the lines of *slow down, mister,* because Walt amended his statement.

"That is, if you're interested."

"On any other day I would probably say it was inappropriate as I'm a married woman," I said wiggling my ring finger to validate my point. "However, given recent events, I'm not sure I much care."

Walt chuckled at my candor. "Well, you just let me know, Lottie. I'm up for a drink whenever you are."

I was tired of always doing the right thing. Always putting everyone else before myself. Serves Charlie right, I thought. I'd been looking forward to this trip and I wasn't about to let him and that snake Alice ruin it for me. Shrugging my handbag onto my shoulder, I turned to Walt. "You know what, lead the way."

"You bet," Walt said, taking my hand to help me up from my seat.

When our hands touched, his innocent gesture sent chills through me. I hadn't felt that kind of zing since Charlie and I first met. One drink, I told myself. Where was the harm in that?

CHAPTER FOUR

Following Walt to the tavern car, I studied the other travelers, wondering where they were headed. There was an older couple contentedly holding hands, the picture of what I'd always aspired for in the future. Fat chance. A young woman with expertly applied makeup and hair sprayed to withstand a hurricane sat diagonal to them. A young family, parents desperately trying to keep their children in their seats filled a section further up the aisle. I wondered where they were all going. What waited for them at their destinations? What was waiting for me when I arrived in Rockland?

Walt stopped at a vinyl booth, ending my musings. Sitting down across from one another on the well-worn seats, I scanned the other patrons. There was a group of businessmen, a few couples, a handful of single men reading the newspaper, and a group of young women.

This car was much livelier than the others we'd passed through. Everyone was talking animatedly, clinking their glasses, and enjoying the company of friends or fellow passengers. I picked up a menu, salivating as I read through the offerings and realizing I was famished. A server, smartly dressed in a navy uniform, arrived at the booth to take our drink orders.

"Good afternoon. What'll you have to drink?" he asked.

"Ladies first," Walt replied, nodding in my direction.

"I'll have a Tom Collins, thank you," I said. "And I'd also like a chicken salad sandwich on rye, please."

"A lady who knows what she wants, very good," he replied with a smile and nod, turning his gaze to Walt, "and for you, sir?"

"That sounds great, make it a double. Thanks."

"I'll be right back with your drinks and sandwiches," the waiter replied, walking away with our order ticket.

"Now that I've finally gotten the chance to sit down and relax for a moment, I realize I could eat a horse!" I declared.

Walt laughed. "Stress will do that to you. I haven't eaten all day and I'm suddenly feeling the same. I received news early this morning that my favorite uncle passed. I'm heading back home for the services."

"Oh, that's terrible. I'm very sorry for your loss," I said.

"Thanks. Uncle Jimmy was like a father to me. Taught me how to play ball and even showed me how to rebuild a motor. We fixed up an old truck together and when I turned sixteen, he told me it was all mine. His plan all along."

"Wow. He sounds like a special guy. You were lucky to have him in your life."

"I really was. He taught me everything I know. Got me to where I am today. I'm really going to miss him."

At that moment, the waiter arrived with our order. Looking at the items on the silver tray, my stomach grumbled loudly, much to my chagrin. I hoped neither of the men had heard it. If they had, they were gentlemanly enough not to let on.

"Here we are, double Tom Collins, chicken salad on rye. Can I get you anything else?"

We shook our heads replying "No, thank you," in unison.

First placing my napkin on my lap, I picked up the heavy glass, taking a long gulp of my drink. Swallowing the cool liquid, I let out an exaggerated, "Whoa!" Walt looked back at me; eyebrows raised. "I think he quite literally made this a double."

I took another sip. I wasn't normally much of a drinker but figured these counted as desperate times. I glanced up at Walt who was watching me, a look of amusement on his handsome face.

"I think you might be right," he agreed after taking a swig. "So, are you going to tell me what happened to you today?"

Exhaling, I began, “First things first, I need to take a bite of this chicken salad before I faint, and then I’ll tell you all the sordid details.”

Cutting my sandwich in half, on the diagonal, of course, I picked it up carefully, so as not to lose any of the chicken salad it held. Taking a bite, I closed my eyes, savoring it. Now that my trip had officially started, I was determined to enjoy every moment, Charlie and Alice be damned. Washing it down with another sip of my Tom Collins, I dabbed at my lips with the cloth napkin before placing it neatly back on my lap.

“Better?” Walt asked.

“Much, thanks for asking. Now, about this morning,” I began, Walt hanging on my every word.

CHAPTER FIVE

Once I had a captive audience, the abridged story came tumbling out of my mouth. Walt remained quiet as I recounted details, ending my tale with the juicy tidbit of how I'd revved my engine at my husband and Alice on the main street of our small town. Walt responded with a long, low whistle.

"Wow," he finally stated, nodding his head. "That's quite the story."

"Tell me about it," I replied, taking another gulp of my drink. I started to feel a little buzz. Taking another bite of my sandwich, I waited for Walt's reaction.

"Now, don't take this the wrong way," he started, "but it sounds like you didn't actually see anything scandalous."

"I know," I said between bites, "and that's what's nagging at me. It certainly could've been worse. But what I did see…" I paused for a moment to think. "There was something there. When we made eye contact it told me all I needed to know," I sighed, putting my head in my hands. I could feel hot tears welling up. I was not going to cry. Especially not here or now.

"Hey," Walt said, placing a hand on my shoulder and handing me a napkin.

I looked up, quickly blinking the tears away. His face showed genuine worry. For a second, it felt like more than just friendly concern. Taking the napkin he offered, our fingers brushed momentarily, sending a tingle up my spine. My body shivered and my breath hitched, revealing my physical reaction to this man's touch. Quickly removing his hand and clearing his throat, Walt took a sip of his Tom Collins. He'd felt it too.

We sat for a moment in silence. Watching the landscape pass by the window, sounds of idle chatter filled the space around us. Pine trees and rolling hills whizzed by. The view was so expansive compared to what I was used to seeing every day from my kitchen window. A reminder of how small my life had been up until now.

The company was entirely different as well. Talking with Walt, I felt like I could be myself. I didn't have to fit any expectations or shrink to build him up. I could just be honest and real. But we'd only just met and maybe that allowed it. Even still, somehow, we already had a strong connection, and though it went unspoken, we were both very aware of it.

Glancing back at him, I realized it had been so long since I had looked at a man other than Charlie. Walt really was an attractive guy. Dark hair, light eyes, a strong jawline. Nice height, strong hands, full lips. Blushing at that last thought, Walt pivoted his head from the view outside the train. Our eyes connected and he looked back at me with an amused smile. I'd been caught. Again.

Mildly embarrassed, I started to look away, but found that I couldn't or maybe didn't want to. Feeling a pull that I could only describe as magnetic; I met his gaze once again. The raucous laughter of a group of women drinking martinis a few tables away broke the spell. I looked over to see that one had dropped her glass, which sent a spray of gin on another of the ladies. There was an ensuing sideshow of hilarity as they clumsily attempted to clean up the mess. Watching the carefree young women, I felt a pang of jealousy. These girls had their whole lives ahead of them. All their decisions were unmade. Nothing holding them in one place.

I thought back to the night I'd first met Charlie. I had gone out to the dance hall with a few of my girlfriends one balmy summer night. It was my favorite place on earth in those days. We'd have drinks and dance the night away with good-looking young men, never tied to anyone. Occasionally, I'd meet a fellow who knew how to dance. Those were the best nights.

I'd twirl and swing my hips to the beat, and if a guy really knew his stuff, I'd allow him to flip me through the air at the high points in the music. Sometimes the crowd would form a circle around us, watching in awe. I loved performing for an audience, all eyes on me. It was such a rush.

On that first night, Charlie watched me dance. I could feel his eyes on me with every move I made. When the song ended and the applause died down, Charlie approached me with a mischievous grin. He was tall and handsome with a swagger about him that I somehow found to be both a turn-on and turn-off simultaneously.

"Nice moves," he said, his eyes slowly traveling the length of my body before returning to mine.

"I've got others," I replied cheekily, one eyebrow arched.

From that night on, we were inseparable. And the rest, as they say, is history.

So many things had changed since then. Over the years, his focus had moved from me to his business. And mine shifted away from the things I loved to loving and caring for my family.

"Hey, where'd you go?" Walt asked, interrupting my train of thought.

"I was just thinking about the way things used to be," I replied. "I'm sorry, I don't know why I'm telling you all this."

"Don't apologize."

Why was I telling Walt about my marital problems? Especially when there was clearly some kind of physical attraction between us. It seemed a little cruel, but he was so easy to talk to.

"So where are you headed?" he asked, changing the subject.

"Rockland," I replied. "It's actually my hometown. I haven't been back in years."

"Going to visit family?"

"No, actually. The phone rang a few days ago and I was offered an opportunity out of the blue that I just couldn't pass up," I explained.

"Lucky break."

"It was. I've got a spot in the Rockland Holiday Show. One of the dancers who'd originally been cast was injured in rehearsal, so I'll be filling in for her. Thankfully, my mother is helping with my girls while I'm away. I have two daughters. I don't know if I mentioned that already. My husband runs a business and can't take any time off," I explained. "He needed some coaxing before I could get him to even consider this trip."

"Sounds like this opportunity came at just the right time," Walt said. "Gives you a break from your everyday life to work things through. After what you saw today, I mean."

"You know, I didn't think of it that way, but you might be right. I'm certainly relieved to have the chance to run away after everything that happened this morning," I sighed.

"No matter what you saw today, I'm sure your husband is still very proud of you."

Looking down to gather my thoughts, I could almost hear Charlie's voice when I'd told him about the show, "You're so good at taking care of us... leave those pipe dreams in the past..." His words echoed through my brain, piercing my heart a second time. I could feel the threat of tears again. What had happened to us that he saw me as a housewife and nothing more?

My eyes started to burn. Walt gently lifted my chin with his thumb and index finger, unknowingly pushing those thoughts from my mind. When our eyes met across the table the rest of the train car fell away. That same rush traveled down my spine, and I gasped at the sensation. My pulse quickened in anticipation.

Looking at each other for another beat, Walt slowly traced his thumb along my jawline, causing my heart to race, as he said quietly, "If it was me, I know I'd be proud of you."

CHAPTER SIX

Heat rushing to my cheeks, I felt flush. Quickly turning my head, I diverted my gaze to the landscape outside the window. Walt's simple gesture and sincere words melted me. I wanted more than anything to tell him just that. Flustered and unsettled by the realization that this man could sense what I needed more than my own husband, I was afraid to look at Walt for fear that he'd read my mind.

"I'm sorry, Lottie," he apologized.

"It's okay, Walt," I interrupted. "I appreciate your kind words. They mean more than you could ever know. Truly."

I smiled. He sighed in relief. Watching his shoulders begin to relax, I placed a hand over his to calm his nerves. It was a reflex. Something I always did when Charlie came home from work agitated.

As our hands touched, I felt what could only be described as electricity run up my arm. Walt cleared his throat as I quickly pulled my hands away, placing them safely in my lap. We were both quiet for a beat, unsure how to proceed.

"I've never had this happen," Walt confided, shaking his head. "It's throwing me off."

"Me either. And I feel the same as you," I agreed. "Even though I shouldn't."

And then we were silent. Neither of us knew what to say or where to go from here. I felt so drawn to Walt. But I just couldn't. I'd be as bad as Charlie.

"Lottie," he paused. I looked back at Walt, trying to keep my composure. "Listen, I don't know what's happening here and I would never presume anything."

"Thank you," I said softly, looking down at my hands.

"I have to say this, because this has never happened to me and I don't know if it ever will again," he began. "Or if I'll ever see you again after today." I nodded, afraid to say anything for fear of the words and feelings threatening to come tumbling out of my mouth. "There's something between us. I really like you. I think it's fair to say that I like everything about you."

"But you've only just met me," I said quietly, looking up at him.

"Exactly. And I want to know you. All of you."

My cheeks burned and heat coursed through me. Not from embarrassment, though that's probably what an onlooker might think, but mostly because I felt the same way. And I knew that I shouldn't.

"I- I'm not sure I know what to say," I stammered.

"You don't have to say anything. Let's just sit here and finish our lunch."

* * *

We ate our sandwiches, downing the last sips of our drinks in comfortable silence. Given the conversation we'd just had, one would think that things would be awkward, but somehow, they weren't.

"Can I get you folks anything else?" the waiter asked, returning to clear our empty plates. Walt looked to me for guidance.

"I think I'd like a ginger ale. With extra ice, please."

"Gladly. And for you, sir?"

"I'll have a Coke, thanks."

"You got it."

He gathered up our empty dishes leaving us without any more distractions. Feeling quite shaken by everything that had happened today, I hoped the ginger ale would settle my stomach.

"So, tell me more about your uncle," I began, shifting the focus off whatever was happening between us. "Sounds like he was a wonderful guy."

Walt smiled, likely remembering a time they'd spent together. "Uncle Jimmy, he was just someone that everyone was lucky to know. And they knew it, too." I nodded in agreement, thinking of my father. Walt was describing him without even realizing it. "He was that guy who could talk to anyone about anything, and he was genuinely interested in what they had to say. He appreciated people and wanted to know their stories. He was real, a salt-of-the-Earth kind of guy."

"Wow. He sounds so much like my father. He was that way too. He was my most favorite person."

"That's who Uncle Jimmy was to me. I lost my dad when I was young. And a boy that age needs his father. Uncle Jimmy jumped in and never looked back. And if you can believe it, I was a real stinker as a kid," Walt said with a laugh. "But he never turned his back on me, even when I was at my worst. I'm really going to miss him."

"I bet. I lost my dad when I was a teenager. I miss him every day."

"I'm sorry. Why didn't you say so before?"

"I didn't want to take away from your loss."

"Well, I guess we were both lucky to have had them as long as we did. I hadn't seen Uncle Jimmy as much these last few years. I should've been better about visiting. I've been so busy trying to get my life in order. You know, get a good job, build my savings, buy a house in a quiet neighborhood, find my wife," he finished, looking pointedly at me.

I blushed, placing myself in the scene he was building, I could see a modest yellow house with a white picket fence. I could picture myself fixing dinner for us or planting flowers out front while he mowed the lawn. What the heck was I thinking? I was already someone else's wife. Charlie Abbott's wife.

"Start a family," he continued. "I wish he'd been around long enough to see it."

"He'll be looking down on you," I said. "I think our loved ones always stay with us. The special ones are always looking out for us."

"I hope so," he said.

"They are. They send us little messages to let us know they're there. I'm convinced of it."

CHAPTER SEVEN

The waiter arrived with our soft drinks, placing them down on the table along with a few napkins and the check. The car was beginning to empty out. We must've been nearing our destination. The time had passed so quickly without my noticing it.

"What makes you so convinced?" Walt asked, returning to our conversation about signs from beyond.

"Oh, I've had a few things happen that seemed more than just coincidence," I replied. "When I was young, my father and I would always watch the birds. He would tell me the different species' names and how to differentiate between males and females. I always found it interesting that the males were brightly colored, while the females were more neutral in tone, to blend into the background."

What a metaphor for my life. I was responsible for all the behind-the-scenes support so Charlie could realize his dream of owning his own business. He was the brightly colored bird while I had been hidden away in the background. I had certainly been the more eye-catching one of the two of us when we'd met all those years ago at the dance hall. I had been such a dynamic young woman, always so full of life and ready for an adventure. I missed it. Suddenly, I felt like an imposter in my own life. Someone playing the role of happy housewife. Why hadn't I noticed sooner? Maybe I didn't want to? Because then I'd have to do something about it.

"I think that's the case with most animals. The males draw the attention from predators while the females are duller to preserve the safety of their young," Walt stated.

"It seems to also be the case with people."

"Lottie. You're anything but dull."

"I should hope so. What I mean is that married women, mothers especially, seem to be expected to take a backseat to their husbands' wishes and desires. It's always been that way."

Tilting his head in thought, he replied, "Maybe. But it doesn't have to be. And you're here now, realizing your dream. So that can't be true for you."

"I suppose you're right. But in fairness to my point, my husband never wanted me to go. In his mind my greatest accomplishment is keeping our home and family."

"Does he know that you want more?" Walt asked.

"I've tried to tell him, but he doesn't ever seem to hear me," I explained.

"Well, I'd be willing to bet your message came through this morning," Walt laughed.

Chuckling in agreement, I continued, "I've gotten off track. My point was that dad and I always loved bluebirds most. I never saw them as often as I did when we were together. It was our special thing. Whenever I see one now, I think he's letting me know he's still with me," I explained. "Keep an eye out. I bet your uncle will let you know he's with you, too."

"I hope you're right."

"I usually am," I joked, placing a few bills on the table to cover my half of the check.

Walt pushed them back toward me. He wouldn't allow it, a true gentleman.

"Thank you," I said.

"You're very welcome. Worth every penny," he smiled.

We got up, making our way back to our seats before our arrival at the station. My legs felt a little unsteady after our drinks, but I forced myself to stand up straight as a rod, refusing to let it show.

Passing through the tavern, I stepped forward into the first passenger car, catching my heel on the toe kick. Losing my footing, I lurched forward into the car. Lunging into action beside me, Walt caught me under the arms before I went any further. My cheeks burned red from embarrassment.

Reflexively, I grabbed onto Walt's broad shoulders as he righted us both to standing. Pressed against him, I could feel a current of attraction running between us. I initially grabbed hold of him to save face, but I held on because it felt so good.

"Are you okay?" Walt asked, looking down at me.

"Yes," I murmured. "Much better now, thanks to you."

"Well, I couldn't very well allow you to fall flat on your face, now, could I?" he winked.

"I'm very glad that you didn't," I laughed.

Neither of us moved. I felt Walt's arms wrap tightly around me, enveloping me in an embrace. Mine did the same, without my thought or knowledge. It felt like a reflex, like something we'd done hundreds of times. Neither of us wanting to let go, we stood still for a moment.

"Rockland station. All passengers prepare to disembark," a voice announced over the loudspeaker.

"I suppose we should return to our seats," Walt said.

"Yes, I supposed we should," I agreed.

We broke apart, continuing to our seats. Sitting down next to the window with Walt next to me, I felt an overwhelming sadness that our journey was about to come to an end.

"What are you thinking about?" Walt asked, breaking the silence.

"Just about how wild this day has been. I've felt every emotion under the sun already and the day isn't nearly over yet."

"I know what you mean."

"You do?"

"Well, yeah. I got the worst news of my life this morning, which was met by the best afternoon I've ever had. With you."

I could feel the color rushing to my cheeks once more. Through my window, I could see the train station looming up ahead.

"Likewise," I replied, twisting my wedding band around my ring finger.

CHAPTER EIGHT

The train pulled into the station with a lurching halt, sending my handbag careening to the floor. Walt and I reached for it in tandem, bumping heads in the process.

"Oh!" I exclaimed.

"Sorry, Lottie. Are you alright?" Walt asked, concern clouding his expression.

"I'm fine," I said, rubbing my head.

Leaning forward, Walt gently pressed his lips to the spot. A warming sensation flooded the area, sending tingles through me. I imagined what it would be like to feel his lips on mine. I felt my pulse quicken at the thought.

"Your bag," he said holding it out to me.

"Thank you," I replied, unable to meet his gaze, as I grabbed it.

We each held one side of the bag like a lifeline connecting the two of us. The other passengers began to file past. Reluctantly letting go, Walt pushed it toward me.

"I suppose we should go," he suggested.

"Yes, we're likely to be kicked off," I said, looking around at the empty train car.

Walt stood, taking a step back to allow me to get out of my seat. "After you," he said gesturing me forward.

"Thank you."

Stepping onto the platform, I watched as Walt exited the train, burning his image into my brain. I knew that this was where we parted ways. I was a married woman with an entire life waiting for me back home. I had children for goodness' sake. I just needed to focus on the show and appreciate this trip for what it was. Just a little blip. Besides, nothing had really happened. Even though I desperately wanted it to if I was being honest. Shaking my head, I banished the notion from my mind.

Silently walking over to our two remaining bags, I bent to grab the handle of my blue case when I spotted something lying on the platform before it. Bending down, I picked it up between my thumb and index finger. Rising to standing, I held it out for Walt to see.

"A feather," he said.

"A bluebird feather," I replied, slipping it into my coat pocket.

"I guess your father is trying to tell you something."

"Yes. I believe he is." What that message was, I couldn't be sure. I had found myself in multiple compromising situations over the course of the day and my head was buzzing. I needed a moment alone with my thoughts to sort through them all.

"Well, Lottie," Walt said, clearing his throat, "I guess this is goodbye."

"Yes, I guess it is. I'm so glad to have met you and to have spent this train ride together," I paused, trying to steel myself to say what I was thinking. "In another time, things might have been different."

"Timing is everything," Walt said, looking down at his feet.

"Yes, it seems that it is."

"Well, I hope you have a great show and enjoy yourself. Not many people get the chance to live out a childhood dream."

"Believe me, I know, and I'm going to savor every second of it," I declared. Unable to stop myself, I blurted out, "You should come out. To see the show, of course, if you'll be in the area long enough."

"If I'm still out here when it opens, I'd love to see you dance."

I blushed.

"And I hope your husband comes to his senses," he continued. "Seems to me that he's a pretty lucky guy."

We paused, both of us avoiding the inevitable.

"Thank you, Walt. For everything."

He nodded, his smile barely covering his regret. Doing my best to conceal mine, I picked up my case and walked toward the station. When I turned back for one last look, Walt was already gone.

CHAPTER NINE

Inside the station, I spotted a young man looking a bit out of his element holding a sign with "Abbott" emblazoned across the front. Walking over, case in hand, I introduced myself.

"Hello, I'm Charlotte Abbott. I believe you're here for me?"

"Yes, ma'am. I'm Robby, uh, I mean, Robert Anderson, from The Rockland Dance Troupe."

"Hello, Robert. I'm your new dancer, replacement anyway. It's very nice to meet you."

"Nice to meet you ma'am. Can I, uh, *may* I take your bag?" he asked, stumbling over his words.

"Thank you," I said, handing it over to him. "Anderson. Any relation to Garrett?"

"Yes, ma'am," he replied sheepishly. "That's my dad. Part-time job."

"Wonderful. Your father is responsible for recruiting me to Rockland. I can't tell you how happy I am that he reached out. Shall we?" I gestured toward the exit.

"Yes, ma'am," he said, leading me to the car waiting outside. He placed my bag in the backseat, opening the passenger side door for me.

"Thank you, Robert."

Closing the door gently, he made his way around to the driver's side and got behind the wheel. "How was the trip out here?"

"Oh, interesting to say the least."

"I guess that's better than it being a drag," he said.

"Certainly," I replied without further explanation.

He maneuvered the car onto the main road and we were on our way. Looking out at the landscape, it was rolling hills and wide-open valleys as far as the eye could see. No snow yet, but maybe we'd get a dusting by the time the show opened.

Rockland was a quaint little town nestled in the mountains. It was known to be a destination spot for summer vacations, weekend getaways, and the like. There were several boutique-style shops and cute restaurants that drew the tourists in. The holiday show was celebrated in the area and throughout New England. I had grown up here watching the show in awe as a little girl and dreaming of one day gracing that stage. It was strange to be going back home after so much time had passed.

"Have you ever been to Rockland, Mrs. Abbott?" Robert asked.

"I grew up here, Robby," I replied. "Is it okay if I call you Robby? I'm not one for formalities."

"Yes, ma'am."

"Please, call me Lottie. 'Ma'am' is reserved for my mother," I laughed.

Robby laughed along with me. "You've got it, Lottie. I guess I don't need to give you the lay of the land as I had planned."

"Probably not. Though it's been a while since I've been back. Things are probably a little different than what I remember."

"Maybe. Things don't change much around here though. We like our traditions here in Rockland."

"That is true."

"So, why'd you leave?" he asked.

"When I was in high school, my father passed away. Everything reminded my mother of what she'd lost. She wanted a fresh start, so we packed up and moved to Western Massachusetts where my aunt lived. I was on track to become a dancer for Rockland back then, but my mother wanted me to graduate high school before putting any focus on dance. We moved before I got the chance. Then I met my husband, and we had our two daughters. And my dreams sat, forgotten, on the back burner. That is until your father called me last week."

"Funny that you ended up right where you were trying to go," he said. "In a roundabout way."

"It is. I guess it was meant to be," I trailed off, transported back to when I was a young girl, and we'd pick up Aunt Jane from the station. She'd come to visit every Christmas. We'd meet her train and take this very road, the scenic route, back home.

"Sounds like it," Robby said, pulling me from my memories. "I'm still trying to figure out what I want to do. My dad wants me to join the business."

"Not your plan?" I asked.

"No. I really want to be a veterinarian. I don't have the best marks in my class, but when it comes to animals, I have a knack."

"If I can give you some advice?" I asked.

He nodded.

"Don't give up on your dreams. Only you know what will make you happy. Life keeps moving. If you don't fight for what you want, you may wake up someday and realize that you're a supporting character in someone else's story. Only the lucky ones get a second chance."

"Like you?" he asked.

"Like me," I smiled.

CHAPTER TEN

"Robby, do you mind taking a quick little detour?" I asked.

"Not at all," he replied. "Where to?"

"Pleasant Street," I said. "That's where I grew up."

"You've got it," Robby said, hanging a left.

Driving onto my old street, a rush of nostalgia hit me. Even though some of the landscaping had changed, for the most part Pleasant Street looked just as it had when we'd left it all those years ago.

"It's just there," I pointed to my childhood home, a white colonial with a wraparound porch and black shutters.

"Would you like me to stop for a minute?" Robby asked.

Momentarily overcome with emotion, I nodded my agreement. Robby pulled the car over to the shoulder. I sat still, memories flooding my mind. A woman stringing lights on the porch spotted us and waved.

"That's Mrs. White. Nice lady. I'm sure she'd let you look inside," he suggested, reading my mind.

"Thanks, Robby, I'll be right back," I announced, already out of the car and closing the door behind me. Rounding the front of the sedan, I called out to Mrs. White, waving as I approached. "Hello, Mrs. White. You don't know me. I'm Charlotte Abbott," I explained, extending a hand when I reached her. "I grew up in this house. I'm in town for the holiday show, performing actually."

"Welcome, Charlotte," she shook my hand. "Nice to meet you. How exciting! I suppose I'll see you on stage very soon then."

"You will," I smiled. "I haven't been back to town since we moved years ago. I was hoping to peek inside the house for old time's sake if it's not any trouble."

"Of course, come on in. I imagine it looks quite different from what you remember, but you're more than welcome," she offered.

"There's just one thing I'd like to see. If it's still there," I trailed off.

"Aha!" she exclaimed, clasping her hands together. "I knew the name Charlotte sounded familiar. I think I know just what you mean. Follow me," she said, leading me up the front steps and into the house. Entering the living room, I noted that the bones of the house remained untouched, but everything else looked entirely different. From the rainbow of colors to the furnishings.

"Wow, it does look different," I mused. "It's lovely. You have a way with color."

"Thank you," Mrs. White chuckled. "Sort of ironic considering my name."

"True," I smiled.

Leading me into the kitchen, she opened the pantry door. Craning my neck around the corner, my shoulders slumped when I saw the clean door frame. Noting my disappointed expression, Mrs. White said, "Don't fret. It's still here."

Extracting a board from a crevice between the wall and cabinetry, she spun it around. Facing me was my father's makeshift growth chart. A board ticked off at irregular intervals marked with my name and the date. Running my fingertips beside my father's handwriting, tears filled my eyes.

"I can't believe you saved it after all these years," I said in disbelief.

"My husband couldn't bear to get rid of it should we ever have a situation like this. He'll be so happy to hear it wasn't in vain. Take it with you," she said, offering the board to me.

"You'll never know how much this means to me, truly. Thank you, I'm so happy I stopped."

"I'm glad to hear it. I'd invite you to stay for tea, but that young man is waiting," she said, nodding toward the door.

"Oh, Robby!" I cried, having forgotten about him for a moment. "I'd better be off. Thank you again, Mrs. White, and your husband too!"

“Our pleasure,” she called. “See you at the show!”

Skipping down the front steps like old times, I smiled, happy to bring a little piece of my past with me. Surely a sign that Dad was with me on this journey.

* * *

Robby pulled the car into an empty space at the Rockland Inn. It looked exactly as I remembered it. Crisp white paint, green awnings, wraparound porch fitted with pairs of rocking chairs. Greenery strung with white lights for the holidays framed the architecture and every windowsill held a single candle. This was to be my home for the next few weeks, and it truly was picture perfect.

“Well, here we are, Lottie,” Robby said. “I’ll get your things. Dad has already arranged your check-in, so everything should be in order. You just need to get your room key.”

“Thank you, Robby. I’ll be sure to let your dad know how wonderful you’ve been.”

“Thank you,” he blushed. “But don’t say too much. Remember, this is a job I have no intention of keeping.”

“Don’t you worry,” I assured him. “I know just what to say.” I got out, noting the familiar creak of the third step as I climbed the stairs to the entrance. Pulling open the front door, I was greeted with the welcoming scent of cinnamon and apples.

“Mrs. Hall’s fresh cider gets me every time,” Robby sighed.

“I’ll say. She always knew how to give guests a warm welcome. It smells like heaven in here. A cup of hot cider sounds like just the ticket.”

“You know Mrs. Hall?”

“I do. Believe it or not, I worked here when I was young. It was my first job. I helped out in the kitchen.”

“Well, then you’ll feel right at home staying here at the Inn.”

“Certainly. It’s been so long since I’ve stepped through that threshold,” I said, taking it all in, “but it still feels the same.”

Robby placed my case and Dad's board next to the reception desk as a middle-aged woman approached with a silver tray holding two mugs of fresh hot cider, one to-go. Upon closer inspection, I recognized her as Mrs. Hall. She looked as I remembered her, though decidedly more mature. Her hair was streaked with gray, and the inevitable lines had started cropping up on her face, evidence that more time had passed than I'd realized.

Mrs. Hall placed the tray down on the reception desk, offering her hand. "Why, Charlotte Dawson, is that you?" she asked, peering at me.

"It's me, Mrs. Hall. I'm back to dance in the holiday show," I replied, taking her hand in both of mine.

"Yes, I've heard. How lucky we are to have you back, even for just a short time," she said. She turned to Robby, "Here you are, young man. I know you're on the clock, so I fixed you a cider for the road."

"Thanks, Mrs. Hall. You're the best," he replied. "That's my cue to get back. Good luck, Lottie, you'll be great. And thank you for the advice."

"Of course, Robby. I'm sure I'll see you around. Thanks again." Robby took his cup and headed for the front door. The jingle of the bell signaled his departure.

"Well, Lottie, you're a sight for sore eyes," Mrs. Hall declared, enveloping me in a hug. "We're delighted to have you."

"I'm delighted to be here."

"I do have to say I feel sorry for that poor girl who was injured. She was so excited to dance for Rockland, but it's all part of show business, I suppose."

"That's show business. I was more surprised than anyone to receive Mr. Garrett's call. I know what it's like to lose that opportunity, so I do feel sorry for her," I empathized, "but I'm truly grateful for the opportunity."

"Well, in any event, I'm glad you were chosen. There's no one more deserving. "Now, have some fresh cider," she said, handing me a mug complete with a cinnamon stick. "You've had a long trip, no doubt, and I'm sure you could use a moment to relax."

"Thank you so much. It's been an interesting day to say the least."

"We'll have to catch up later when I have a free minute. Maybe over tea. I want to hear all about what you've been up to since you left for

Massachusetts."

"That sounds wonderful," I said, sitting down in an armchair facing the bustle of Main Street. "It's quite a story," I said, absentmindedly swirling my cider with the cinnamon stick.

CHAPTER ELEVEN

Turning the key in the lock of room number 22, I opened the door to my home away from home for the next few weeks. I knew Mrs. Hall had given me an upgraded room. What I didn't expect was how luxurious it would be.

"The Hollywood Suite will be just perfect for you, Charlotte," she'd said, handing me the key.

I felt as if I'd just stepped into the Beverly Hills Hotel. The bed was fitted with a rose-colored satin coverlet and matching upholstered headboard. Monogrammed pillows sat atop it with "RI" embroidered across the front. The walls were dressed in embossed fan-print wallpaper in a warm beige tone. Art deco-style sconces cast a soft glow about the room. To top it all off, a framed movie poster for The Belle of New York, featuring my treasured icon, Vera-Ellen, was hanging on the wall. This room couldn't have been more perfect if I'd designed it myself.

Having taken it all in, I collapsed onto the bed, stretching my arms behind my head, and letting out a long sigh. This was the first moment I'd gotten to myself all day and there was a lot to digest. The thought of dissecting it all was exhausting. Perhaps better to soak in a hot bath. I got up to start running the water. A claw-foot soaking tub awaited me, along with a selection of soaps and plush towels. A small chandelier hung in the center of the bathroom adding to the glamorous feel of the space.

Turning the handle, the tub began to fill. I added a few drops of rose-scented bubble bath to the running water. As the bubbles multiplied, the floral aroma filled the room. Taking a deep breath, I imagined myself in a rose garden on a sunny spring day. Tying up my hair, careful not to leave any strands hanging loose, I stepped into the steaming hot water.

Easing into the tub, the cloud of bubbles enveloped me. I felt my shoulders finally begin to sink away from my ears, my tension melting away in the hot water. Closing my eyes, everything I'd been pushing down all day suddenly came rushing back up to the surface. A sob escaped my lips and hot tears streamed down my cheeks. All these years I'd spent supporting Charlie, caring for our girls, keeping our home… the endless loads of laundry and piles of dishes to wash. And this was what he'd been up to. Sneaking around with Alice Baker. What a fool I'd been.

I sat up, wiping my face with a washcloth, smudging my mascara in the process. What a mess. Looking at the black streaks smeared across the fresh white towel, I couldn't tell whether I was angry with him or myself. I lay back down again, looking up at the ceiling in hopes of divining some answers. Of course, none came. I replayed the events of the day in my mind. Everything felt so mixed up. So many questions swirled through my head and I couldn't begin to come up with a single solution. My life had been turned upside down in a matter of hours and I didn't know what to think of it all. For now, I was safe from facing any of it thanks to the show, but in a few weeks, it would be back to reality.

Maybe Mrs. Hall could help me sort it out over tea. She'd always been a great listener, even when I was a young girl with much smaller problems. I envied the days when deciding which dress to wear or how to style my hair were my biggest worries.

Standing up, I rinsed off the bubbles clinging to my wet skin. I stepped out onto the plush pink bathmat, wrapping the thick, white robe hanging on the nearby hook around me. The monogrammed pocket caught my eye as I tied the sash. Mrs. Hall didn't miss a single detail.

Wiping the remaining mascara streaks from my cheeks, I peered at my reflection in the vanity mirror. I almost didn't recognize myself. The person I felt I was on the inside didn't always match the image in the reflection. Was it possible for the same person to look different from herself on any given day? There were so many separate pieces of me that no longer seemed to fit together.

I'd played the roles of wife, mother, and housewife for so long that, somewhere along the way, I had lost sight of who I really was and who I wanted to be. I looked closely at the reflection of the woman before me. She looked familiar but felt like a stranger. All the features were the same, but something was missing.

I thought about the advice I'd given Bobby. It was so easy to identify a problem and the matching solution when it belonged to someone else, but another thing entirely when it was yours. It was time that I started living with intention, just as I'd suggested to Bobby. Serendipity had brought me here, but from today on, I would choose my path instead of blindly following the one neatly set before me. It was about time I figured out what I truly wanted and there was no better place to do it than here in Rockland.

* * *

Sitting at the vanity, I pulled out my cosmetics case and got to work on my face. This was one problem I could fix. Smoothing on my eye cream, I wiped away the last remnants of my melting mascara. I applied a fresh coat to my lashes, and then patted on some powder and a little rouge.

Admiring my handiwork, I noted the frizzy fly-aways on top of my head courtesy of the steamy bathroom and got to work with my boar bristle brush. I had my mane smoothed and tamed in no time.

Dressing in my favorite navy and white polka-dotted dress and matching navy pumps, I slicked on a fresh coat of lipstick, blotting my lips on a tissue. I pulled out my string of pearls, fastening it around my neck. Twirling before the mirror, a little of that excitement I'd felt when Mr. Anderson had called with the offer came rushing back. I was really and truly here. I had made it to Rockland despite all the drama.

"Lottie, you've still got it," I told my reflection, turning on my heel and closing the door behind me.

Descending the stairs to the lobby, I ran my hand along the railing lost in thought. I'd never really taken the time to think about what I wanted from my life after getting married. Finding a husband had always been the goal. I'd said I do and then it was happily ever after, the end. As much as I loved my family, a part of me was unfulfilled, bored. The day-to-day monotony was stifling. While there was some satisfaction in checking things off a to-do list, there was no challenge. I couldn't take pride in how deftly I folded a fitted sheet or made the floors gleam. I needed to move, to create.

These few weeks without my usual daily family responsibilities were going to be a bigger blessing than I'd originally thought. I vowed to use this time wisely and to pay attention to what made me happy. Reaching the lobby, I smiled when I caught Mrs. Hall's gaze. She was well-prepared, teapot in hand. Somehow, she was always impeccably ready for everything.

"Charlotte, perfect timing. I've just brewed my favorite English Breakfast tea. I've brought a few warm scones fresh from the oven for us as well. Come and join me."

"Thank you, Mrs. Hall. Tea sounds wonderful. I was hoping to catch you before the dinner rush."

"Oh, not to worry, I have a new assistant manager who takes care of dinner. I decided to cut my hours down a bit last year. I'm not getting any younger, you know."

"Sounds like a smart idea. You should take some time for yourself."

"My thoughts exactly," she said, pouring some tea into each cup. "Milk, cream, sugar? I also have honey if you'd prefer that."

"Just milk is fine, thank you," I replied.

"Now Charlotte, tell me what you've been up to. Are you still living in Massachusetts?" she asked, handing me my cup.

"Yes, I am. In the same town as my mother. Aunt Jane moved to Florida a couple of years ago."

"Well, good for her. I wouldn't mind pleasant weather year-round."

"Yes. She's really enjoying herself."

"And you? Are you enjoying yourself? What's been keeping you busy?"

"Well, I'm married," I said, displaying my wedding ring. "My husband owns an automotive garage. I've been supporting him at home taking care of the house and our two girls, Kathy and Penny."

"Wonderful. Two girls, you're truly blessed. What's the husband's name?"

"Oh, I'm sorry. Charlie. Charlie Abbott."

"Charlie and Charlotte. Almost too cute." Mrs. Hall chuckled.

"Yes, exactly. I usually go by Lottie these days, so the joke isn't always so obvious," I laughed.

"Well, why didn't you say so? Lottie. That might take some getting used to. I'm a creature of habit, and I'll always think of you as the young Charlotte who baked such delicious pies. And now look at you, married with two girls. Seems like just yesterday you were a teenager working for me."

"I loved working here. The place looks amazing by the way. I absolutely love my room. Thank you so much."

"Of course, dear. I had you in mind when I put it together," she revealed.

"Well, you got it exactly right. Down to the Vera-Ellen poster."

"I wanted to do a few specialty themes in the larger guestrooms and remembered she was your favorite."

"She is. From the second I saw her dance I knew I wanted to be a dancer myself."

"You've always seemed the happiest while dancing."

"It's true. Something takes over and I'm just in it," I explained. "Everything else just falls away."

"And you haven't done any dancing until now?" she asked.

"Not unless you count nights out at the dance hall before I met Charlie," I replied.

"In that case, can I ask a question, dear?"

"Certainly."

"Why did you give it up?"

Why did I give it up? I parroted her question in my mind. *Why did I give it up?* "You know, Mrs. Hall, I've been asking myself that same question ever since I received Mr. Anderson's phone call."

"And what did you come up with?"

"Well," I began, pausing to collect my thoughts, "I suppose because I met Charlie, and we got married soon after. He'd always wanted to open a garage, so I supported him. As he was getting it up and running, we found out we were expecting Kathy. And then Penny came along. Life got busy and somewhere along the way, I lost sight of myself."

"Tale as old as time," she sympathized. "But look at you now. You're going to be starring in the holiday show."

"I don't know about starring. But I'll finally get to dance in it. I'm happy to be in the show at all."

"And your husband? What does Charlie think of all of this? I can imagine it came out of left field, especially if he's accustomed to you taking care of everyone."

"You've got that right. His first reaction to the news wasn't great," I began. "Until I baked a batch of my famous cookies to soften him up. Worked like a charm."

"You always had a knack for baked goods. I'm sure he's happy for you. He's probably just worried about caring for the children on his own."

"That was part of it," I started, ashamed as I recalled his immediate reaction. "I'm embarrassed to say this out loud, but when I told him the news, he actually referred to dancing as a pipe dream and went on to tell me that I make a great homemaker."

"Oh boy," Mrs. Hall replied, eyebrows raised. "Charlie certainly put his foot in his mouth."

"Yes. I was quite upset by it, but that was nothing compared to this morning," I began.

"What happened this morning?"

Taking a deep breath, I continued, "I thought it would be nice to leave on a high note and bring him a little surprise before I left. I made a special trip down to the garage to bring him his favorite coffee and a donut. When I got there, I caught him with his arms around another woman. The one woman in town that I despise."

"Oh my!" Mrs. Hall exclaimed. "What did you do?"

"I ended up spilling the hot coffee on myself and when I cried out in pain, they both spotted me. I was so enraged at what I'd seen, I chucked the donut at the shop window and marched straight to my car." Mrs. Hall didn't say a word. She continued to sip her tea, listening intently. "Charlie came running after me with Alice nipping at his heels. By then, I had already gotten into my car and pulled up to a red light. They were in the crosswalk when the light turned." Pausing for effect, I concluded, "So naturally, I revved my engine and peeled away, leaving them standing there in shock. Haven't spoken to him since."

CHAPTER TWELVE

"Oh dear," Mrs. Hall chuckled. "Some things never change. You always were a firecracker."

"Me?" I asked, a hand pressed to my chest feigning innocence.

"No matter how many years pass, I'll never forget the time that Johnny Wilson dared to cross you."

"Ah yes, that was the first time I was burned by a man. Well, a boy really. How is Johnny?"

"Why don't you ask him yourself? He's back in the kitchen preparing dinner."

"*Johnny* is your chef?" I asked, somewhat shocked.

"He sure is. He's quite the cook, you'll see. Besides, I had to give him a second chance after you humiliated him here all those years ago," she teased.

"To be fair, he had it coming."

"If you say so," she said. "Just promise me one thing."

"What's that?"

"Before you do the same with your Charlie, talk to him and get to the bottom of what's really going on. Things aren't always as they appear at first glance."

She had a point. Charlie and I had problems long before Alice came into the picture if I was being truthful, but I needed time to sort out my own feelings first.

"You're right," I agreed. "I'll talk to him. Just not quite yet. I refuse to let him ruin this trip for me."

"Okay, dear. But don't take too long. That Alice sounds as if she's up to no good. I hope your Charlie has a good head on his shoulders."

"He does," I stated. "Or I thought he did. I'm not so sure anymore," I trailed off. "There's one other thing."

"There's more to that story?" she asked incredulously.

"Oh yes, a lot more."

"Well, out with it then," she said, swiping her famous honey butter over a scone and handing it to me.

"Thank you," I said, taking a bite of the warm scone. "Delicious."

"Stop keeping me in suspense, girl," she chided.

"Yes, sorry," I started, afraid to divulge the rest. "Well, I met someone on the train."

"What kind of someone?"

"A man. And I know what you're going on say." Her single raised eyebrow said it all. "But I swear I have never met someone and felt an immediate connection like I did on that train. Ever."

"Charlotte. This sounds like dangerous territory if you ask me," Mrs. Hall warned.

"I know. I really do. And maybe it's only because of what happened with Charlie just before. I don't know."

"Did anything happen between you and this mystery man?" she asked tentatively.

"Oh! No! Nothing like that. I would never," I exclaimed. "But if I was a single woman... Well, there's no doubt in my mind that it would have."

"Oh, boy. You've certainly had a day. Don't forget, there's a difference between love and lust. One is built over time and the other is immediate, but it's not usually lasting. And the two don't generally go hand in hand. Unless you're lucky."

"I've been telling myself all afternoon that it's wrong to have thoughts about another man. Since we married, I've never even considered anyone else, but with this guy I could see it. I could imagine myself happy with him. I don't know what's wrong with me."

Mrs. Hall took a sip of her tea, carefully placing the cup back down on the saucer. "Charlotte. I'm sorry, I can't get used to calling you Lottie just yet. Marriage is complicated. As time passes your relationship changes and your needs change. And sometimes it can be enticing to think about a life with someone new. But in any relationship, there will always be challenges. While the grass may look greener with this new fellow now, it's only because you haven't encountered any challenges yet. That's always the draw of someone you've just met, their vices are still hidden. Does he have a name?"

"Yes, I know," I replied, hanging my head. "I just felt such a pull. It was magnetic. I can't think of any other way to describe it. It was such a strange and thrilling sensation. He really saw me, the real me, and listened to what I had to say and seemed to want to understand me. He treated me respectfully, as his equal, and valued my opinions. It's been so long since I've talked with a man and felt that he genuinely cared about my thoughts. His name is Walt, by the way."

"Walt," she repeated with a smile. "Well, now that changes things for me. I miss my Walt every day."

"I knew you'd say that. I didn't want to upset you."

"You could never upset me by bringing him up. Everything wonderful is wrapped up in that name. I shared my best years with my Walter, you know that."

"I do," I said, placing a hand over hers.

"Charlotte, all I can tell you is that I wouldn't trade my years with Walt for anything. It was cut short, but I cherish that time as the most joyful period of my life. As for your dilemma, I don't have the answer. That's up to you. I do know that we get one life and it's meant to be enjoyed and lived. And if I know you, you're the last person to squander it."

"Except that's what I've been doing these past years, just going through the motions," I said, letting out a long sigh. Resting my chin on the heel of my hand, I mused, "I have the girls to consider and, honestly, I don't know what I'm thinking. I share lunch with a stranger, and now I'm questioning my entire life? Have I lost my mind?"

"Maybe," she joked. "Life doesn't always work out the way we expect it to, my dear. There are surprises at every turn, but that's what keeps things interesting. Just follow your heart and you can't go wrong. Besides, you're here now doing exactly what you were always meant to. I'd hardly call that going through the motions."

"I suppose you're right," I agreed.

"Things will work themselves out, Charlotte. They always do," Mrs. Hall said, glancing at the grandfather clock in the corner of the room. "In the meantime, Johnny should have dinner ready any minute now. Why don't you go on and meet the rest of the girls, and enjoy a meal you didn't have to prepare?"

Standing up to head to dinner, I smiled, "Thanks Mrs. Hall, that's the best advice I've heard all day."

CHAPTER THIRTEEN

Poking my head in the doorway of the kitchen, I was hit with an overwhelming sense of déjà vu. Little had changed over the years. The same cherry-printed wallpaper hung on the walls and the old worn table where I used to roll my pie crust sat in the same spot. I was picturing my younger self working at the table alongside Mrs. Hall when a voice interrupted me.

"Excuse me, miss? Can I help?"

I turned, finding myself face-to-face with Johnny Wilson. "Hi Johnny," I said sheepishly.

"Hello," he started, working out how I knew him. A flash of recognition crossing his face he asked, "Charlotte?"

"It's me," I replied, flashing a smile.

"Wow! Look at you, back in Rockland," he said, swooping me into a hug. "It's great to see you!"

"Is it?" I asked. "I wasn't sure you'd be keen on seeing me."

"Well, I have matured, believe it or not."

"Stranger things have happened," I joked. "Mrs. Hall mentioned you were the chef. I had to see it for myself. And I wanted to be sure you wouldn't tamper with my meal," I winked.

"Well now that you mention it…"

"Johnny Wilson, don't you dare. I still have a few tricks up my sleeve."

"I wouldn't dream of it, Charlotte. You stay away from my pie filling, and we'll be just fine."

"You have my word," I said bowing my head.

"That blueberry filling stained my hair for weeks you know. I never went anywhere without a cap."

"I remember. And I also seem to remember that Betty refused to be seen with you. So, I'd say it was a success on my part."

"I was a stupid kid. But thanks to you, I've been a one-woman man ever since," he smiled.

"Happy to help. I take it you're married?"

"I am. Seven wonderful years."

"That's great, glad to hear it. Whatever happened to Betty?"

"I married her."

"Oh! Well, then I forgive you for being a cheat all those years ago. Looks like you two were meant to be."

"The heart wants what it wants," he replied.

"I'm starting to realize that."

"How about you? Are you hitched? Any kids?" he asked.

"I am. My husband, Charlie, and I have two beautiful little girls. I live in Massachusetts now. I'll be out here for a few weeks dancing in the holiday show."

"That's great. Your dream came true. I wonder why Mrs. Hall never mentioned you were coming to stay?"

"Knowing her, I bet she preferred to watch the drama unfold," I laughed.

"Well, none here. I hope I can say the same for you," he teased. "Charlotte Dawson always was a bit of a wildcard."

"Abbott now and not anymore, I promise."

"Good to know. Listen, it's been great to see you, but I've got to get back to plating these meals. We'll have to have you over while you're here. Betty would love to see you."

"Sounds great," I agreed. "Can't wait to try your food. Head chef, impressive."

"I hope you like it. I've got a little something planned that I know you'll enjoy."

"This is the first time in a long time that someone is preparing a meal for *me*. Don't you worry, I'll enjoy every bite," I called, walking out of the kitchen.

Johnny and Betty, married. Who would've guessed? And still together after all these years. Things had worked out after all and maybe in the way they were always supposed to.

Were Charlie and I a true match? I had thought so in the beginning. I wanted to be with him every second in those days. We were inseparable.

Back in those early days, he took me to the drive-in and out for milkshakes. I'd find flowers on my front porch for no reason other than he'd been thinking of me. We would drive to The Point to gaze at the stars and to be alone, alongside the other young couples with the same idea. Sometimes we would just walk aimlessly downtown, content to be going nowhere in particular. It didn't matter what we did if we were together.

My favorite times were the nights we went to the dance hall with friends. Dancing wasn't his strong point, but he tried his best because he knew I loved it and always made me laugh with his efforts. We had so much fun together back then. It had been years since we'd done anything like that, just the two of us.

Snapshots of those carefree days filtered through my mind and warmed my heart. We did have something real. Maybe I was wrong about what I thought I'd seen. Maybe Mrs. Hall was right and this was all a misunderstanding. This was one time I really hoped I was wrong. I'd call Charlie after dinner and sort it out once and for all.

CHAPTER FOURTEEN

As I entered the dining room, Mrs. Hall appeared, ushering me over to a large table with several young women already seated, chatting animatedly among themselves.

"Excuse me, ladies," Mrs. Hall interrupted the chatter, "if I may, I'd like to introduce your new troupe member. She's an old friend of mine." All eyes turned to me as Mrs. Hall continued, "This is Charlotte Daw-, Abbott, I'll get that someday," she laughed, patting my arm, "and she will be a fabulous addition to the show. Please welcome her accordingly."

"Hello, ladies. I'm so happy to be here with all of you," I said, looking at the expectant faces of the women seated at the table.

"Hello!"

"Hi!"

"Welcome!"

I smiled at the warm response. Out of the corner of my eye, I spotted an icy blonde, arms crossed over her chest, lips drawn in a straight line, her blue eyes burning a hole through me.

Well, I thought to myself, apparently, not everyone is happy to have me here. Naturally, I looked right at her, flashed my biggest grin, and said, "It's so nice to meet all of you." Her eyes began to roll, but she corrected herself, forcing a tight smile, ever-so-slightly nodding in my direction.

"Please, sit here next to me, Charlotte," a redhead gestured to the open chair beside her. Offering her hand, she introduced herself. "I'm Judy. We're all so thankful to have you with us on such short notice."

"Thanks so much, Judy. I'm truly happy to be here and I appreciate the warm welcome," I replied, shaking her hand as I sat down.

"I'm Nancy," the brunette to my left introduced herself, continuing around the table with the rest of the troupe. "And next to me is Linda, and that's Mary L. and Mary M., Kay, Bianca, Jean, and Barbara."

"Hello, everyone. I'm looking forward to getting to know you all."

"Likewise," Bianca said with a haughty tone.

"Bianca, is it?" I asked.

"Good memory," she replied.

"I always try to remember names when I meet someone new. Makes it much easier when someone has such a unique name as yours."

"I was named after my grandmother, it's a family name."

"Well, look at that, something we have in common."

"You don't say," she flatly replied.

The smart response I was prepared to come back with was interrupted by the arrival of our dinner plates, my stomach rumbling in anticipation. The waiter placed each plate down with a flourish. As he placed mine down, he tilted his head, studying my profile.

"Oh my! Can it be? Charlotte Dawson has graced us with her presence. Watch out Rockland!"

"Billy!" I exclaimed, jumping up from my seat. "I was so preoccupied with the food. I didn't even see you! How are you?"

Placing the last plate down in front of Nancy, he immediately grabbed me in a bear hug. "Charlotte, it's been too long! I'm so happy to see you!" he said, releasing me from his tight grip. "After my shift, you and I are having a drink to catch up. It's been what, almost ten years? I won't take no for an answer, so don't bother arguing with me."

"I wouldn't think of it," I laughed. "I'm all yours."

"How I always wanted to hear those words," he quipped.

I raised an eyebrow, giving him a knowing smile. He winked, pulling my chair out to allow me to sit. I returned to seated, Billy gently pushing my chair back in to meet the table.

"Ladies, we have lemon roast chicken and veggies this evening. Is there anything else I can get anyone?" he asked.

"No, thank you," we replied in unison.

"In that case, enjoy," he announced. "I'll see you later," he said to me, bending down to plant a quick peck on my cheek.

I blushed as all the girls looked to me for an explanation, wondering how I knew Billy and what our relationship was.

Judy elbowed me with a smirk and said, "Charlotte, just how well do you know our handsome waiter?"

"I've known Billy forever. We grew up together. We've always been close."

"I'd say," she replied cheekily.

"Oh, nothing like that," I laughed. "Billy was like a brother to me. We lost touch when I moved to Massachusetts."

"Well, it's nice that you two are able to reconnect. I can already tell that we're going to have so much fun. Even despite that wet rag over there," she whispered, gesturing toward Bianca.

Placing my napkin in my lap, I was eager to try Johnny's cooking. "I noticed, but I refuse to acknowledge it. I won't give her the satisfaction."

"Oh, she's just mad that you took Jade's place," Judy explained. "That's her cousin and best, or maybe I should say only, friend. They do everything together and had big plans for this show to jump-start their careers."

"Ah, well that makes more sense. At least it's not personal."

"For her, it may be. She has no real friends here now. Those two alienated themselves from the rest of us since day one."

"Well, I'm not going to worry about Bianca. I'm here to dance, and that's what I plan to do," I decided.

"That's the attitude. She's flying solo now anyway, so she'll have to shape up. I doubt she'll have such bravado without her sidekick to back her up."

"She sounds like trouble."

"She is. But she's an exquisite dancer, so we tolerate her."

"Good to know," I replied, cutting a small piece of roast chicken, and popping it into my mouth. The zing of the lemon paired with the earthy herbs was heaven. Johnny Wilson was the real deal. I took a sip of my chardonnay, sitting back to observe the ladies and wondering what other characters from my past would crop up during my stay. I hadn't thought about rekindling old friendships when I agreed to come back to town. This trip was already proving to be so much more than I had imagined.

CHAPTER FIFTEEN

Billy returned to clear our plates, all picked clean, except for Bianca's. She had simply moved the food around her plate without making much of a dent.

"Was everything to your liking, Miss?" Billy asked, retrieving her half-full dinner plate.

"Yes, it was delicious. I'm just very mindful of how much I consume," she replied.

"Understood," he nodded. Addressing the table, he said, "Dessert will be out in a few moments, ladies."

Bianca raised her index finger, calling out, "Minus one. No sweets for me." Billy nodded his understanding, judgment hidden from everyone but me, before disappearing into the kitchen.

"Bianca, you barely ate anything," Barbara noted.

I was quickly working out the who's who of the group as I watched the ladies interact. Barbara was the mother hen, an interesting role as she was the youngest of the women. It had already been established that Bianca was the Alice of this group, much to my chagrin. I made a mental note to keep my eye on her. Just when I thought I'd escaped that snake another popped up in its place.

"You need to keep your energy up for rehearsals," Barbara chided. "You can certainly have a bite of dessert."

"Barb, I'm perfectly fine," Bianca assured her. "It's a small sacrifice for the good of my career."

"You won't have a career if you can't stand. You're already too thin as it is," Jean quipped.

"Mind your own beeswax, Jean," Kay jumped to Bianca's defense. "Bianca can make her own decisions."

"Really, Kay? I think we all know why you're piping up now," Jean shot back, eyebrow raised.

"Ladies," Nancy announced. "May I remind you that this is Charlotte's first evening with us," she scolded, effectively shutting down further discussion regarding Bianca's eating habits.

Sipping my wine, I silently watched the scene unfolding before me. It was better than a television sitcom. I could see a divide forming among the group. With Jade's departure, Bianca had seemingly found new supporters in Barbara and Kay. From where I was sitting, she loved the attention. I had a feeling she would use them to her advantage.

Jean was proving to be the unedited voice of the group. Whatever she thought, she said. Not the most tactful in her delivery, but so far, she wasn't wrong. I liked her. She was genuine. Linda and the Mary's were the nice girls as far as I could see. They stuck together, never said a bad word about anyone or anything, and stayed out of the fray. Nancy was the leader of the pack keeping everyone organized and on task.

Judy was the most like me. I could tell she had a good sense of humor and was enjoying this exchange just as much as I was. I had a feeling we'd have a lot to talk about over the next few weeks. As we made eye contact, I hastily turned away for fear that I'd burst out laughing. From the look on her face, I knew that Judy and I were on the same page. Thank goodness I would have at least one friend in the troupe. It looked as though I'd benefit from having an ally among this group of women.

At that moment, Johnny emerged from the kitchen with a tray of ramekins and a devilish grin. He made his way over to our table, headed straight for me. "Evening ladies," he said, nodding to the table. "I wanted to personally deliver your dessert for this evening. I made a last-minute change to the menu in honor of a special guest," he paused for effect, looking right at me.

Everyone turned their attention to me for the second time that evening. What must these girls think of me and my dealings with the men of the

Rockland Inn? "Johnny, you're going to make me blush. Don't forget our conversation earlier," I said, wagging a finger at him.

"Charlotte, how could I?" he asked in mock horror, placing a darling dish of blueberry cobbler before me. "I present to you, Charlotte's Cobbler." I laughed out loud as he continued, "I'll allow you to share the story with your new friends if you so choose, but try not to make me look bad," he said to me. "Ladies, enjoy," he addressed the table and then retreated to the kitchen.

"My, my, new friend," Judy said. "I'm going to stick by you. You certainly seem to be acquainted with all the fine-looking gentlemen Rockland has to offer."

"I knew I liked you, Judy," I chuckled. "I hate to burst your bubble, but Chef Wilson is married, and our waiter is..." Just then, Billy appeared with coffee and tea for the table. Placing the cream and sugar down, he noted our table's dessert special. I saw him smirk, but he kept quiet. "Unavailable," I finished my thought.

"Well, you must have others up your sleeve," Judy retorted. "We've only been here an hour or so, and the two best-looking men I've seen tonight have drifted right over to you like moths to a flame."

"They're both old friends. I really didn't expect to see either of them, but so far, my return to Rockland has been filled with familiar faces." I continued, "I promise you that if any others crop up, I'll send them over your way," wiggling my occupied ring finger to exaggerate my point.

"Well, that's more like it. Who knew all the attractive men were hiding in Rockland? I'm counting on you," she said.

"At your service," I replied with a salute. "I'll do my best."

"Now, what's the story behind the cobbler?" Judy asked. "Seems juicy."

"Well, that's one way to put it," I laughed, picking up my dessert spoon and tucking into the cobbler bearing my name.

CHAPTER SIXTEEN

"Remind me to stay on your good side," Judy laughed.

I wrapped up my story about Johnny and the blueberries, never mentioning the true reason for it. I didn't want to harm him any more than I already had. Blue hair had been punishment enough. "I had my reasons," I quipped.

"Which were?" Judy asked.

"I'll never tell," I said, zipping my lips in gesture.

"I bet I can guess," Judy said, eyebrows raised, "but I'll respect your privacy since I've only known you a couple of hours."

"Thank you. Johnny has suffered enough at my hands," I joked.

Ding! Ding! Ding! Nancy tapped her glass with a spoon to cut through the chatter. "Ladies, I want to remind you that we're days away from opening night. I'm counting on all of you to get Charlotte up to speed. Get some rest, and I'll see you first thing for rehearsals. It's going to be a long day."

"Thanks, Nancy. We will!" the Mary's sang out in unison.

Judy leaned over, whispering, "A couple of us are going to the dance hall for a bit if you want to join. Don't tell the director over there," she nodded in Nancy's direction.

"I think I'll take a rain check. I still need to get settled, call home to check in on my girls, and I promised Billy a drink. After that, it's lights out for me."

"You're a mom? I never would've known. I hope my body holds up as well as yours did. But first, I need to find my man," she announced. "No time like the present."

"Well, thanks. I was worried that I was going to be out of my league with all you young ladies."

"You fit right in," she assured me. "I would venture to say you look younger than a couple of these girls, but don't tell them I said so."

"I wouldn't dream of it, but I love that you think so."

"On that note, I'm going to go back up to my room to freshen up. I'll see you in the morning. Breakfast is at 7."

"Sounds good. Have fun tonight and good luck with your search."

"I'll fill you in tomorrow morning over tea and toast," she replied, pushing her chair in and making her way toward the exit.

"Night," I called back.

The rest of the girls began filing out of the dining room, heading to their rooms. I followed suit, anxious to call home and hear what Charlie had to say.

"Charlotte," a voice called out behind me.

I turned around to see Bianca approaching. She stood a few inches taller than me and looked much thinner upon standing. Sidling up next to me, she grabbed my hand. Her bony fingers were ice cold even though the packed dining room was quite warm.

"Yes, Bianca?" I asked.

"I just wanted to wish you luck for rehearsals tomorrow," she said in a sickeningly sweet voice, loud enough for Barbara and Kay to hear. Leaning in closer, she hissed under her breath, "you're going to need it."

"Thank you for thinking of me, sweetie," I began, squeezing her hand with a little extra force, "but luck is irrelevant when you have talent."

Bianca let my hand drop, her mouth gaping open, not having anticipated a matching response from me. I would be damned if I was going to put up with this garbage. She'd picked the wrong day to goad me.

"You're going to catch flies like that, B," I said quietly, then called out to the rest of the girls, "Goodnight, ladies! See you bright and early."

"Goodnight!" Barbara and Kay sang back.

"She seems so nice, don't you think, Bianca?" I overheard Kay ask enthusiastically.

"Very," Bianca flatly replied.

Smiling to myself, I headed toward my room to set things right.

* * *

Sitting down on the bed, I dialed my home number. After a few rings, my mother answered in her usual chipper voice.

"Good evening, Abbott Residence."

"Hi, Mom, it's me," I said.

"Charlotte! I'm so happy you called. I was just getting the girls ready for bed. How was your trip?"

"It was great, mom," I fibbed. "I just had dinner with the other ladies and rehearsals start early tomorrow, but I'm ready. Oh! You'll never guess who works at the Rockland Inn now!"

"Let me see, Johnny Wilson and Billy Jones?" she mocked, clearly already informed.

"How did you know? And why didn't you tell me?"

"I still keep in touch with Mrs. Hall, dear. We thought it would be more fun for you to be surprised."

"For me or for you?" I asked.

"Well, both really," she laughed. "I'm glad you're having fun. Let me get the girls on the line." I waited as she called Kathy and Penny over.

"Me, first. I'm older," Kathy announced. "Mommy?"

"Hi, Kitty Kat! How's everything going with gran? Are you having fun?"

"Gran is the best. She let us have ice cream before dinner!"

"That sounds terrific. I knew she would spoil you girls. I miss you, but I'm glad you're having a good time. Listen to your grandmother and do a good job while I'm away, okay?"

"I miss you, too. I know, Mom. I'm always good, remember?"

"Yes, you are. Sweet dreams, honey. Can you put your sister on for a minute?"

"Okay, goodnight, Mommy." I heard the exchange of the telephone receiver as Penny came to the line.

"Mommy?" she asked.

"Hi Penny, I miss you," I said.

"Miss you. Love you, Mommy."

"Love you too, sweetie. Get ready for bed and have sweet dreams, okay?"

"Okay, bye."

Through the receiver, I heard my mother say, "Now, girls, let me say goodnight to mom, and then we'll go read our bedtime story. Why don't you go choose a book together?" she instructed. "Charlotte?"

"I'm here, Mom. Thanks again for helping out. I really appreciate it."

"No problem, honey. Happy to do it."

"Can you put Charlie on quickly?"

"Oh, he called before dinner and said he'd be late at the shop. Something about closing out the month and getting paperwork in order."

"Oh, okay. I didn't even think of that," I lied, trying to mask my surprise and disappointment. "Just let him know I called when you do see him. I'm in room 22 at the Inn if you need to reach me for anything."

"I will, dear. Break a leg tomorrow! You're going to dazzle them," she said.

"Thanks, Mom. I'm certainly going to try. Goodnight."

"Night, Charlotte."

I placed the receiver back on the cradle, cheeks burning. Charlie was at the shop doing paperwork at this time of night. Convenient. Don't jump to conclusions, I warned myself. Maybe he is doing paperwork after all. Goodness knows he'd do anything to avoid my mother, especially after this morning.

I picked up the handset again, quickly dialing the number to the shop. Listening to it ring and ring and ring, my heart dropped. Replacing the receiver with a thud, I grabbed my key and went off to find Billy. As I reached the end of the hallway, I thought I heard a phone ringing and paused for a moment. Maybe it was mine, Charlie could be calling back. Should I turn back? Shaking my head, I kept going. I had already tried. He could wait for me this time.

CHAPTER SEVENTEEN

Taking a seat at a table for two by the window, I wondered if it had been Charlie phoning me back. I hoped so. Let him wonder where I was. Served him right. So much for my earlier sentiments. I was right back to being spiteful. Moments later, Billy arrived with a steaming mug, placing it on the table in front of me.

"My famous Cider Toddy, my lady," he said, gesticulating as though he was announcing the arrival of the Queen.

"This looks delish," I replied. "May I ask what's in it?"

"You may, but you won't get an answer. It's my secret recipe. Just trust that it will knock your socks off."

"In that case, I'm going to stick to just one. I have to be up early for rehearsal," I said. "Where's yours?"

"I wanted to get you started first. I'll be over in a jiffy; I just need to close out my last table. Hang tight," he said, hurrying off to the dining room.

I picked up the mug, cradling it in my hands and soaking up its warmth. I rolled my neck, trying to work out the kinks, and took a sip of cider. Billy wasn't kidding, this was tasty. If I didn't know better, I would guess it was a virgin drink.

Through the window, I watched Judy and a few of the girls on their way to the dance hall. They were all dolled up, dressed to the nines, joking and laughing. I envied them. In truth, it wasn't all that long ago that I had been doing the same, but it felt like a lifetime. Placing the mug down on the table, I rested my head in my hands, eyes closed.

"Penny for your thoughts?" Billy asked, sitting down with a mug of his own.

I looked up, sighing, "I don't even know where to begin..."

"At the beginning, of course," he quipped.

I smiled. He was the same old Billy. "I'm glad to see that you haven't changed a bit."

"Why would I? I've always been fabulous, darling."

"And humble as ever," I laughed. "This drink is to die for, by the way. I can't even taste the liquor."

"Why, thank you. It's my special recipe. I'm working on signature cocktails for the Inn. I haven't told Mrs. Hall yet, but I think they'll be a moneymaker."

"That's an amazing idea, Billy. She'll love it!"

"Once I perfect them, she will. Until then, this stays between you and me."

"My lips are sealed," I assured him. "I'm happy to be your guinea pig for the next few weeks."

"You've always been good at keeping a secret. And I do love a sidekick."

"I never share secrets that aren't mine to tell," I said. "Happy to be the Robin to your Batman."

"I love that I'm Batman in that scenario; a cocktail superhero," he chuckled. "In all honesty, I'm so thankful it was you that saw us that day. When I think about what could've happened if it had been anyone else," he shuddered, taking a sip of his drink.

"It was the beginning of a beautiful friendship," I said, grabbing his hand. "We might never have become so close if that didn't happen. I always had a crush on you and thought you wanted nothing to do with me."

"Well, I didn't," he laughed. "But mainly because you were a girl."

"Yes, there's that," I chuckled. "I have to admit it was a relief to find out that it was nothing personal. I didn't have the confidence then that I do now."

"Who are you kidding? You've always been confident. That's just the difference between being a girl and a woman. On a serious note, though, thank you for keeping my secret all these years."

"Well, I don't spread gossip. What goes on between two people is none of my business," I paused. "Unless, of course, one of those people is my husband," I revealed.

"That's a loaded comment. I knew that you needed this drink. I have a sixth sense about these things. What happened?"

"Well, a lot actually, and just before I caught the train here. I haven't even really had time to process it." He nodded, waiting for me to continue. "I thought I'd surprise Charlie, my husband, with a little treat before I left. I stopped at the bakery for a coffee and donut."

"That's not the kind of treat I thought you were referring to," Billy frowned, disappointed.

"Oh no, that wasn't all. I was also wearing new lingerie under my overcoat, and nothing else."

"Well, that's more like it," he said, eyebrows raised in approval. "How could you go wrong with a surprise like that?"

"That's what I thought. Until I reached the shop window."

"What was in the shop window?" he asked, leaning forward in anticipation, sensing the drama to come.

"My husband. Locked in an embrace with a woman that I cannot stand. Alice Baker, owner of the bakery across the street from his shop, and our town busybody."

"What did you do?"

"I was shocked. At first, I couldn't move. I couldn't look away. I was like a deer in headlights. And then someone honked a car horn startling me out of my stupor. I ended up spilling Charlie's hot coffee all over my legs. I cried out, which got their attention. When they spotted me, I was so angry and embarrassed that I hightailed it out of there as fast as I could."

"Oh, Lottie. That doesn't sound like you. Why didn't you confront them?" Billy asked.

"I couldn't. I was humiliated. I got into my car as they came running out after me. Of course, I got stuck waiting at a red light. By the time it turned green, they had just about reached me. So, I glared at them both, revved my engine, and burned rubber. I haven't spoken to Charlie since."

"Wait. Back up," he said, a smile beginning to form at the corners of his mouth. "You revved your engine at them?"

"Yes. I did. He was trying to talk to me, and I wasn't going to have that."

Billy burst out laughing. "There she is. There's the girl that I know and love."

Smiling, I had to admit that it was a little bit funny. Apart from the reason behind it. "I did manage to scare the wits out of Alice, which was very satisfying."

"I bet. If only I could've been a witness. What a scene."

"She's lucky I didn't swerve and flatten her," I said.

"I don't blame you. But running someone down in your car is never the answer."

"I suppose you're right, but it sure was tempting," I replied.

CHAPTER EIGHTEEN

"Well, that's quite the morning and such a waste of good lingerie. I hate to ask, but has anything like this ever happened before?" Billy asked.

"No, never! Charlie would never, at least I don't think he would." I paused, questioning the entirety of my marriage.

"Well, as you said, you didn't see Charlie do anything but remove Alice's hands from his neck. So, he could be innocent in all this," Billy offered. "She might just be after your man."

"True. But from what I did see, I think there was a part of him that liked it."

"That might be true. But who doesn't enjoy a little flattery from time to time?"

"I suppose."

"How have things been with you and Charlie? How did he feel about you coming to Rockland?" Billy asked.

"Well, that's another story. He was against it from the get-go and suggested I stay at home 'because I'm such a great homemaker,'" I said, imitating Charlie.

Billy's eyes grew wide, "I can imagine how that went over with you."

"Not well. I mean, I know that I'm a great homemaker. I make it a point to be a good wife and mom. But that's not all I am."

"Of course not."

"But I get the feeling that's how he sees me now."

"Then you need to show him. You're here for a reason. You were meant for the spotlight. If he can't handle it, he'll have to step aside."

"You're right. God, Billy, I didn't realize how much I've missed you or our talks. Promise me we won't lose touch again."

"Done," he said. "So, tell me about these kids of yours. What have you got?"

"I have two beautiful little girls, Kathy and Penelope, Kitty Kat and Penny. They're the lights of my life and such opposites. Kathy is very serious and a strict rule follower. Penny is still little, but we already know that she's got a temper and knows what she wants. She going to give me a run for my money."

"Funny, she sounds just like someone else I know," Billy replied, eyebrows raised.

"The similarities were not lost on me. Believe me, my mother likes to point it out all the time," I laughed.

"Well, you know what they say, your most challenging child is the one most like you."

"Then I've got my work cut out."

"Those girls are lucky to have you as their mom. I bet you have a lot of fun with them."

"We really do. I wouldn't trade it for anything, but I do sometimes feel like I've lost a part of myself."

"Understandable. I don't see why you can't do both. If anyone can find that perfect balance, it's you. You know that, right?"

"Thanks," I smiled. "You're the second person today that's said that and I'm just now realizing how badly I needed to hear it."

"The second?" he said, feigning horror. "I thought I was the one with the sage advice. Who was the first?"

"Walt."

"Walt?"

"A man I met on the train."

"Interesting, it feels like there's a story here. Tell me more," he chided, resting his chin on the heel of his hand, waiting.

I blushed. Billy always knew just what I was thinking, which in this case was dangerous. But if there was anyone I could trust to spill the whole story to, it was my oldest friend. No matter how many years it had been, we had picked up right where we'd left off. And I desperately needed to tell someone the truth of what had happened.

"Well," I said stirring my cider, "he was my seatmate and asked if I'd like to have a drink to pass the time. After the situation at the shop, I thought, why not?"

"Naturally," Billy agreed.

"We had lunch and got to talking and," I paused, looking around to be sure no one was listening, even though Billy and I were the only two in the reception area. Billy looked at me curiously, having already noted that there was no one else in the room.

"And?" he asked.

"And I felt something," I whispered.

"You, what?" he asked, unable to make out what I'd said.

"I felt something," I repeated.

"Oh, I see" he replied, nodding his understanding.

"I've never felt electricity like that with anyone, Billy. Not even Charlie."

"Wow. Did something happen?"

"Not really, no."

"Okay, you're going to need to give me the real story here. No skimming over the good parts!"

I took a deep breath. "Fine. We just clicked. I felt so comfortable with him, almost immediately. We talked about so many things. At one point, he wanted me to look at him and placed his hand under my chin, like this," I demonstrated.

"Nice move."

"It wasn't like that, Billy. I was upset about Charlie and fighting back tears. He traced his thumb along my jawline, and I thought I'd melt to the floor. I told him about Charlie's misgivings about my coming out here to dance and he said that 'if he were my husband, he'd be proud of me.'

"Whoa," he breathed, placing a hand over his heart. "That's forward. What did you say?"

"I didn't say anything. What could I say?" I asked, throwing my hands in the air.

"I don't know. I've never had such a romantic exchange."

"Neither had I. Thankfully, he understood and changed the subject."

Billy took a sip of his drink. I followed suit, hoping that it would give me the courage I needed to tell him what happened next.

"We talked about our dreams for the future and the most important people in our lives. It was like we'd always known each other," I continued. "And he was truly interested to hear about all of it."

"I hate to say it, but this is a pretty romantic story," Billy noted.

"I know!" I cried. "Then, as we returned to our seats, I tripped, and he caught me. I instinctively grabbed his neck so as not to fall. Once we stood up, we stayed like that longer than necessary, just holding each other. I didn't want it to end."

"Lottie, this sounds like a motion picture."

"Except it's my actual life, Billy."

"I guess it's not as romantic when you put it that way."

"Tell me about it," I sighed. "I feel like a hypocrite. One minute I'm storming off like a bat out of hell after seeing Charlie and Alice and in the next I'm cavorting a with handsome stranger on the train."

"All's fair in love and war. That's a cliché for a reason."

"True. It has me questioning everything."

"Of course, it does. This story has me questioning everything!" he exclaimed.

I laughed, "Well, I guess I'm in good company."

"How did you leave it?"

"I just told him that in another time things could've been different."

"That's a pretty clear ending," he said.

"And then I invited him to the show if he's still in the area when we open," I blurted out.

"Okay, maybe not so clear," he added.

CHAPTER NINETEEN

Billy took a long sip from his mug, thoughtfully considering my dilemma. I was hoping he'd have some helpful advice for me. I looked back at him, waiting. After a few minutes passed, I could no longer take the suspense.

"Well?" I asked.

He sighed. "I don't know. I'm at a loss with this one."

My shoulders dropped as I finally exhaled, just realizing that I'd been holding my breath in anticipation.

"There are just so many variables to consider," he continued. "You have your girls to think of."

"Of course. My girls always come first."

Considering my response, he replied, "Well, maybe that's part of your problem."

"How so?"

"Maybe that's a factor in your marriage. Charlie used to be number one and now he's taking a backseat to the girls."

"Billy, they're his children," I scoffed.

"Yes, but men need to be taken care of, Lottie. We need to feel important and appreciated. From what you've said about Alice, it sounds like she's giving Charlie the attention he's been missing from you."

I could feel heat creeping into my cheeks. Billy had hit a nerve. "Guess what, Billy? Women need the same damn thing. Yet we're expected to take care of everyone and everything, before even considering our own needs and, God forbid, wants. I gave up everything I wanted for myself so that

Charlie could open the garage. That was his dream. I wanted him to have it... but the one time I ask for something, the only time, he can't even try to be supportive?"

"Do you want to know what I do all day, Billy?" I ranted on. "Let's see. I get up early to make sure that Charlie has a hot meal to start the day. I make his lunch and a thermos of coffee. I'm not sure why I bother, with Alice bringing coffee over to him every afternoon. Then I get the girls up. I feed them, get Kathy to school, and make sure Penny has an activity to do while I plan meals for the week and make a shopping list. I start the laundry. I vacuum and dust. I scrub the bathrooms. And that's all before lunchtime!"

"Lottie," Billy interrupted, gently placing a hand over mine. "Calm down, honey. Nobody is making light of everything you do. I'm just trying to show you another perspective. As your friend."

I exhaled, raking my fingers through my hair. "I'm sorry, Billy. I'm just so tired of holding it all together on my own."

"You have a lot on your mind," he empathized. "To be honest, it sounds like all this has been a long time coming, and maybe Alice isn't the real issue here," he suggested. "Maybe she just brought everything to the surface."

I looked down at my half-empty mug of cider, stirring it with the vanilla bean Billy had garnished it with, a detail I knew Mrs. Hall would appreciate. Watching the caramel-colored liquid swirling inside the mug, I considered his take on the situation. Was I focusing my attention on the wrong person? Alice was a snake and an opportunist to be sure, but I had been treating Charlie like one of the chores I needed to cross off my to-do list for longer than I cared to admit.

"There might be some truth to that," I agreed begrudgingly. "You always see things so clearly. Where have you been all this time when I needed you?"

"Right here in Rockland," he said, gesturing like a ringmaster introducing the main event. "And none of us like to reveal our faults."

"I suppose I've just been going through the motions for a long time now."

"My guess is that Charlie's probably feeling the same way as you. But let's be honest, men, me excluded, of course, are not always great at communicating. It sounds as though you two need to talk."

"We do," I agreed. "I thought I'd fix things and tried calling after dinner, but he wasn't home. He had already called my mother with an excuse. She's staying at mine to watch over the girls while I'm away," I said as an aside. "Anyway, he still hadn't returned from work, which isn't like him. He's home at 5 p.m. on the dot every day. And he's never worked late to 'close out the month' as he claimed."

"Oh, I see," Billy replied, a line of concern wrinkling his forehead. "Well, don't jump to conclusions just yet. Talk to him first."

"Easy for you to say," I said, slumping back in my seat.

"Until you do talk to him, let's get back to Walt. You never told me what he looks like."

At the mere mention of Walt, I felt that familiar tingle shoot up my spine, a smile forming at the corners of my mouth without my knowledge. I pursed my lips, eyes drifting skyward, imagining him as I'd seen him last, standing on the platform in his suit. His dark hair in stark contrast with his light eyes. His strong hands...

"Lottie Dawson!" Billy exclaimed, interrupting my daydream.

"Abbott."

"Abbott, Dawson, who cares," Billy cried. "You're smitten!"

And I was.

CHAPTER TWENTY

I awoke to the shrill ring of the alarm clock, swiftly pressing the button to stop the offending sound. Plopping back down on the pillow, I took a cleansing breath, saying a quick prayer to whoever was listening for a good first rehearsal.

I quickly dressed, brushed my teeth, and fixed my hair. It was early still, but I always made a point to arrive a few minutes ahead of schedule whenever I had an appointment. You only have one shot to make a first impression. Best to make it a good one.

Grabbing my room key, I tossed it into my tote bag when I heard a lovely chirping at my window. Pulling the shades open, I spotted a bluebird sitting in the tree just outside.

"Well, I'll take that as a sign that my message was received," I said out loud. "May you bring me luck, little bird."

He chirped back a response as I threw my bag over my shoulder, heading down to the dining room. I was the first one seated, the other girls still sleeping off their night out. Billy approached with a hot cup of tea and a basket containing the day's bakery item wrapped up nicely in blue gingham cloth.

"Good morning, sunshine. You're here bright and early," he said. "And looking quite chipper if I may say so."

"It's just my nerves. I can't wait to work all of this out in rehearsal," I replied, rolling my head from side to side. "Our talk definitely helped."

"I'm glad. Fresh-from-the-oven blueberry muffins," he said, placing the basket on the table. "Made especially for you."

"Johnny is really rolling with this theme," I laughed. "Works for me. Blueberry muffins are my favorite."

"They're fabulous. Hey, break a leg today, Lot. Show these girls how it's done in Rockland."

"You know I will," I said, placing a warm muffin on my plate.

"I'll see you later. I want to hear all about your first day. Maybe I'll test out another cocktail on you later if you're lucky," he said, retreating to the kitchen.

"Can't wait," I called after him.

"Can't wait for what?" Judy asked, pulling up a chair beside me and looking flawless despite the late night.

"Good morning," I said. "Billy wants to meet later to hear about my first day. I'm nervous. It's been a while since I've been on stage."

"Stick with me. I'll show you the ropes," Judy said, placing a napkin on her lap.

"Thank you. I'm so glad you're here. I wasn't sure what I'd be walking into."

"I knew we'd get on as soon as I met you," she replied. "You're my kind of people."

I handed Judy the basket of warm muffins and the honey butter. Billy passed through with a cup of tea for her and a pitcher of fresh-squeezed orange juice for the table. Pouring a glass for each of us, I said, "I could get used to this treatment. I'm not used to being waited on."

"It is a nice perk of the job," she agreed.

"So, how was your night out?" I asked. "Did you find any suitable gentlemen?"

"I did. I started out the evening talking to a lovely man. A real handsome guy," she said.

"Oh? That's exciting!"

"It was. Until I mentioned that I was in the show, and he asked if I knew you."

"Oh, Judy, not again," I cried. "I'm almost afraid to ask. Who was it this time?"

"His name was Walt." I felt my eyes instantly grow wide, and my cheeks flush. "So, I take it you know him?" she gathered.

"You could say that," I began. "He was my seatmate on the train."

"He seemed quite taken with you, Lottie. He was disappointed when I told him that you hadn't come out with us. I spent the night dancing with his friend, Jack, who was another looker. You sure know how to pick 'em, lady," she said with an approving glance.

"I can't believe Walt was there. He told me he was going back home for a funeral."

"Jack said he dragged him out. Said his uncle wouldn't want him moping around on his account. I told him that I'd try to get you back over there tonight."

"Tonight?!" I panicked. "Judy, you recall that I'm married?"

"I do. But when's the last time you let loose? Everyone needs to let their hair down from time to time, Lottie. There's no law that says you can't have a good time just because you're hitched."

I remained silent, unable to think of the last time I went out on the town. "You're right," I agreed, popping the last bite of muffin into my mouth. Washing it down with some orange juice, I blotted my lips with my napkin.

"So, it's a date then?" she asked, buttering half of her muffin.

"I guess it's a date," I confirmed, wondering what I had just gotten myself into.

CHAPTER TWENTY-ONE

Judy and I walked the few blocks from the Inn to the rehearsal space at the community center together. The production was to move over to the theater once dress rehearsals began and the sets were finished. Walking into the building, memories of the time I spent here as a young girl flooded my mind. The same old-fashioned black wooden bench sat by the main entrance, exactly where it had been all those years ago. The walls had been given a fresh coat of paint and new flyers had been posted on the bulletin board. In comparison to what I recalled; the lobby seemed to have shrunk down over time. It had felt so much larger back then, as things often do when you're a kid.

All my Girl Scout meetings had been held here in the main assembly hall; the space now reserved for our rehearsals. Billy's mother had been our troop leader back then. He'd join us at meetings under the guise of assistant, pretending not to be interested in arts and crafts or selling cookies, but secretly enjoying every second of it. I would watch him with curiosity, my first attraction to a boy. He was one of the most sought-after boys by the girls in our school, as he was both handsome and smart.

At one of our Thursday evening meetings, Mrs. Jones taught us a course on hand tools. Afterward, we were tasked with the job of building birdhouses to be hung outside in the community garden. Billy had gone out to his mother's car to get the necessary supplies as well as the Handywoman badges we'd earn upon completion.

I wasn't feeling particularly well and had excused myself to the restroom. When I sat down on the toilet, I spotted a few drops of fresh, red blood on my panties. Luckily, I caught it early enough that it didn't bleed through to my skirt. Panicked and alone, I cleaned up as best I could. I was ill-prepared for my entrance into womanhood. Worrying that everyone would know that I had just started my monthlies, I went searching for a sanitary napkin.

I peeked my head out of the bathroom, making sure that the coast was clear, before creeping down the hallway to the health office. Silently opening the door, I flipped the light switch, gasping at the realization that I wasn't alone.

Billy Jones and Bobby Dean stood entwined before me, badges and supplies in a box at their feet. They quickly separated, averting their eyes to the linoleum.

"I'm..." I began, having no more words to finish my thought. I turned on my heel, hastily flicking the light switch, and taking off down the hallway.

"Charlotte! Wait!" Billy called, chasing after me. I stopped, turning to face him, cheeks flushed with embarrassment. "Charlotte, that wasn't-" he stammered. "We weren't-"

"I didn't see a thing," I quietly replied, looking down at my saddle shoes.

Billy exhaled, running his fingers through his thick hair, his shoulders slumping as he leaned against the wall. "I... thank you," he finished, catching his breath.

The next thing I knew, hot tears were splashing onto my cheeks. I turned my head, hoping he hadn't noticed. I was now officially a woman, alone with my first love interest who didn't even like girls. This was turning out to be a fantastic day.

"Hey," he said, grabbing my hand, "are you okay?"

"I just, there's something I need in the office," I explained.

"Okay, c'mon," he said, pulling me back down the hall. "Let's go get it. I have to go back for the supplies anyway or my mother will have my head."

I smiled. Mrs. Jones was a stickler for getting things done in a timely fashion. If she knew what Billy had really been up to, I shuddered at the thought. "Thanks," I said, and we walked back together, still holding hands, both a little shaken after having experienced big firsts that evening.

* * *

Judy and I entered the rehearsal space, placing our things along the back wall. After changing into our tap shoes, we began to stretch. The other girls filed in shortly after.

"Anything I should know before we start?" I asked.

"The choreographer can be a bit full of himself, but he's a genius."

"Okay, got it."

"Just be sure your form is on point, and you'll be fine."

"Will do."

A cacophony of rapid-fire claps echoed through the hall, quickly garnering our attention. "Ladies! Ladies! We don't have much time to get this show in tip-top shape, so let's get down to business. I see that Charlotte has arrived," the choreographer nodded in my direction, "so I will be counting on all of you to get her up to speed. We're going to start with the first number on 8. Places, please."

As I looked at him, I realized I had seen him before. I might not always remember names, but I never forgot a face. Who was he?

"Charlotte, why don't you join me up front for the first run-through, and then you'll jump in," he called out. "And 5, 6, 7, 8!"

Walking toward him as the girls burst into action, the image of Billy and Bobby flashed before my eyes. I knew exactly where I had seen him before! Bobby Dean was choreographing the show?! Why hadn't Billy told me?

"Charlotte," he said, extending a welcome hand, "so pleased that you could be here. I recommended you to Garrett, even though I knew it was a long shot with you having been away so long."

"Wow, Bobby, I had no idea you were on choreography," I replied.

"Mr. Dean," he said conspiratorially, "at least while we're working. I have to live up to my reputation."

"Mr. Dean," I corrected myself. "This is wild. Thank you so much for the recommendation. I can't begin to tell you how grateful I am to be here."

"Thank Billy. It was his idea. Anything to get his old friend back, but don't tell him I told you so," he explained. "He didn't want you to think that was the only reason you're here. To be honest with you, I only made it happen because I know you have the talent we need."

"I hope so. I'm a little rusty, but I'll do whatever it takes to prove that I deserve to be here."

"Good answer," he said. "Now get out there and show me what you've got."

CHAPTER TWENTY-TWO

"Let's take five, ladies!" Mr. Dean commanded. "That's lunch! Be back in an hour!"

Quickly wiping the sweat from my forehead, I headed over to my bag, desperate for a drink of water.

"So, what do you think so far?" Judy asked.

"I think I'm out of shape for starters," I said somewhat breathlessly.

"Oh honey, you're doing great out there. It's only your first day and you've kept up the entire time."

"Thanks," I said, grateful for Judy's positive attitude. "You're right. Maybe I'm being too hard on myself."

"Give it a minute. You just need to acclimate," she assured me. "And going out dancing tonight will be just the ticket for you to blow off some steam and relax." I had momentarily forgotten about our plans for the evening. Mixed feelings of dread and excitement were suddenly coursing through me. My face must've reflected how I felt. "Don't tell me you've changed your mind," Judy chided.

"No. I just," I began, resting my head on my knees. "Oh, Judy, I've really gotten myself into it."

"What's going on?"

"I'll fill you in on the walk over to the Inn," I said, changing into my Keds. "This isn't something I want the other girls to hear."

"I won't say a word," she promised. "Let's take the long way, just to be safe."

Picking up our bags, we headed for the exit. We stepped out onto Main

Street, hanging a left and heading away from the Inn. As we rounded the building, away from the rest of the girls, I began to fill Judy in on everything that had happened the day I arrived in Rockland.

* * *

"Well, that's quite a story. I'm surprised you've been holding up so well since you arrived. I never would've known you were dealing with all of that," Judy said.

"I don't like to let anyone see me sweat," I replied. "Besides, there were lots of distractions to keep my mind off things."

"So, what now?"

"Darned if I know. I'm just trying to focus on the show," I said. "I'm hesitant to see Walt again."

"I can understand that. I'm sorry I pushed you to meet up with him. If I'd known all of this, I might've thought twice."

"Judy, it's not your fault. I could've said no. There's a part of me that didn't want to."

"Well, I'll be right by your side tonight, so if you want to leave, you just say the word."

"I appreciate that. Walt is a gentleman, so I'm not concerned about anything untoward happening. I'm just worried about how I'm going to feel when I see him."

"It sounds like he's had an effect on you for sure," she mused. "What if you were supposed to meet him? What if this is destiny?"

"I'd be lying if I said that thought hadn't crossed my mind," I confided in my new friend. "But I'm married with a life and a family hundreds of miles from here. This isn't my real life. Even if I wanted it to be," I said wistfully.

"Well, why don't you see how tonight goes?" Judy asked. "We'll keep it casual, a group hangout."

Reaching the Inn, we climbed the front steps. Mrs. Hall was tidying the front porch, making sure the rockers were evenly spaced.

"Good afternoon, ladies. Lunch is on," she called.

"Thanks, Mrs. Hall," we sang back in unison.

"Charlotte there's a message for you at the front desk. Ask Billy for it," she hollered to me.

"Will do, thanks!" I replied.

The heavenly scent of freshly baked bread greeted us as we stepped through the door. I also detected the savory aroma of beef and wine, hoping that Johnny had prepared beef stew for lunch today. My stomach grumbled loudly at the thought of a piping hot bowl.

"Hungry?" Judy laughed.

"Apparently more than I realized."

"Let's eat!" she said, leading the way to our table in the dining room. The rest of the girls had already begun their meals and I was happy to see that my hunch was correct.

"That looks amazing," I said, sitting down next to Nancy.

"Oh my gosh, Lottie, it is. The chef here is great," she replied.

From the other end of the table, Bianca said, "Glad you two made it, we were going to send a search party."

"Not to worry," Judy jumped in before I could respond. "Just taking in a little fresh air on this lovely day."

"I see," Bianca replied. "I hope rehearsal wasn't too much for you, Charlotte."

"Not at all," I assured her. "I just thought it would be fun to take a little walk around my hometown. It's been so long since I've been back. It was nice to see all my old haunts, and to share that with Judy."

"I loved seeing this place through your eyes," Judy agreed.

"Cute," Bianca said, turning to Kay, clearly no longer interested in our conversation.

"Judy, she's not coming tonight, is she?" I asked, nodding toward Bianca.

"No way. She never comes out with us. She's probably sewing up voodoo dolls in her room instead," Judy laughed.

"I wouldn't be surprised," I chuckled.

Billy appeared with two bowls of beef stew, freshly baked rolls, and green salads tossed with homemade balsamic vinaigrette. "Bon appétit, ladies," he announced, placing our meals before us. "Oh, and Lot, this is for you," he said handing me a folded note card. "Charlie called," he quietly informed me, eyebrows raised.

"Thanks," I said tentatively taking it from him.

"Read it later," he instructed. "How's rehearsal so far?"

"It's going great," I replied. "We have an amazing choreographer."

"Oh?" he said implying ignorance.

"Yes. I think you'd really be impressed with him," I hinted.

Billy smiled, "I'll have to check out his work."

"Uh-huh," I mumbled sarcastically.

As Billy went back to work, I shook my head, tucking into my bowl of stew. The savory flavors of beef stock and wine warmed me through. From the first taste, I was reminded of winter afternoons playing in the snow as a little girl. At the first snowfall each year, my mother would set her stew to simmer on the stove all day, so the meat fell apart in your mouth. I would come inside frozen to the core and after one bite, that chill was gone.

Billy's stew was wonderful, on par with Mom's. It brought me right back to that time and made me feel closer to her. This was the next best thing while we were so far apart, especially since my world felt like it had been turned upside down. Even as an adult, I still needed my mom sometimes. But this particular dilemma was one I wasn't sure she'd understand.

CHAPTER TWENTY-THREE

Moving through the steps of the routine I'd learned that morning, I was holding my own alongside the rest of the troupe. It felt great to be dancing again. I didn't realize how much I'd missed it all these years. We came together for a kick line, Bianca to my left. As we raised our left legs in unison, she swiftly hip-checked me, almost knocking me off my feet. Luckily, Judy was on my right side and kept me balanced and upright.

"Whoops lost my footing there," Bianca explained, an angelic expression on her face.

"You're lucky Mr. Dean missed that. Watch it," I shot back.

"I don't know what you mean, Charlotte. It was an accident," she demurred.

I managed to make it through the afternoon without further incident. I certainly wasn't in the fighting form of my younger years but refused to let on. I assumed Bianca's attempts to sabotage me wouldn't stop anytime soon, so I'd need to stay alert.

"Ladies, great rehearsal!" Mr. Dean bellowed out to the troupe. "Kay, Barbara, I need you to put some more power behind your kicks! Mary M., posture! Jean," he called, pantomiming a showbiz grin with index fingers pulling at each corner of his mouth," I want to see those pearly whites! Remember, you're having the time of your life out there. We want the audience to feel your enthusiasm." Turning his attention to me, he said, "Charlotte, I have to admit it, I'm impressed. Still at the top of your game."

I felt a reassuring hand on my shoulder. "See, honey?" Judy whispered.

"You've still got it and she knows it," she nodded in Bianca's direction.

"Great work, ladies!" Mr. Dean continued. "Enjoy your Sunday morning off and I will see you back here tomorrow at 1 p.m. sharp."

"Thanks, Judy," I replied.

At that moment, I caught Bianca's eye. She looked none too pleased. Flashing my sweetest grin in her direction, I was met with an icy glare and a sour grimace. Bianca looked as though she'd just bitten into a lemon.

Judy caught the exchange calling out, "Great rehearsal today, Bianca. Your form is really improving! Lottie here could probably give you a few pointers to really perfect your footing though." Stifling the laugh that threatened to escape my lips, I reached back to whack Judy.

"Troublemaker," I whispered back to her.

"I guess that's something that comes with age," Bianca retorted in her measured tone.

"Oh, I don't know honey, I think for Lottie it's just natural, much like her flawless skin. One would think she was your age if she didn't know better" Judy cracked back. "But don't worry, there's always practice. You'll catch up." Bianca glared at Judy. I wouldn't have been surprised if actual daggers had shot out from her stare. "Rehearsal room is still free for another hour," Judy announced, glancing at the clock. "No time like the present."

Gathering my things, I called out, "See you all at dinner!"

"See you later!" a few of the girls called back.

Hoping to escape this tête-à-tête between Judy and Bianca, I stood up and motioned toward the exit. Judy joined me, linking her arm through mine. "You're terrible," I said quietly, leaning in so no one would overhear.

"She was being a pistol. She asked for it," Judy rationalized. "Besides, no one picks on my friends but me."

"Good to know," I chuckled. "You know, I've really missed spending time with girlfriends. There's nothing quite like it."

"Especially when you've got a common enemy," she laughed. "That's when the real fun begins."

* * *

CHAPTER TWENTY-THREE

Back at the Inn, I flopped down on the bed, exhausted from the whirlwind of new choreography and nonstop rehearsing. Even still, my day was far from over. We'd be heading out to the dance hall tonight. My anxiety and, dare I say, excitement, at the thought of seeing Walt again was enough to quell any fatigue I felt.

I began unpacking my tote when the message Billy had passed to me at lunch slid out onto the coverlet. I opened the note card containing a dictated message from Charlie in Mrs. Hall's sprawling penmanship.

Lottie, ring me as soon as possible. Please let me explain. - Charlie

Folding the note card closed, I placed it on the night table next to the telephone. Well, that was to the point. No apology. No *Love, Charlie.* Not the groveling note I'd expected.

It was almost a quarter to five. If I called the shop now, I might catch him before he headed home for the day. Reaching for the telephone, I dialed the number to the shop, tentatively listening to the ringtone.

"Charlie's Garage," a gruff voice said over the line.

"Yes, I'd like to speak to Charlie," I replied.

"Just a second, ma'am. Let me see if he's still here."

"Thank you," I said. I could hear mechanical sounds and tools clanging and then a voice calling out for Charlie. Moments later the same person picked up the handset again.

"Looks like you just missed him. Care to leave a message?"

"No, thanks. I'll try back another time. Thank you," I said, replacing the handset on the cradle.

It was early still to call home, so I decided to get washed up for dinner and the evening out. Running the water until I could see the steam begin to rise, I stepped into the shower. The ringing of the telephone in my room was swallowed up by the sounds of the shower and the vent fan in the bathroom. I stood there, hot water raining down on me, relishing the calm.

CHAPTER TWENTY-FOUR

I awoke to a soft knock at the door. For a moment I forgot where I was, disoriented from my impromptu nap. Tightening the sash on my robe, I opened the door a crack to see who was there.

"Honey! You're still in your robe? Dinner is in thirty minutes!" Judy cried.

I let the door swing wide, allowing Judy into the room. She wore a royal blue A-line dress with a square neckline and pearl button detailing. A thin belt in matching blue fabric circled her trim waist. Her hair was set perfectly, not a strand out of place, and her lips were stained a deep crimson color.

"Judy, you look amazing!" I cried. Looking down at my robe I said, "I'm going to need some help if I'm going to be ready on time."

"No worries, I'm here now," she assured me. "Wow. They really like you around here, huh? This room is fabulous!"

"Thanks. Perks of joining the troupe late when there aren't many rooms to choose from," I explained. "But Mrs. Hall and I go way back, so she definitely took care of me."

"I'd say. I feel like a Hollywood starlet in here," she mused, taking in the decor. "So, what are you wearing tonight? Let's see what you've got." Judging by the look on her face as she peered into my closet, it was clear that I wasn't prepared for many nights out. My simple dresses paled in comparison to Judy's fashionable look. I turned to her, shrugging my shoulders. "You packed light, huh? Lucky for you, we're about the same size and I always have options. I'll be right back," Judy called over her shoulder as she exited my room.

Sighing, I sat down at the vanity to put on my face. As I got to work applying facial cream in upward strokes in the constant battle to keep gravity at bay, my nerves came back in full force. I had no idea what to expect this evening. What was I thinking going along with this? I couldn't see Walt again. I was asking for trouble.

"Knock, knock," Judy interrupted my thought as she entered the room with various frocks. There were solids, florals, lace accents, cap sleeves, an off-the-shoulder style, and even a strapless dress.

"Judy," I breathed, getting up to take a closer look. "These are beautiful. You've brought a boutique to my room."

"Fashion and dance are my first loves, especially since I've yet to find a man who can compete," she chuckled. "Now let's see which of these says 'Lottie'." Judy held up an ice blue and cream number with a lace bodice and chiffon skirt. Tilting her head to the side, she considered it. "Too formal," she decided. "And not enough flounce in the skirt for dancing. Let's try this one," she said, holding up a strapless floral option with a full skirt.

"I don't know about strapless. I need something I can really move in without constantly worrying that my dress is covering everything it's supposed to."

"Noted," Judy replied. "In that case, I think we skip the off-the-shoulder, though I think that ruby shade would've knocked their socks off."

"What about this one?" I said, running my fingers along the skirt of an emerald green dress with black piping at the neckline.

"Yes, this one is perfect. Here," she said handing it to me. "Try it on and show me."

I took the dress into the bathroom and slipped it over my head. The emerald color brought out the green flecks in my hazel eyes and worked well with my complexion. Not bad, I thought.

"Well, come on out. Let's see," Judy called. When I opened the door, she gasped in delight, clutching her hands together. "It's perfect! Let me zip you up." Judy zipped the back, and I was instantly transformed. The dress looked as though it was tailored especially for me. It perfectly skimmed my curves and highlighted my best assets. "Lottie. You may need to keep this dress. It's never looked this good on me."

"Oh no, Judy, I couldn't. I seriously doubt that. I do love it though," I said, twirling in front of the mirror, watching as the skirt billowed out around me.

"Between the sweetheart neckline and the black sash," she said, straightening the bow on the sash at my waist, "you've got killer curves, Lottie. I'm a little jealous, to be honest."

"Judy, give me a break!" I laughed. "You're a knockout, who are you kidding?"

"All I know is that we make a pretty impressive pair," she said, examining our reflection in the floor-length mirror. "Those men better watch out tonight!" Laughing, I retrieved my black peep-toe dancing shoes from the wardrobe and slipped them on. "Now, about your hair..." Judy started. "Let's get those rollers out and get to work."

"Yes, ma'am," I said with a salute.

"I'm glad you know who's boss," she joked.

"I wouldn't dream of defying your orders," I laughed. "I'm just happy to have my hair done. No one ever fusses over me."

"Well, it's about time someone did. Here's your Cinderella moment, Lottie. After I work my magic, all eyes will be on you" she said with a wink.

That's what I'm afraid of, I thought, an image of Walt as Prince Charming popping into my head. As Judy brushed my hair and pinned it into place, I couldn't help but wonder if my luck would run out at midnight.

CHAPTER TWENTY-FIVE

Studying myself in the mirror, I almost didn't recognize the glamorous woman, perfectly coiffed and dressed to kill, peering back at me. I turned my head, considering every angle.

"Flawless. My work here is done," Judy announced, snapping my cosmetics case shut.

"Well, I have to say, you definitely have a knack for this stuff. If dance doesn't pan out, there's always the beauty field. I don't recognize myself. In a good way," I added with a laugh.

"You look exactly like yourself," she said. "I've just highlighted your cheekbones, accented those hazel eyes, and exaggerated your already full lips. You're a great subject. It's you that made me look good."

"Happy to oblige," I smiled. "And for the final touch," I said, opening the small jewelry box on the vanity. "My string of pearls." Carefully lifting the necklace out of the box and closing the lid, I handed it to Judy. "Mind doing the honors?" I asked.

"Of course," she replied. "These are beautiful."

"They were a gift from my father when I turned sixteen. He passed away shortly after. This necklace is the last thing he ever gave me."

"What a wonderful keepsake. This way, he's always with you," she said, fastening the clasp at my neck. I placed a hand over the pearls, remembering the day my dad had given them to me.

"You're a young woman now, Charlotte," he had said, standing behind me to fasten the clasp. "Every woman should have a string of pearls. They signify wisdom, honesty, and dignity; all traits I see in you. I'm so proud of the woman

you're becoming, and I look forward to seeing all the things you'll accomplish," he beamed. *"This necklace belonged to my mother. I've been saving it all these years for your sixteenth birthday. I know you'll care for it and pass it on to someone special someday."*

Recalling his words brought tears to my eyes. I hoped that wherever he was, he was proud of me.

"Honey, no tears," Judy said giving me a little squeeze. "You don't want to ruin your makeup."

"You're right," I said sniffling. "It just took me back for a minute. I really miss him."

"I know. I bet he's looking down on you and so proud of everything you've accomplished," she said. "You're living your dream! How many people can honestly say that?"

Patting me on the shoulder, she exited the bathroom to allow me a moment alone to compose myself. I knew she was right. Dad loved to watch me perform and was my greatest supporter. He'd be happy to see that I'd returned home to finally reach my goal. Frowning, I wondered what he'd think of this business with Charlie and Walt. I wasn't sure how dignified it all was. Hopefully, he didn't see that sort of thing. There were some things fathers didn't ever need to know about their daughters.

"We'd better get down to dinner before Bianca actually sends a search party," Judy called from the bedroom.

"Coming," I called, checking my reflection one last time, and vowing to do my best to live up to everything this necklace symbolized.

* * *

As Judy and I entered the dining room I heard a low whistle call from behind us. I turned to see Billy heading in our direction carrying a tray of drinks.

Blushing, I said, "Hi, Billy."

"Hi, indeed. You two look fantastic! Big plans?" he asked.

"We're heading out to the dance hall tonight, care to join?" Judy asked, batting her lashes at Billy.

"I just might take you up on that," Billy replied. "It's been ages since I've been for a proper night out."

Leaning in close, I whispered to Billy, "Walt's going to be there."

Gasping audibly, a wide-eyed Billy wrapped an arm around my shoulders and said, "In that case, count me in. I'll meet you two in the lobby once my shift is over, and we can head over together. Lucky for you, I always keep a change of clothes here should an opportunity such as this present itself."

"Always be prepared," I laughed, replicating the Girl Scouts Promise hand sign and quoting Mrs. Jones.

"Mom still says that to me," Billy chuckled, shaking his head.

"Once a scout leader always a scout leader. We'll meet you then," I paused. "Billy, I'm nervous."

"You'll be fine," he reassured me. "Plus, Judy and I will be there, what could go wrong?"

"So many things."

"Relax, Lot. Go and enjoy your dinner and we'll talk later. Think of this as a long-overdue night on the town with your best childhood pal."

"And fab new girlfriend," Judy chimed in.

"When you put it that way, I'm almost excited," I quipped.

"I've got to get back to my tables," Billy announced. "I'll see you two later."

Judy and I continued to our table. As we approached, I heard someone mutter, "Well, well, look what the cat dragged in."

Bianca.

"Wow, girls. Look at you two!" Nancy exclaimed.

"You look amazing!" the Marys said in unison.

"Thanks, girls," Judy said. "We just felt like getting dolled up and treating ourselves to a night out after a long day of rehearsals."

"Sounds fun, can we join?" Jean asked.

"Sure, everyone's welcome," Judy replied. "The more the merrier, right?"

"Right," I tenuously agreed, unsure of how I felt about all the girls seeing me with Walt.

"Great, I could use a night out," Jean said. "I'm in."

"Us too!" Mary M. responded for herself, Mary L., and Linda.

"Don't forget about afternoon rehearsals tomorrow, ladies," Nancy warned, always the voice of reason of the group.

Bianca, Barbara, and Kay expressed no interest in joining, which was fine by me. Barbara and Kay seemed harmless, even nice enough, but Bianca was another story. I could feel her steely gaze trained on me like a cat patiently waiting for the perfect opportunity to pounce.

"Not very subtle, is she?" Judy asked, nodding in Bianca's direction.

"I'd say no," I agreed.

"Well, at least she's not coming tonight. And don't worry, we'll just tell the girls that Walt's an old friend, just like Johnny and Billy. It's no biggie, Lottie," Judy said in a hushed tone. "You're from Rockland. No one will even think a thing of it."

"Okay," I nodded. "I hope you're right."

"If anyone can put a spin on things, it's me. You just focus on having a good time tonight. Leave the rest to me," Judy said.

CHAPTER TWENTY-SIX

In the lobby, Judy and I sat at a table by the window while Billy changed for our night out. I was charged with nervous energy, absentmindedly drumming my fingernails on the table.

"Honey," Judy said, pressing her palm down on my hand, "you're going to bore a hole through the table if you keep that up. Relax."

The breath I hadn't noticed I was holding in came out in a huff. "I'm sorry, Judy. I'm just so anxious."

"This guy has really gotten under your skin," she observed.

"He has," I admitted reluctantly. "To tell you the truth, I'm afraid I'll feel the same as I did on the train, and then what will I do?"

"Well, at least you'll know either way. Maybe it was only the stress of just having seen Charlie and that other woman that made you romanticize the train ride?"

"Maybe." I replied skeptically.

"Ladies," Billy announced, strutting in wearing a navy suit and wing-tipped shoes. He ran a hand through his hair, flashing a dazzling grin and regarding us with what could only be described as bedroom eyes.

"As humble as ever," I laughed.

"You clean up real nice, Billy," Judy said, admiring his look.

"Why, thank you, miss," he replied, grabbing Judy with both hands, and twirling her into a spin. He gently dipped her before returning her to her seat.

"My, my," she said, sitting back down and smoothing her hair. "You sure know how to impress a lady."

"Billy is the king of impressing the ladies," I noted.

"Too bad I'm not interested in them," he laughed, pulling a chair over to our table. "Now, shall we have a drink before we head over? Looks like my old friend could use one," he said, nodding in my direction.

"She certainly could," Judy answered for me. "A little liquid courage should do the trick."

"Coming right up," Billy said, disappearing behind the bar.

"It's a shame that he's batting for the other team," Judy said, eyebrows raised. "He's a good-looking guy, smart and fun too. The trifecta."

"Tell me about it," I commiserated. "He was my first crush, and boy was I crushed when I found out." Billy emerged with a tray and 3 glasses garnished with a cinnamon stick and a vanilla bean.

"What is this concoction?" Judy asked.

"This is my Gingerbread Fizz. It's the perfect winter drink and has the added benefit of calming the stomach."

"I like how you think," she said, casting a pointed look at me.

"Thanks, Billy. It'll be a miracle if this can calm my nerves," I said, taking a glass. "Nice touch with the garnish per usual."

"Try it," he prodded. "And be honest."

"Mm," we responded in unison, tasting the subtle hints of ginger, nutmeg, and vanilla.

"This tastes like Christmas in a glass!" Judy exclaimed.

"It really does! This may be better than the last drink you made for me. You really know what you're doing behind the bar."

"Oh, I'm so happy to hear you say that! I've been tweaking this recipe for weeks trying to come up with the perfect ratios," he explained.

"Well, it looks like you did it," I assured him.

"Bottoms up, ladies! We have a night to begin!" Billy exclaimed, throwing back his drink. Judy and I followed suit, draining our glasses, ready to see where the night would take us.

* * *

The illuminated sign for The Rockland was like a beacon on Main Street. Groups of young people hurried toward the dance hall, eager to get the night started. Billy opened the door and a rush of sounds hit us; jaunty music, laughter, and lively conversation filled the air. Judy immediately perked up, ready to take on the night.

"Come on, Lottie," she called, grabbing my hand and dragging me into the crowd. "This place is really hopping tonight!"

Propelled toward the dance floor with my friend, my head swiveled left and right searching out Walt. "Judy, wait. Shouldn't we find the other girls first?"

"I suppose you're right; I forgot my manners once I heard the music. Let's go see if they've gotten a table." We headed toward a row of tables flanking the dance floor. Searching the crowd for familiar faces, I recognized a few girls from the troupe.

"I see Linda and the Marys," I yelled over the music, pointing in their direction.

"Ah, I see them now," Judy replied. "Let's go and say hello, and then I'm back on the dance floor."

"Sounds like a plan," I said.

As we approached the girls, arm-in-arm, I heard my name. Half-expecting to see Billy, I spun back, whipping Judy around with me. I stopped dead in my tracks when I locked eyes with Walt. Frozen in place, I couldn't move or speak. Recognizing my apparent paralysis, Judy jumped in to save me.

"Walt!" she cried, "great to see you again! Isn't it, Lottie?" I nodded in agreement.

"Evening, Judy, nice to see you as well," Walt said. "Lottie, I'm glad I ran into your friend and happy to see that you made it out tonight."

I smiled, "It's nice to see you again, Walt."

"Yes, well I was just heading over to get the rest of the girls. It seems like you two have a lot to catch up on," Judy explained, pushing me toward Walt. "Why don't you find a table on the balcony level where you can actually hear one another talk?" she suggested, pointing toward the stairwell.

"Good idea, Judy," Walt agreed. "As long as that's alright with you, Lottie."

"Uh, yes," I managed to reply. "It is quite loud by the band."

Feeling an arm circle my waist, I looked up to see Billy. "There you are, Lottie. I lost you two for a second there." Billy made the connection that we were standing in front of Walt and offered his hand. "Billy Jones, childhood friend of Charlotte here."

"Nice to meet you. Walter Beckett, but you can call me Walt."

"Nice to meet you, Walt. I've heard great things," Billy announced, catching my gaze, and nodding his approval.

"Walt, is your friend Jack here tonight?" Judy asked.

"He's around here somewhere. I think he was hoping for a dance."

"I think I can spare one," Judy laughed. "If you see him, let him know I can be found on the dance floor."

"Will do," Walt chuckled.

"Come on, Billy. Let's get the girls. There's a night to be had." At that, Judy dragged Billy off to the dance floor, leaving Walt and me standing on our own.

"Hi," Walt said.

"Hi," I replied. It was as if we were the only two people standing in that crowded room. My instincts were right. I did have something to be afraid of. Things felt exactly the same and if I wasn't careful, I was going to have a hard time honoring the promise I'd made earlier.

"Shall we?" Walt gestured to the stairwell leading to the second-floor balcony level.

"Yes, let's." Climbing the stairs, I instinctively reached for the string of pearls around my neck, hoping for some guidance from above. I was really getting myself into a pickle. Rolling the pearls between my fingers, I remembered my dad's words, "Dignity, honesty, wisdom."

Here goes nothing.

CHAPTER TWENTY-SEVEN

I chose a table overlooking the dance floor, imagining a visual lifeline connecting me to my friends. Walt pulled out a chair for me to sit on, gently pushing it in toward the table before sitting down himself. We sat, smiling at one another for a beat.

"So," he started.

"So," I replied, a smile teasing at the corners of my mouth.

"Well, I'm just going to say it," Walt began, "this is awkward."

I burst out laughing. "Agreed," I said, thankful that he'd broken the tension. "At least we're on the same page. I wasn't sure what to expect after the train."

"Same here. To be honest with you, I was hoping to run into you last night when Jack dragged me out. It was just a coincidence that I met Judy."

"When she said she'd met you I couldn't believe it. Interesting coincidence," I mused, tilting my head.

"How so?"

"Well, of all the people you could've talked to who were out on a Friday night during the busiest season of the year, you just happened to talk to the one person I've become good friends with. Like I said, interesting coincidence."

"Maybe it was one of those signs you were telling me to look out for."

My cheeks flushed. What was I doing? Why was I flirting? I couldn't help myself around this man. This was going to be harder than I thought. Switching to a more neutral topic, I said, "Speaking of signs, I actually had another bluebird sighting the morning before rehearsals."

"Ah, so your father is here with you."

"Seems like it."

"And how are rehearsals going?" he asked.

"It's tough. I'm not in the shape I used to be, but I'm keeping up. The choreographer gave me some really positive feedback today so I'm feeling good about the show."

"That's great," Walt said, his voice deepening as his eyes swept over me, "you look to be in perfect shape if you ask me." Blushing once more, I turned my gaze to the dance floor. "Lottie," he said, waiting for my attention. "You look beautiful tonight."

"Thanks, Walt," I said quietly. "You look very handsome yourself."

"Thank you."

We watched the crowd below moving to the music. Carefree pairs and raucous groups moving in harmony on the dance floor. It was such a contrast to our quiet conversation. We were in our own little world, yet again.

"Lottie?"

Looking up at Walt I saw that he'd been watching me with a nervous, yet determined expression set on his chiseled face. I was almost afraid to hear what he had to say, but at the same time couldn't wait to hear it.

"There's something I need to say," he confided. "I told myself when I left the platform that day that if I ever saw you again, I would be honest with you."

"Okay," I tentatively replied.

"This is going to sound crazy, but ever since the train, I haven't stopped thinking about you. I know that we've only spent a few hours together, but I've never felt this way before. I've found myself imagining a life with you, Lottie." I sat silent, barely breathing, as he voiced everything I had been thinking. "I know that probably sounds crazy and nothing can come of this, but I just wanted you to know that meeting you has made me feel," he paused, searching for the right word, "alive."

It was the most romantic thing anyone had ever said to me.

"I know."

Walt grabbed my hand in both of his. The warmth of his hands on mine somehow gave me chills. I shuddered. He smiled, recognizing his effect on me, and pulled my hand closer to him. Bending his head, he gently kissed the back of my hand. It was a sweet, old-fashioned gesture, so unexpected that my heart caught in my throat for a moment. When his soft lips met my skin, I felt a warm tingle travel through my body. An overwhelming desire to kiss him came over me.

"Walt," I whispered. He looked up and I could see everything I needed to in his eyes. My body felt like it was on fire. I had never wanted anything or anyone so badly. "Can we go somewhere?" I asked. "I think I need some air."

"Of course. Fresh air would do us good."

* * *

The cold night air rushed over my bare arms. I took a deep breath, it's briskness burning my lungs. Shivering, I wrapped my arms tightly around myself. In my haste to get outside, I hadn't grabbed my overcoat. Noticing my goosebumps, Walt removed his jacket, carefully draping it over my shoulders. "Thanks," I said. "But won't you be cold?"

"I'm perfectly fine. Don't worry about me," he said. "Now where to? Do you want to take a walk?"

"Yes, I know the perfect spot," I said leading Walt away from the dance hall.

"Won't your friends be worried?" he asked.

"Knowing Judy, she's tearing up that dance floor and won't have any plans of leaving soon. Besides, it's not far. We won't be gone long." We walked side by side in silence. As we moved away from the dance hall, the quiet of the night surrounded us and I was finally able to relax. "I'm sorry if I've been acting strange this evening," I began, "I've just been so anxious about seeing you."

"It's okay. I understand. You're in a much tougher spot than me."

"True," I agreed. "But I can't pretend I'm not feeling something very real." Flurries began to fall around us. The first snowfall of the season. Trying to catch snowflakes on my tongue, I laughed at how ridiculous I must've looked until Walt joined in. "Here we are," I said. We had reached the old bridge. The sound of the river below was always so soothing to me. "I used to come here when I was a girl. It was my favorite place to think. I've always loved the sound of rushing water."

"Soothing," he replied, reading my mind.

"Exactly." Walking to the middle of the bridge, I looked over the railing down to the river rushing beneath our feet. I watched as the water surged over the rocks, crashing into the banks.

"What are you thinking now?" he asked. I looked at Walt who was awaiting my response, hands in his pockets, standing in the cold in his dress shirt as snowflakes fell lightly around us. How could I possibly tell him what I was thinking?

"I'm not," I breathed, and in a split second I was reaching up to gently pull his face toward mine. Our bodies automatically came together as if by some magnetic pull. He pulled me closer until there was no space between us. My hands slid behind his neck, my fingertips trailing up into his hair. Our eyes locked and there was no stopping what I'd just started. When our lips met, the familiar spark of warmth and electricity we created together buzzed through me. At that moment, nothing else mattered. I needed to be wrapped up in Walt's arms. I needed that electricity coursing through my veins. I needed to feel alive again.

CHAPTER TWENTY-EIGHT

The snap of a twig breaking underfoot brought me back to reality fast. Pulling away as quickly as I had initiated the kiss, my head swiveled, trying to locate where the sound had come from, but there was no one around.

Walt followed suit, replying, "Don't worry. There's no one here but us."

Relieved, yet still shocked by my behavior, I cried out, "I'm sorry!" Distraught, I wrung my hands, pacing. It was as though my body had gone on autopilot, blocking any input from my brain. *So that's how these things happened.*

"Lottie. I'm sorry," Walt said, gently resting his hands on my shoulders to calm me down. "I shouldn't have let that happen."

Placing my hands down on the railing, I hung my head. My left hand reached for my pearls and instantly my father's words ran through my head. What had I done?

"Lottie," Walt gently prodded, placing an arm around me. "It's okay."

"What have I done, Walt?!" I cried.

"What have *we* done," he corrected.

"Oh, God. I don't know what came over me. I'm so sorry."

"It's okay. I usually have great self-control," he said. He looked truly upset with himself, shouldering the blame for my action. "I just couldn't stop myself, but I should've tried harder for your sake."

"And now I've ruined a perfect moment."

"You couldn't, Lottie," he assured me. "I won't forget this as long as I live. No matter what happens between us. Most people hope to experience a connection like this with another person, though I suspect most never do."

"How has no one snapped you up? Even after all this, you're doing everything you can to comfort me."

"It's a mystery," Walt laughed, trying to lighten the mood.

"I'll say," I said, cracking a smile.

"One dance?" Walt asked. I nodded as he placed a hand on the small of my back and began leading me in a waltz. We moved slowly, in time with each other. Alone on this bridge, dancing in the moonlight, I could see glimpses of a future with Walt. It was a happy one. But what happened when we returned to the real world, to our lives and the people in it?

"What do you say we head back to the dance hall before Judy and Billy notice we've gone?" he asked, dipping me.

"Good idea. We should probably get back. Maybe we can have another dance before the night is over?" I asked, righting myself. "I can teach you a few things."

"For you, I'll give it a try. You may need to lower your expectations of me," he joked.

"So far, all you've done is exceed them," I replied. And that's precisely the problem.

* * *

Walt and I returned to the dance hall, noticing that the crowd had thinned since we'd sneaked off. Scanning the dance floor for Judy and Billy, neither was to be found. I noted the clock on the wall read 10:20 p.m., almost closing time. "How long were we gone?" I asked Walt, nodding at the time.

"I thought just a short time, but the clock says otherwise," he replied.

"I think they've left. I don't see them or any of our group," I shouted over the music.

"I'll have to take a raincheck on that dance," he called over the horns. "I'll walk you home and then see if I can find Jack."

"Let me just grab my coat," I called, heading toward the bank of tables flanking the dance floor. Slipping it on, I headed for the exit. Back out in the cool night air, I felt revived. Walt and I walked the few blocks back to the Inn in comfortable silence, both of us content to be together, walking more slowly than usual.

"Well, this is me," I said when we'd reached the Inn.

"Looks nice," he said, looking at the building's facade. "I've always loved a wraparound porch."

"Me too," I agreed. "Someday I hope to have a home with one."

"Someday," he said. "Goodnight, Lottie."

"Goodnight, Walt," I said, planting a kiss on his cheek. "Thank you for an unforgettable evening." I turned to head inside, stopping halfway up the stairs to holler back to him, "Don't forget about the Holiday Show if you're still in town."

"I wouldn't miss it," he called back with a wave.

I watched for a few moments until he rounded the corner and then practically floated up the rest of the stairs. Stepping into the lobby, I was met with the familiar scent of apples and cinnamon, and the warmth of logs burning in the hearth. All my senses felt heightened. Closing the door quietly behind me, I leaned back on it, replaying the events of the evening in my mind. What a night. It felt like falling in love. Righting myself to standing and rounding the corner, I heard a familiar voice call my name.

"Charlotte."

I froze, the voice belonged to my husband.

CHAPTER TWENTY-NINE

"Charlie?" I said, cautiously turning around to find my husband seated at a table with Judy and Billy. "What are you doing here?" I asked, shaken by the close call.

"I needed to talk to you," he replied. "And seeing as we kept missing each other and the shop is closed tomorrow, I figured I might as well make the trip."

"Oh," I said in response, dumbfounded at the turn of events.

"We kept Charlie company for you, honey," Judy said, "while you went back to gather your gloves," she fibbed, raising her eyebrows to convey the message.

"Thanks, Judy. Luckily, they were right where I left them. And now they're right where they should be," I replied, patting my handbag.

"Good," she said, tapping Billy on the shoulder. "Well, it's getting late. I think Billy and I will leave you two to it. I need my beauty sleep and we've got rehearsals in the afternoon."

"And I've got the breakfast shift," Billy said, standing up. "Goodnight, Lottie," he said with a look of concern, "and very nice to meet you, Charlie."

"Night all," Judy said, pushing her chair in. Passing me, she whispered, "Good luck." I nodded almost imperceptibly. I was going to need it.

"Good night to you both, it was nice talking to you," Charlie replied. Walking over to the table, I sat down across from my husband. He looked worn out. Suddenly, I felt the same. The magic of the evening had fizzled out.

"Hi," he said.

"Hi."

"I tried calling but could never seem to get you on the line."

"I did too. But you were never home. Or at the shop," I replied.

"Charlotte, I know that I owe you an explanation," he began.

I remained silent, staring back at him expectantly.

Charlie placed his head in his hands, elbows resting on the table, before exhaling with a huff. Looking up at me, he popped his knuckles and reluctantly began to speak. "I'm not sure where to begin, or even how it started," he said, regretfully. "I'm sorry, Lot."

How it started. He had been with Alice. I knew it. A wave of nausea washed over me at the thought.

"At first, it was just Alice bringing a coffee to the shop here and there," he began. "Eventually, we'd gotten to talking in the afternoons. I guess I liked the attention."

"I see," I said, lips drawn, nodding my head slowly. "Go on."

"I guess I've been feeling like you're not interested in me anymore. You don't care to hear about the shop or what I'm working on. She was so focused on me. It was nice for a change. You've got the girls and now all this," he said, motioning around us, referring to Rockland. "It feels like you don't really need me any-."

"Wait a minute," I interrupted. "Let me get this straight. You're saying that this happened because of how *I've* been treating *you*?" I asked, incredulous.

"No. I mean. Well, what I'm trying to say is I don't think you and I have been happy for some time."

"And what does that mean, Charlie? That any time some two-bit hussy gives you some attention, you've got carte blanche to do whatever you please?" I cried. I could hear my voice climbing higher and louder, but I didn't care.

"Calm down, Lottie. That's not what I'm saying at all," he insisted. "I'm saying that I'm sorry. I know I was wrong. I've been kicking myself ever since."

"Why? Because you were caught?"

"No. Because I regret ever getting involved with Alice. I was trying to end it when you showed up."

"Well excuse me for interrupting you. And do not say that name around me. Just so you know, I showed up that day to bring you something special before I had to leave," I spat. "I'm sure you can guess what I mean. I don't know why I even bothered since it looked like you were all set in that department."

"Oh," he said, hanging his head. "I had no idea. It seemed like you couldn't wait to get away from me."

"Because I wanted something for myself? Because I wanted to pursue my dream?" I practically yelled. "Charlie Abbott, I have supported you in building your business since day one! I have scrimped and saved doing anything I could to help you succeed. I take care of our home and our girls, and I never ask you to lift a finger. The one time I get offered something just for me, for my talent, you try to dissuade me and tell me I make a great homemaker??!!"

Rage coursed through my veins. How dare he blame me for his indiscretions. Once again, it was all about Charlie. I had had enough. Slamming my palms down on the table, I bolted upright, sending my chair toppling over behind me. "I'm not going to let you do this, Charlie. I'm not going to let you ruin this for me," I cried, tears dangerously close to falling.

"Lottie! Stop!" he commanded, standing up. "I know that I've messed up here. I'm not here to ruin this opportunity for you."

"Then why are you here?" I demanded. "Because all you've done so far is make excuses."

"I wanted to apologize," he began, advancing toward me slowly, as one might approach a frightened animal. "I needed to see you. To talk to you. I miss you, Lottie. I miss us. The old us."

Looking at him I could see that he was being genuine. He was finally saying the words I hadn't realized I'd been waiting to hear for years. If only he'd said them sooner. Before I kissed another man. *Oh God, I kissed another man.*

Charlie gathered me up in his arms. Collapsing into him, his familiarity comforted me as hot tears cascaded down my cheeks. Everything I'd been holding in since that dreadful morning, and for the past few years, came pouring out. I held on to my husband as tightly as I could, fighting the feeling that my knees might buckle at any moment. We stood that way until I had nothing left.

"I'm so sorry, Lottie. I never meant for this to happen," Charlie said.

"I know. I just don't know where we go from here," I replied.

"For now, maybe we just call it a night. Is it alright if I stay with you?"

"It's fine. I suppose we can talk more in the morning. My room's this way," I said, heading for the stairwell and wiping my eyes.

CHAPTER THIRTY

Rounding the corner to the stairwell, I nearly crashed into Bianca, seated on the third step, her overcoat folded neatly across her knees.

"Oh!" I cried, raising a hand to my heart, not expecting to run into anyone at this time of night. "Bianca? What are you doing here?"

"Good evening, Charlotte," she stood to let us pass. "Evening, Charlie," she purred with a satisfied smirk.

That witch had been eavesdropping on our entire conversation. If I hadn't been so distraught, I would've given her a piece of my mind. But I had more important things to worry about. Like my marriage. And the fact that I'd kissed Walt just hours before.

"Night, Bianca," I said with a sigh, continuing up the stairs.

"Sweet dreams," she called after us.

When we reached my room, I slipped the key out of my bag and into the lock. Turning the handle, I lost my grip on my handbag, the contents spilling out onto the floor. I quickly gathered my cash, compact, lipstick, and mints. Briskly shoving the items back into the bag, I prayed that Charlie hadn't noticed the absence of my gloves. I stood up, catching him looking at me with a careful gaze. He looked as though he wanted to say something, but kept his mouth clamped shut.

"Still clumsy as ever," I blurted out, effectively cutting him off. "Here we are," I said, opening the door wide to allow him to enter.

"Wow," Charlie said, looking around the room. "They really took care of you."

"Mrs. Hall, the proprietor, and I have known each other for years. I worked here when I was young. I don't know if I ever told you that."

"No, you never did."

"It's been nice seeing faces from the past and reconnecting. I'm enjoying my time here."

"That's good, Lot. It looks like you have a good thing going out here. Your friends seem nice."

"They are," I agreed. "Make yourself comfortable. I'm just going to get changed for bed. I'll be right back."

Grabbing my pajamas from the wardrobe, I hastily headed for the bathroom. Closing the door behind me, I took a deep cleansing breath, replaying the events of the evening in my mind. I had thought I'd feel better, or at least closer to a resolution, once I knew the truth about what I'd seen at the garage. But I was more confused than ever.

Unzipping my borrowed dress, I carefully hung it back on the fabric-covered hanger, placing it on the door hook. After slipping into my pajamas, I sat down at the vanity feeling for the clasp of my necklace. Removing the string of pearls, I placed them gently on the vanity table.

"Dad, what have I done?" I said, quietly regarding the necklace.

Charlie had been unfaithful, but he recognized his wrongs and had tried to right them. He wanted to fix our marriage. He had a point about us. I'd been feeling unfulfilled too and hadn't said anything. We spent so many years together and had a family. That had to count for something.

But I couldn't get Walt out of my head. Was I just as bad as Charlie? How could I be angry about Alice when I'd just kissed Walt and lied about where I'd been. I didn't have any plans to tell Charlie the truth. Even worse, I didn't even regret it.

I felt so alive with Walt. Mundane things became exciting, and we both truly enjoyed the other's company. He respected me. But we'd just met. We really didn't even know each other. I didn't even know his middle name or where he worked or whether he liked dogs or cats. But he made me feel things I'd never felt before. My body came alive in a way it never had before. And we'd only just kissed. I blushed at the thought of what it would feel like if we moved beyond just kissing.

Looking at my reflection, I hoped to garner some hint of what to do. Some semblance of what I wanted. I didn't know. Because either choice was a loss. A loss of what I'd known or a loss of what could be.

"I really wish you were here, Dad. I don't know what I'm doing anymore."

"You okay in there, Lot?" Charlie called from the bedroom. "You talking to me?"

"Fine, just talking to myself. I'll be out in a minute."

* * *

"You okay?" Charlie asked when I climbed into bed.

"Fine."

He rolled onto his side, one arm propping up his head. He looked at me and for a minute it felt like the old us. It had been so long since we'd even talked in bed. He was usually fast asleep before I'd even finished my nightly routine.

"Lottie, I know you're not fine. You don't have to pretend."

"I don't know what else to do, Charlie. I don't even know how I feel or what to say." I reached over to the nightstand, turning off the bedside lamp. We lay there in silence for a few moments.

"I don't know how we got here," Charlie said in the darkness.

"I think I do," I began. "We were so excited to start a family and to get your business up and running. So, we jumped in and somewhere along the way we started to grow apart. We stopped doing things together and started living mostly separate lives to make the plan work."

"You've got a point there."

"I gave up the things that make me who I am to be the perfect mother and housewife. I wanted to help you chase your dream, so I let go of mine. And I lost myself. And you didn't even notice. Maybe at first, I didn't either. You were so focused on your business, and I had to take care of the house and the girls, so there was no time for anything else. And then we lost us."

Charlie rolled onto his back. I could just make out his profile staring at the ceiling. We lay there in the quiet, barely moving, listening to the sounds of the night. "So how do we get it back?" he finally asked.

"I don't know," I replied quietly. "I don't know if we can."

"But we have to at least try, don't we?"

I rolled over with my back to Charlie, and whispered, "I don't know. I don't know anything anymore."

He leaned into me, placing his arm over mine, holding me like he used to, before the girls and the garage. Before the house. Before responsibilities. "If anyone can figure it out, it's us," he said, kissing my shoulder.

I'm not so sure, I thought to myself, wishing I was alone. His presence stifling me.

"Night, Lot," Charlie yawned, falling asleep immediately after speaking the words.

"Night," I whispered, staring into the shadows, visions of the bridge invading my mind and holding tight to my heart.

CHAPTER THIRTY-ONE

Opening my eyes, I stretched my arms wide, patting the empty bed and realizing that I was alone. I turned my head to see the vacant pillow beside mine. Relief washed over me. Had last night been a dream? I sat up, groggy from a fitful sleep. Rubbing my lids, my eyes felt swollen. Yawning, I glanced at the clock, and then my gaze landed on Charlie's wristwatch. It wasn't a dream. A sinking feeling washed over me. The click of the lock broke the silence. I stifled a groan as Charlie entered, freshly showered and bright-eyed, carrying a tray.

"Morning. I thought you might like breakfast in bed today," he explained, hopeful. "Figured it'd be easier for us to talk in private."

Fluffing my pillows, I shifted back to receive the tray. "Thanks, that's probably best," I agreed.

"Sure," he said placing it down. "They have quite the spread downstairs. Hey, what's the story with Bianca? Strange girl."

"Ugh. Let's just say that Bianca isn't very pleased to have me here. Her cousin is the dancer who was injured. I'm her replacement."

"Ah, I see," he replied. "I ran into her downstairs. She was watching every move I made. Gave me the creeps. I could feel her beady eyes tracking me. She finally came over and was asking questions about you and suggesting sights I should see while I'm here."

"What kinds of questions?"

"Something about going out to the dance hall," he said, sliding some scrambled eggs onto a plate. "And she mentioned a bridge I should visit." At the mention of the bridge, I inhaled quickly, choking on a sip of orange juice. "You alright?" Charlie asked.

I regained my composure, croaking, "Fine. Just went down the wrong way." Had Bianca been at the dance hall? She'd said she was staying in, but maybe that was just a ruse. Had she seen me with Walt? What if she'd followed us to the bridge? The sound of the snapping twig popped into my head. Oh God. Had Bianca seen me kissing Walt?? I thought back to almost bumping into her on the stairs. *She'd had her coat with her. OH GOD.*

"Where'd you go?" Charlie asked, watching me as he buttered a warm slice of banana bread.

"Sorry. Just thinking about rehearsals," I fibbed. "Bianca really has it out for me."

"You can handle her. She's just a scared kid."

"You're probably right. I just feel a little out of my element. I'm the only mom in the group. And the oldest by quite a few years."

"They don't know that. Besides, what does it matter? You've got natural talent."

"Thanks," I said, surprised at the compliment. Making a plate for myself, I took a bite of scrambled eggs. "Ooh, he added cheddar and chives."

"The food here is great. You've got a nice little setup."

"The chef is an old friend," I explained, breaking off a chunk of some warm banana bread. "He's amazing. And I must admit I like having someone else cook and serve me for a change," I laughed.

Charlie's expression softened. "You know, I never really thought about all the things you do. You make it look so easy. I never thought of it as work."

"I just have a system. There are some days when I'd like to just skip all of it, but if I did everything would fall apart." He nodded. "Charlie, I know that you've put everything into the garage to make sure that the girls and I are cared for, and I appreciate it and you. I should've told you all these years. Maybe things would've been different."

"I guess we both could've done things differently. I really wish we'd had this conversation sooner. Before..."

"Before Alice?" I finished his thought.

"Yeah."

"Would've made things easier," I said, matter of fact.

"I don't know what to do other than to tell you how sorry I am, Lot," he said, wringing his hands.

"I know you are," I sighed. "I just don't know how to be okay with it. I'm sorry, too." *For more than you know.* "Things feel different between us. I don't know if we can go back to the way we used to be. So much has happened."

Charlie put his head down, hyper-focused on his plate. He pushed the last few bites around with his fork before placing it down gently on the tray. I took the last sip of my orange juice, draining the glass. Carefully wiping my mouth with the cloth napkin he'd brought; I cleared my throat to get his attention. Charlie looked up at me tentatively as if he was afraid of what I might say next.

"If I'd never come to the garage that morning, would you have told me about Alice?" I asked, my gaze trained on my husband. Watching Charlie's face, I saw doubt in his eyes. He sat for a moment, mulling it over.

"You know, Lot, I don't know if I honestly would've."

"I thought so."

"Well, I ended it. What good would it have done?"

"I don't know, Charlie," I said, shrugging.

"I hope we can get past this, Lot. I can't lose you. Or the girls."

I could see tears filling the corners of his eyes. Sitting there, I wanted nothing more than to run from the room. Away from my husband. Away from thinking about this any longer. Away from talking about it. Away from my guilt. But I sat there, silent. Charlie brushed a loose strand of hair from my eyes and tucked it gently behind my ear.

"I want you to know that I love you," he said, sadness clouding his eyes. "And that I'm going to head back home to give you some space." I looked up at him, surprised at his decision. "This is your chance to follow your dream and I finally understand how important it is to you. I'm not going to attempt to ruin this a second time. All of this will still be here after the show is over. We can figure things out then," he suggested.

"Okay," I agreed softly.

Charlie leaned over, placing the tray on the bedside table. He gathered me into his arms, leaning back on the stack of pillows and holding me tight. I rested my head on his shoulder. We lay there like that for a few minutes, finding comfort in our familiarity and avoiding whatever was to come.

CHAPTER THIRTY-TWO

Watching from the front porch as Charlie expertly maneuvered his Ford pickup out of a tight parking space, relief filled me. He beeped the horn twice as I held a hand up in farewell until he rounded the corner. I could finally breathe.

Lowering myself down into an old rocking chair, I felt a crushing exhaustion creeping over me. I closed my eyes and exhaled, slowly rocking. I was no closer to a resolution than before. Things were starting to feel even more complicated. Somehow, in my mind Charlie's transgression was absolutely wrong, yet mine was justified. Was I being a hypocrite? All signs pointed to yes, but it didn't feel like it. I had experienced a very real and true connection with Walt that I couldn't deny. How could something so genuine ever be wrong?

"Why, hello, Charlotte," an unwelcome voice interrupted my thoughts. A voice that I unfortunately recognized. I slowly opened my eyes to see Bianca rocking next to me.

"Hi, Bianca," I said flatly.

"Late night?" she asked. "You seem tired."

"You could say that," I replied, resting my head back on the chair.

"I imagine it's exhausting," she sweetly commiserated, eyes trained on me. "I saw you last night. On the bridge."

"I figured as much," I flatly countered.

"I'm sure Charlie would find it quite interesting; don't you think? His wife cavorting at all hours of the night with another man while her children are safely tucked in bed miles away. You should be more careful," she threatened.

"Really. And what is it that you're saying exactly?"

"I'm simply saying that if you want to keep your spot in the show you should probably be a little more discreet."

Stomping both feet down onto the porch, I sat up stick straight stopping the rocker on a dime. Turning to Bianca who was peering back at me wearing a smug look, I spat, "Listen, Bianca. My personal business is no concern of yours. I'm truly sorry that your cousin was injured. You're quite obviously struggling with that, and I understand how hard it is to do this alone. You're lucky that you don't have someone gunning for you, as I obviously do," I said, implicating her with my gaze. Bianca looked a little taken aback that I had empathized with her and remained silent.

"Furthermore, I'm dealing with some very serious, very complicated adult problems. This isn't a game. This is my life, and I don't have time for your childish schemes. I'm very aware of the choices I've made. Believe me, I don't need you to remind me. Why don't you grow up and focus on why you're here? Are you that threatened by an out-of-practice veteran dancer? You should try putting as much energy into your craft as you do into being spiteful. You could have a very promising career ahead of you, but if you keep your focus on taking down anyone else with an ounce of talent, your only success will be continuing to be this lonely, miserable person for the rest of your life," I said, gesturing in her direction in disgust. "Jealousy is not a good look."

Bianca's eyes grew wide. I had touched a nerve. I watched in shock as a single tear rolled down her cheek. She did have feelings under that hard exterior. She quickly wiped it away, embarrassed to have shown any vulnerability. "I'm sorry," she whispered, bolting out of the chair, and disappearing inside the Inn as quietly as she'd first shown up.

I sat back down, thankful that she'd gone, but left with an overwhelming sense of guilt. This seemed to be a common theme for me in the last 24 hours. Maybe I'd been too hard on her. Charlie had probably been right. She was just a scared kid, and I'd essentially just knocked her out with my bluntness. Instead of feeling triumphant at finally putting the girl in her place, I felt ashamed. I wasn't this person. Sighing, I left the comfort of the rocking chair and headed inside the Inn. I found myself walking in the direction of Bianca's room. I could at least try to resolve one issue today.

* * *

Knocking on the door of Room 29, I waited for Bianca to answer. The door opened a hair, and I could see her splotchy, red face looking back at me. "Bianca," I began. "I'm sorry I was so harsh. Can I come in?" She considered my question for a moment and then let the door swing wide. I took in her meticulous room. Everything was in its place. "May I?" I asked, motioning to the armchair.

"All yours," she quietly replied.

"Look, Bianca, I think we got off on the wrong foot. I apologize if I took it too far out there. I'm just dealing with a lot right now, and you pushed the wrong button. I'm sorry."

"Thanks," she said, sitting down on the bed. "I guess I never really gave you a fair chance. And I was sort of asking for it."

"You were," I agreed. "Now what's going on with you? You haven't known me long enough to be this upset with me."

Bianca shifted on the bed, folding her legs underneath her. Taking a deep breath she began shakily, tears threatening to fall. "Jade is all I have. My parents passed away when I was very young. Car crash. My aunt, Jade's mom, took me in. Jade and I grew up together, she's like a sister to me. I've never been good with people," she continued. "Before I moved in with my aunt, I never really had any friends. Jade's the friendly one. She can talk to anyone. She's the only real friend I've ever had. We did everything together. She and I started dancing when we were little and always planned to climb to the top together. We had it all figured out. We were going to get an apartment in New York City and dance on Broadway someday," Bianca trailed off, twirling her long blond hair around her index finger, lost in her daydream.

"That sounds like a lovely plan," I said. "I can see you're there now, in your mind." Bianca blushed. "You know, I do the same thing," I confided. "Ever since I got the call from Mr. Anderson, I've been picturing myself onstage, my name in lights. Imagining the costumes, the music, the audience going wild. You and I probably have more in common than you think."

Bianca nodded, sadness crossing her features. "After her injury, Jade says she doesn't know if she even wants to dance anymore. She keeps talking about getting married and starting a family with her boyfriend, which leaves me alone. Just like you said."

Listening to Bianca tell her story, I realized how young she sounded. She really was just a scared kid. "Bianca, I'm so sorry. I had no idea. But you know that you're not alone, right? You have the whole troupe. You just have to work with us, instead of plotting against us," I said, eyebrows raised, "like you've been doing with me since I arrived. You can't base your whole future on another person. You need to figure out what you want and what will make you happy. And the rest will come together."

It was amazing how easily I doled out this advice when it was exactly the guidance I needed.

Bianca quietly contemplated what I'd said before replying, "But how do you know, Charlotte? Forgive me for saying so, but your life looks like it's a bit of a mess right now."

I laughed. This girl was blunt. "That's true, it is a mess. And that's because I didn't follow my own advice."

"Oh," she said, satisfied with my answer. "Well, I hope you figure it out."

"Me too. Friends?" I asked hand outstretched.

"Friends," she agreed, shaking on it.

CHAPTER THIRTY-THREE

Sitting down next to Judy, I couldn't wait for lunch to be served. With the stress of last night and this morning, I was famished. "Hi," I said, resting a hand on Judy's shoulder.

"Oh! Lottie!" she cried. Dropping her voice to a whisper she said, "I've been dying to talk to you all morning. What happened? Tell me everything."

"A lot," I said. "But not here. I'll tell you tonight. Maybe Billy can join us? That way I only have to go through the whole story once."

Her face fell. "You mean you expect me to wait the rest of the day?" she asked in mock horror.

"I do," I laughed. "But everything is okay."

"Fine. You're lucky I like you so much," she replied with a wink, handing me a glass of water with a fresh lemon slice.

"So, how was your night?" I asked. "Did you see Jack?"

"Oh, did I," she replied. "We had a few dances, and he plans to meet me again Tuesday night for a drink."

"That's wonderful. I'm glad you had a good time. I'm sorry I missed the whole evening. But more on that tonight," I smirked.

"Lottie," she narrowed her eyes at me, "You'd better tell me the whole story if you're going to make me wait. I can already tell by the look on your face that there are some details I don't want to miss." Smiling, I took a sip of my water and shrugged my shoulders, reveling in my secret.

Just then, Billy approached with our lunch. Homemade chicken noodle soup and green salad. Rolls fresh from the oven and Johnny's now-famous honey butter to go along with them. "Charlotte how are you today?" he asked cautiously.

"Good, Billy. Really," I began, pulling him closer. "Come up to my room tonight after your dinner shift. Judy will be there too. I'll fill you both in on everything."

"I'll be there. The suspense has been killing me!" he exclaimed in a hushed tone. "But I'm glad that everything is okay."

"I have some things to work out, but for now I'm just concentrating on the show," I said.

"Smart." To the table, he announced, "Ladies, enjoy your meal."

Grabbing my soup spoon, I tasted the soup and wanted to hug Johnny. The broth was perfectly seasoned and so flavorful, and the homemade thick-cut noodles took it to another level. It was exactly what I needed. There was nothing like chicken soup to heal the soul. Or to at least help you forget your troubles for a few minutes.

"Is everyone ready for rehearsal?" Nancy asked, passing the basket of rolls. "I hope last night wasn't too wild."

"We're ready!" the Marys announced, buttering their rolls. Always in unison.

"I may need a coffee first," Jean quipped. "But it was worth it. What a great night."

"It was fabulous," Linda agreed. "Some very good-looking men, too!"

"Speaking of good-looking men," Jean began, turning her attention to me. "Who was that dish you were with all night, Lottie? And where did you two disappear to?"

The questions I was hoping to avoid. I could feel the heat creeping into my cheeks. "Oh, just another old friend," I explained nonchalantly. "We were just catching up."

"This one's having a regular Rockland reunion," Judy added in support.

"Can't blame you," Jean replied in a sassy tone. "I'd like to catch up with him, too."

"Jean!" Judy laughed. "Who knew you had a naughty side?"

"I did," Linda joined in. "You missed her flirting last night. It was impressive. I think she even made the gentleman blush."

"Happy to give pointers next time," Jean announced with a chuckle. "And it worked by the way. He'll be back to meet me on Tuesday. So there," she laughed, sticking her tongue out at Linda.

"You're awful," Linda joked.

"I'm actually meeting someone Tuesday evening as well," Judy said. "Maybe we should do another night out?"

"Yes, let's!" Linda agreed. "I could use a lesson in how to catch a man."

"Works for me," Jean said. The girls began chatting about what they might wear and the men they might meet. That was a close call. I didn't need the entire troupe knowing my personal business.

"Can anyone join?' Bianca asked from the other end of the table, effectively silencing the chatter.

"Of course!" I answered a little too quickly, noting Judy's quizzical look. "The more, the merrier. Why don't we all go," I suggested, "as a sort of troupe outing?"

"That's a great idea, Charlotte," Nancy agreed. "It will be a nice way for us to bond as a group, which will make the show even stronger. I love it. Let's all plan for Tuesday."

Bianca smiled at me from across the table. I returned the sentiment. I could feel Judy staring at me, one eyebrow raised in suspicion, trying to figure out what had just happened.

"What is going on there?" she whispered, gesturing from me to Bianca. "I thought you two were enemies?"

"Not anymore," I said. "We're friends now."

"What? You're joking. Friends? You and her?"

"I'll fill you in tonight."

"I really missed a lot more than I thought last night," she mused. "It seems like we have a lot to cover, in which case, I'm going to suggest that Billy test out a few more cocktails on us."

"I'll ask him to rustle up some snacks, too. I think we're going to need them. There's a lot to talk about," I agreed.

Soaking up the last of the chicken broth in the crock with my dinner roll, I took a healthy bite. My mind wandered back to the bridge as I thought about kissing Walt for the first time and found myself hoping that it wasn't the last.

CHAPTER THIRTY-FOUR

From the hallway, I could hear the faint trill of the telephone ringing inside my room. I hurriedly swung open the door and rushed inside, dropping my tote on the floor, and launching myself onto the bed. Reaching over to the nightstand, I snapped up the receiver. "Hello?' I said breathlessly into the handset.

Hello, Charlotte," my mother's voice sang into my ear. "Is this a bad time? You sound as though you've just run a marathon."

Catching my breath, I laughed, "It's fine. I heard the phone ringing as I was coming in, so I dashed to grab it. I've just gotten back from afternoon rehearsals, so I was already a little out of breath. I didn't realize how out of shape I was until I had to keep up with these younger girls."

"You'll snap back in no time. How is everything else going?" she asked pointedly.

"Things are great, mom," I fibbed. "I'm glad you called. I'm overdue for a chat with the girls. The last time I called you were out for an ice cream dinner, I believe."

"Well, dear, they don't call me grandma for nothing. It's my job to spoil."

"And I'm sure you're doing just that, mom," I joked.

"Now, tell me the truth," she began. "What's really going on? Charlie has been acting quite strange since you left, and I know he made an unplanned trip out there." She knew. Trying to keep my composure and build up the courage to tell my mother about my husband's affair, I took a deep breath, exhaling slowly. "Charlotte? What's happened?"

"If I tell you, you need to promise me you won't say a word," I warned.

"Not one word."

"I don't like the sound of this, but you have my word," she promised.

"Are the girls nearby?" I asked.

"No, they're upstairs building a fort," she explained. "We've been making blanket forts for our afternoon story time. They've been having a ball."

"I'm glad. I feel much better just knowing you're there with them."

"Charlotte."

"Okay," I sighed. "Long story short, I caught Charlie with another woman before I left. He was ending it at the time, but something had already happened between them. I didn't pry for details. He made the trip out here to apologize in person."

"Oh, my!" she exclaimed, before bringing her voice back down an octave. "I had a feeling something of the sort had happened."

"How so?" I asked.

"Just a hunch," she replied. "You're a headstrong woman. That can be difficult for an old-fashioned man like Charlie. Your father was the same way."

"He was?" I asked. My mother never mentioned anything that could be construed as negative when it came to my dad.

"He was. There are things I've never shared about your father because I didn't want to tarnish your memory of him."

"Oh."

"Charlotte, every marriage has its ups and downs. You'll get through this. If Charlie ended things of his own accord, he recognizes his mistake."

"True," I agreed tentatively.

"Is there something else?" she asked. I sat silent for a moment weighing whether I wanted to share the rest of the story with her. After a minute, I realized that my silence had essentially answered her question. There was no use trying to deny it now. June Dawson would press until she found out the truth. She was relentless when she had a hunch.

"Yes, there is. I don't know how it happened, but I met someone on the train," I blurted out the truth.

"You did what?" she asked in disbelief.

"I met a man, and we had an instant connection, Mom. I've never felt electricity like I did with him."

"Did you tell Charlie about this?" she asked.

"No."

"And why not?"

"I'm not entirely sure."

"It sounds like you're playing with fire, Charlotte." I remained silent. "I understand that you were probably crushed after catching Charlie with another woman. And the attention of a stranger can be intriguing after a situation like that. I also know how thankless being a homemaker can be. All your hard work goes unnoticed. But trying to find yourself in the arms of another man isn't the answer. You made a vow."

"I know. But Charlie also made that vow, and broke it," I argued.

"I agree. What he did was wrong, there's no way around it. Just please think carefully before you make any rash decisions. You have the girls to consider," she said. "Once you cross that line, there's no going back." She spoke as if from experience. What else had my mother kept to herself over the years? I wasn't sure I wanted the answer.

"For now, I just want to focus on the show. Charlie suggested we talk things through after it closes. He wants me to take advantage of my time here."

"Well, I think that's a good idea. It sounds like maybe he realizes he wasn't supporting you at the outset," she said. "Maybe this has opened his eyes. He's a good man, Charlotte. People make mistakes."

"I know."

She cleared her throat, decidedly finished with this line of questioning. "Well, I'm glad that you trusted me with all of this. I won't let on that I know a thing. Try not to worry, it will all work itself out. These things always do."

"Thanks, Mom."

"And enjoy yourself. You're doing what you've always dreamed of. Not many people can say that."

"You're right. I have to just put the rest out of my mind for a couple of weeks," I decided. "Will you put the girls on? I need to hear their voices."

"Certainly, let me get them on the line," she said. "I love you. I know you'll make the right choice."

"I love you too, Mom," I replied, as she hollered for my girls to come to the phone. The right choice. I knew exactly what she meant by that, but right for whom? I didn't even know what was right anymore.

"Mom?" Kathy's voice called out over the line.

"Kitty Kat!" I cried. "You have no idea how much Mommy misses you."

CHAPTER THIRTY-FIVE

"Open up, Charlotte!" Billy cried, tapping at the door with the toe of his wingtips. "Room service has arrived!" Chuckling, I tightened my robe and opened the door.

"Well, if I'd known it was a pajama party, I would've dressed the part," he announced, giving me a once-over.

"Last-minute decision," I said. "I'm beat. Between rehearsals and all the drama in my life, I just couldn't stand the thought of wearing a dress any longer."

"Understandable. You'll feel better after getting everything off your chest. And I came prepared," he said, displaying the contents of the large tray he was carrying. "A variety of libations, a mix of snacks, and a few tea lights for ambiance."

"I wouldn't expect anything less."

A soft knock at the door announced Judy's arrival. She looked fabulous in a satin striped pajama set and marabou slippers, her hair tied up with a floral headscarf. "Party's here!" Judy exclaimed, executing a spin to show off her attire.

"Well, look at you!" I admired. "Always the best dressed for any occasion. Even in pajamas."

"I try," she laughed, sailing past me into the room. "Billy! I see you've brought everything we discussed. What would we do without you?"

"You'd probably be raiding the kitchen right about now," he quipped, placing the tray down on the bed. "Now Charlotte, I think you've made us wait long enough. What happened last night??"

I sat down, motioning for them to join me. Where to begin? My mind raced just thinking of everything I needed to cover.

"And start at the beginning," Judy commanded. "I don't want to miss a single detail."

"First, I'm going to need a cocktail. Where would you suggest I start, Billy?" I asked, motioning to the spread he'd brought.

"You're just going to move clockwise around the tray, Lot. I've got everything paired and in order."

"Naturally," I replied, picking up the first cocktail, a pink concoction. Taking a sip of the frothy liquid, I began to retell the events of the prior evening to my very captive audience.

* * *

"Wow," Billy breathed once I'd finished regaling them with my story.

"My thoughts exactly," Judy agreed.

Draining the last of the pink drink, I placed the empty glass back on the tray. I took a handful of pistachios, discarded the shells, and popped them into my mouth. "So now the question is, what do I do?" I asked.

"That's a tough one, honey," Judy began. She had moved on to the second drink, this time a blue one. "Only you know the answer to that."

"She's right, Lottie," Billy sided with Judy. "We can't answer that for you. But I will say that after meeting both gentlemen, you've got a hard decision to make."

"Tell me about it," I commiserated.

"Let me ask you this," Billy started. "If Charlie came out to apologize as he did last night, but you'd never met Walt on the train, would you have forgiven him?"

"Good question," Judy nodded approvingly.

I reached for the blue cocktail, taking a sip, and feeling as though I'd been transported to the islands. Flavors of pineapple and coconut invaded my taste buds, overpowering the hint of grapefruit left behind by the last drink. I removed the little yellow umbrella Billy had garnished with fresh pineapple and a cherry. "What a fun little drink," I mused, spinning the tiny umbrella. "I feel as I've been whisked away to Hawaii."

"That was my intention," Billy smiled, satisfied with his artistry. "Now stop stalling and answer the question."

"Well," I began, carefully considering my answer. "To be honest, I think I might have."

"Oh," he replied knowingly. "This is really about Walt."

Dropping my head into my hands, I exhaled a long breath. Was this about Walt? I hadn't stopped to consider how I'd feel about things with Charlie if I'd never met him on the train. As much as I wanted to say it wasn't about Walt, Billy had hit a nerve with that question.

Meeting Billy's gaze I tried to explain my feelings as best I could. "Charlie and I had problems long before I came here. I think Walt opened my eyes to possibilities I hadn't considered… or didn't know existed for me. I just accepted my life for what it was before, without realizing I had any choice."

"That makes sense," Judy said. "I imagine it's normal to feel that way once you're married and have a family. Your responsibilities are beyond just yourself. So, you feel you've already chosen a path."

"Exactly."

"Lot, do you think you could be happy again someday with Charlie?" Billy asked. "I'd hate to see you throw away everything you've built together over the possibility of someone new. Have you thought about the reality of what life would look like with Walt?" he paused, letting that thought sink in. "I know you're a dreamer and I love that about you, but in the real world a relationship with him might not be anything like what you're seeing in your head."

Visions of Walt and me working outside together at the little house with the white picket fence were replaced by us shuttling the girls between me and their father. It was hard enough to be away from them temporarily. I couldn't stomach the thought of not seeing them every day on a permanent basis.

"You're right, Billy. I've definitely let myself get caught up in the magic with Walt," I said wistfully. "If only being with him didn't affect me the way it does."

"Listen Lot, I'm just playing devil's advocate here because I care about you. If you really think Walt's the guy for you then I support you, no questions asked. I just want you to really understand what it would mean for your life, and how everything would change," Billy explained. "For everyone, not just you."

"He has a point, Lottie," Judy said. "Right now, you're basically on holiday. These things happen on vacation for a reason. And usually they stay there."

"True," I said, considering the reality of my friend's comments. "Whatever I decide, I just don't want to go back to the way things were. And I think it would be really easy for Charlie and me to fall back into old patterns."

"Then don't," Billy replied. "This is where you choose something different for yourself. Remember why you came here in the first place. To dance. It seems like your focus has been on everything but since you arrived."

"This is your time, don't make it all about them," Judy added.

"It's time to put yourself first," Billy argued. "Ladies first, my friend."

"Ladies first," I repeated, lifting my glass to cheers.

CHAPTER THIRTY-SIX

"Now that that's settled," Judy announced, "I'm going to need you to explain to me what in God's name is going on with you and the Ice Princess."

Smirking, I reached for the last drink, which looked like a classic White Russian.

"Ice Princess?" Billy asked.

"Bianca," Judy and I called out in unison, bursting out laughing.

"Ah, yes. That little blond who barely eats anything. Am I right?" Billy guessed.

"Right-o friend!" Judy exclaimed.

Billy raised his eyebrows. "I see this one is enjoying herself," he laughed, nodding toward Judy.

"What's in this thing?" Judy asked, raising her glass. "It's delish!"

"That's my twist on a White Russian. I'm thinking of calling it a White Chocolate Cherry."

I took a sip, noting the hints of white chocolate, vanilla, and cherry. It was so smooth, like boozy chocolate milk.

"What about Boozy Cherry Chocolate Milk?" I suggested. "You could serve it with a malt shop straw. Ooh, this would be amazing with my cherry chocolate chip cookies, Billy. Maybe we should do a collaboration?"

Billy looked at me thoughtfully, pursing his lips, head cocked to one side. "You know, I actually like that," he said considering my suggestion. "I may get you into the kitchen to whip up a batch when I present all of this to Mrs. Hall. Or what if each cocktail has a signature cookie pairing? *Cookies and*

Cocktails. You might be on to something."

"Hello!" Judy interrupted, laying on her back and waving her hand in the air. "Are you going to tell us how you tamed Bianca or what?"

"Sorry, I got sidetracked by this fabulous drink," I said, winking at Billy. "Long story short, she threatened that she'd seen Walt and me on the bridge and made pointed comments to Charlie suggesting as much. Thankfully, they went right over his head. Anyway, after he left, she approached me on the porch and started in on me. I had had enough and really let her have it. She left in tears."

"Yikes," Billy said. "I bet she knows better than to cross Charlotte Abbott."

"I wish I'd been there for the takedown," Judy added wistfully.

"Honestly, I felt terrible afterward. Charlie had pointed out that she's probably just a scared kid and I realized he was right. I went to her room to apologize. We talked and she opened up to me. I feel a little sorry for her. She's had a tough life and just needs a friend."

"You're a softie," Judy proclaimed. "I still don't trust her, but I believe that you're a better person than me, Lottie."

"Lottie's been known to tame the worst of foes," Billy shared. "Usually after taking them down a peg," he laughed. "I could tell you stories."

"Billy Jones, I could tell stories about you. Watch it," I warned with a chuckle.

Judy sat up, looking at me with a questioning gaze, "Hey, have you ever thought about teaching? Dance, I mean."

"Teaching? Me? No," I said shaking my head.

"Why not?" Billy jumped in. "You'd be a natural. You're fun, you know your stuff…"

"Lottie," Judy interrupted. "You somehow befriended Bianca after she threatened to blow up your life. You obviously have people skills."

"I guess so," I conceded, shrugging my shoulders.

"You know, I really love that for you," Billy exclaimed. "Think about it. You've been feeling like you don't have anything for yourself. And that's been the problem, right? So, make something. You could bring the girls along. It's honestly perfect. Judy, you're a genius."

"Yes, well, I have to agree," she half-joked.

"Humble too," I added.

"Seriously, Lottie. Think about it. Maybe it's not what you originally saw for yourself, but it could work," Billy said.

Could I teach? It had never crossed my mind. I'd always pictured myself on a big stage, name in lights, but having my own studio could be interesting. I could create my own shows, focusing on choreography. "I'll think about it," I said.

* * *

Drinks drained and snacks devoured, the three of us lay back on the bed chatting. The alcohol made us a little silly and prone to oversharing.

"You mean to tell me that Mr. Dean is your boyfriend??!" Judy cried.

"I shouldn't say," Billy replied, nodding an emphatic yes.

"Well done, Billy! He's quite the catch," Judy exclaimed. "I take it you already knew about this?" she added, looking in my direction.

"Since we were kids," I confided. "I was crushed once I realized Billy would never be my sweetheart."

Billy put a hand to his heart, touched by my admission.

"He's *that* boy?! How sweet," she said. "And you've been together all this time?"

"No, Bobby, uh Mr. Dean as you know him, left for years and worked in the city. We ran into each other again a few years back, on the bridge actually, and it was like he'd never left."

"What is it with that bridge?" Judy asked. "Maybe I'll bring Jack over there for luck."

"It's a magical spot," he agreed. "He and I are this town's best-kept secret. Mum's the word, ladies."

"You got it," Judy said covering her mouth with her palm, as I pantomimed zipping my lips and throwing away the key.

"Unfortunately, not everyone is as progressive as you two," he added.

"Progress is my middle name," Judy cried, dissolving in a fit of giggles.

"What'd you put in her drinks?" I asked.

"Nothing more than in ours," he said dumbfounded. "That's all her."

"Judy, are you alright?" I asked a little too loudly as if the drinks had somehow affected her hearing. "Did you take something?"

"Just a muscle relaxer," she slurred. "I tweaked something at rehearsal, but I'm fine."

Seeing that she wasn't fine, Billy got up. "I'll go get a carafe of water. I'll be right back," he said grabbing the tray and heading for the door.

"Thanks! Looks like she'll be sleeping it off in here tonight," I called after him.

"Now you've really got yourself an old-fashioned pajama party!" he laughed, closing the door behind him.

CHAPTER THIRTY-SEVEN

I woke to the twittering calls of the little bluebird in the tree outside my window. Peering at the clock through the sleep in my eyes, I saw that it was early, a few hours until rehearsal began. Judy was fast asleep next to me with no signs of waking. I figured it better to let her sleep off the evening's cocktails.

Rolling out of bed, I crept quietly to the wardrobe, gathering my things for the day. In the bathroom, I washed my face, brushed my teeth and hair, and applied my face cream. Grabbing my key, I waved a silent goodbye to sleeping Judy and headed for the stairwell. The halls were quiet as it was still early for a Monday morning. Relishing the calm, I took a satisfying breath, feeling truly relaxed for the first time in days. Getting everything off my chest had worked wonders. I'd just needed a good old-fashioned venting session with my friends.

Reaching the front door, I lightly skipped down the steps and onto Main Street. It was a perfect morning for a walk. Brisk, but not cold, and sunny with clear blue skies. One of those New England days where the weather is unseasonably warm for the calendar month.

Rounding the corner, I noted a familiar birdsong. I looked up to see the little bluebird hopping along the windowsill attached to my room. "Trying to tell me something, are you little fella?" I called up to him. The bird looked at me, seeming to understand, and took a quick flight, landing a few branches above my head. He hopped about singing. "I see," I said to him with a chuckle. Satisfied, he flew back up to the windowsill to continue his hopping dance. Realizing I probably looked crazy talking out loud to a bird,

I did a quick survey of the area, relieved to see that I was the only one out and about.

Smiling to myself, I continued on my way, passing storefronts and a few passersby getting an early start. Studying the buildings lining the main road, I found that the town itself seemed much smaller than I had remembered. This street had always felt so sprawling when I was a young girl. Hit with a sense of nostalgia as I passed the Rockland General Store, I could almost see my younger self skipping down the sidewalk, clutching a nickel. Mr. Smythe always kept the penny candy fully stocked for the kids in town. On any given day, you were bound to bump into a friend in front of those bins.

I hadn't understood how much I truly loved this town until returning as an adult. There was such a sense of community. In just a few days, I really felt as though I was a part of something. I had people outside of my family who were connected to me, and who cared. I never felt that back home.

Turning onto First Street, I passed a young mother pushing a restless baby in a carriage. I could see her exhaustion in the way she carried herself, pressing on, probably silently praying that the child would finally doze off to give her a moment's peace. Remembering those days, I felt a pang of sadness. It seemed so long ago, but at the same time like yesterday. I missed my girls.

My heart ached at the thought of them. I'd been consciously focusing on other things to avoid thinking about being away from them. They'd been my little sidekicks since they entered the world and it was strange to suddenly be without them, even if for just a few weeks.

Kathy had always been a bit of a challenge as a baby and toddler, much like the child I'd just passed in the carriage. I'd always gotten the sense that she had plans but was too young to communicate or execute them. She was constantly restless and frustrated, unable to achieve whatever goal she had in her mind. Now that a few years had passed, my Kitty Kat had proven to be a very clever and independent little girl. Thinking up projects all on her own and presenting her creations when they were complete. I smiled, thinking of the hat she'd fashioned for Bun-bun, her prized stuffed bunny. She'd been so proud of herself.

And my little Penny. More easygoing than her sister, but still stubborn nonetheless when something was important to her. Probably a trait passed on from me, I thought with a smirk. Penny was young yet, but she already knew what she wanted and wasn't afraid to ask for it. She was always ready with a hug, possessing an innate ability to sense whenever someone needed a little extra love.

On the outside, I already had everything most women wished for. A successful husband, a nice home, two beautiful children. I was blessed. Yet I wasn't satisfied. Why couldn't I just be happy with what I had?

Looking up, I found myself at the bridge. Focusing on the old structure before me, I suddenly saw Walt and me in my mind's eye. Under the moonlight in a lover's embrace, my lips seeking out his, needing to know the truth of what was between us. At the memory, a rush of warmth flowed through me. That kiss had been magic. Intoxicating. Awakening me in a way I hadn't ever felt before. Putting fingers to my lips, I closed my eyes, yearning for that feeling again.

I stepped onto the bridge's wooden floorboards, walking over to the railing, and watching the rushing water below. It felt like a metaphor for everything I was feeling. Unease washed over me. While the novelty of being on my own was nice, and the heady feeling of being with Walt was intoxicating, I still found myself missing my family.

Resting an elbow on the railing, I propped my head in my hand thinking back to my life as I knew it just a few days earlier. Right now, I would be fixing Charlie's breakfast and packing his lunch. Then I'd get Kathy up and ready for school, though she usually did that on her own nowadays. Next up was waking Penny, never an easy job. She preferred to stay in pajamas all day, a true lover of leisure. I'd fix the girls' breakfast, bring Kathy to school, and then Penny and I would go about the daily chores, mixing in some fun along the way. As much as I sometimes resented my role, I somehow missed it, too. But the fact remained, I still needed a little something for myself.

Out of the corner of my eye, a flash of blue caught my attention. Turning my head, I watched as my bluebird flitted around the foliage surrounding the bridge until finally coming to rest on the railing a few feet from where I stood.

"Hello, again," I began, as the little bird bobbed on his tiny legs, regarding me with his head cocked to one side. "Is that what you've been trying to say all this time?" I asked, suddenly understanding.

Maybe that was it. Balance. The scales had always been tipped one way or the other. There had to be a way for me to even things out to find happiness in all my roles. I needed to figure out a way to tie it all together. Maybe not the easiest task, but I was determined to do just that.

CHAPTER THIRTY-EIGHT

Balancing the breakfast tray in one hand, I unlocked the door to my room with the other, gently nudging it open with my foot. Once my eyes adjusted to the darkness, I saw a Judy-sized lump under the coverlet. She looked as though she hadn't moved a muscle since I'd left, still lost in dreamland.

I opened the curtains halfway, allowing a little light into the room. Placing a hand on Judy's shoulder, I said, "Honey, it's time to wake up." She barely stirred. I could see I had another Penny on my hands. "Judy, there's only an hour until rehearsal," I continued, shaking her a bit. "It's time to get up. I brought breakfast."

Slowly opening her eyes, Judy mumbled, "Did somebody say breakfast?"

"Yes, me," I replied with a laugh. "Now sit up and have something to eat." I sat down next to my friend, placing the breakfast tray between us. Pouring a cup of coffee, I added two sugars and a little cream. "Here," I said, holding the steaming cup in front of her. "Start with this. Looks like you're going to need it today."

Taking a sip of the coffee, Judy looked bewildered. "What happened last night?" she asked, finally waking up enough to realize where she was. "Why am I still in your room?"

"Well, what happened is that you failed to mention to Billy and me that you took a muscle relaxer before coming over here," I began. "You told us after you'd polished off a few drinks. The cocktails had quite the effect on you."

"Oh God," Judy cried, throwing her head back, "please tell me I didn't do anything horribly embarrassing."

"Not really. Just a few funny comments and some fits of laughter. You had a grand time, but nothing to be concerned about."

"No blackmail material then?" she asked.

"Definitely not," I chuckled. "Besides, I would never blackmail you, or anyone for that matter."

"You're too nice."

"Well, that, and the fact that you already know too much about me."

"Good point," she agreed. "If anyone's getting blackmailed around here, it's you." We had a laugh, digging into our breakfast. It was stacks of blueberry pancakes this morning, fluffy and buttery-crisp at the edges. "These pancakes are just what the doctor ordered," Judy muttered through a mouthful.

"They're amazing," I agreed, pushing a bite into my mouth. "It's like Johnny knows what we need. He's really going all out with the blueberries though."

"You've got to know what the customers want," Judy quipped. "It's the key to any successful business. I think it's cute that he's giving you a hard time. I'd take this as payback any day."

* * *

"Ready to go?" I called, opening Judy's door a crack.

"Be right there," she hollered back. "Just fixing my hair." Judy emerged from the room, freshly showered, and impeccably put together.

"Honestly, how do you do it?" I said in awe. Just minutes ago, you looked as though you rolled out of the back of a truck."

"Charlotte!" she exclaimed. "I would never ride in the back of a truck. Unless of course it was parked," she grinned, elbowing me in the ribs and laughing wickedly.

"Oh, Judy, what will I do without you?" I chuckled, shaking my head.

"Without me? Don't tell me you're leaving, Lottie" she scolded.

"No, I mean after the show closes. When this is all over and we go home."

"I don't even want to think about that. I'm having so much fun in Rockland, more so now that you're here," she confided, threading an arm through mine. "I take it you've made a decision?"

"I think I have," I replied. "The strangest thing happened this morning. While you were asleep, I went for a walk and ended up at the bridge."

"Naturally," she commented.

"Anyway, I had an epiphany of sorts, a sign from my father."

"What kind of sign?" she asked.

"A bluebird," I began. "Since he passed, I've seen bluebirds more than ever. When I was young, they were our favorite species of bird to watch together. They've always held a special meaning for us. Anyway, when I got off the train, I found a bluebird feather on my luggage and a bluebird has been perched outside my windowsill here at the Inn since the first morning of rehearsals."

"Interesting."

"Anyway, I saw him this morning singing at my window and then he showed up at the bridge just as I realized that I miss my family and my life back home. I just need to figure out a way to also carve out something for myself and I think it would make all the difference."

"So, you think he was affirming that thought?" Judy asked.

"Yes."

"And you're absolutely sure it couldn't mean something else?"

"Like what?" I asked.

"Well, you found the feather after the train, right?" I nodded. "Where you met Walt," she continued. "And you saw him today on the bridge where you had your first kiss, with Walt." I could see where Judy was going with this. "I'm just saying that after having seen you with both Walt and Charlie… I mean, I've never seen two people with the sort of obvious connection you have with Walt. It's the stuff of films, the type of thing teenaged girls' dreams are made of. That doesn't come around every day, Lottie."

I took a deep breath and exhaled, considering her words. What she was saying rang true.

"But then again, you can't make life-altering decisions based on the actions of a bird," she laughed, trying to lighten the conversation. "Lottie, all I'm saying is that you seem to always make the best choice for everyone else's sakes. Make sure that you also think of yourself equally and about what will make you happy."

"I am Judy, and I agree with you. You're right about all of it. But the fact of the matter is my choices don't just affect me. I have to think about everyone involved, Walt included."

"True," she agreed.

"In another time, it could've been like a Hollywood romance. If I'd met Walt first," I began, shaking the thought from my head. "But now it would just be tarnished by a broken marriage and after that, I just don't think it would ever be the same."

CHAPTER THIRTY-NINE

"And 5, 6, 7, 8!" Mr. Dean commanded with the music. "Keep in time ladies! Straighten those legs! I want to see those kicks reaching well over your heads!"

I kicked my legs in time with the count, pushing myself further with every lift. Judy was supporting herself on my shoulder as she kicked, rather than just resting her palm there in formation, and I could feel the pressure of stabilizing her with each kick.

As the music changed, we shuffled into two lines from downstage to front, each opposite pair consecutively fanning her arms in and back out. The back of the line filed through the center heading upstage, breaking apart to stage left and right respectively until we formed a triangle, with the apex front and center, the sides gradually angling closer to the backdrop.

"STOP!" Mr. Dean hollered. "Cut the music please!" he yelled to his assistant, Miss Barker. She was also in charge of costumes, scheduling, and set design. A woman of all trades. The troupe came to a halt, each of us looking puzzled, wondering why we'd stopped mid-number. "Judy," Mr. Dean called, motioning for her to come forward. "Can I speak to you for a moment?"

"Yes, of course, Mr. Dean," she replied. Watching as Judy approached him, I noticed an almost undetectable limp. She was quite good at masking it, but it was there.

"The muscle relaxers," I whispered to myself.

"Everyone take five," Mr. Dean ordered as everyone dispersed, parched after the rigorous numbers we'd run through so far. Leaning against the wall,

I took a long sip from my thermos. The cool water was so refreshing, giving me a renewed sense of drive to keep going. Bianca approached, taking a seat next to me.

"Hi, Charlotte," she said.

"Call me, Lottie," I replied good-naturedly.

"Lottie," she corrected herself. "Is Judy okay? It looks like she's nursing an injury out there."

"I hope so. I noticed something too."

"It was barely noticeable, but after Jade's injury I'm just tuned in to those things," she explained.

"She's quite adept at hiding it if so," I agreed. We watched as Judy walked over, carefully landing her right foot with each step. Disappointment clouded her expression. "Oh Judy, are you hurt?" I asked as soon as she reached us. "I should've paid more attention."

She looked from me to Bianca, sizing up whether it was safe to speak freely. I nodded my head, giving her the okay.

"I noticed it myself," Bianca said, trying to prove her allegiance. "I hope you'll be alright."

"Well, girls, it seems that I've tweaked something in my back. Probably just a pulled muscle, but Mr. Dean wants me to have the doctor check it out before continuing," she told us. "So, looks like I'm out for the rest of the day."

"Honey, I'm sorry," I empathized. "But he's right. Better to make sure nothing else is going on and get you back to tip-top shape."

"I know," she said, packing her things into her tote. "I was just so looking forward to running through my solo today. He asked me to recommend a stand-in," she revealed, meeting our collective gaze. Glancing at Bianca, I could see the fire in her eyes. I would've loved to dance it myself, but I was still learning the main numbers and my own small feature.

"Why not Bianca?" I proposed. "I'm sure she already knows the steps and her form is impeccable." Judy looked from Bianca to me, pursing her lips as she thoughtfully considered my suggestion. I knew that Judy would've recommended me in a heartbeat, she was the kind of girl who always put her friends first, but Bianca needed it more than me.

"Bianca?" Judy asked. "Are you up for it?"

"Yes!" Bianca cried, launching forward and nearly squeezing the life out of Judy. "Thank you so much!"

Judy reciprocated the hug, though not quite so aggressively, choking out her words, "Bianca, remember my back."

Releasing Judy from her grip, Bianca apologized, promising, "I'm sorry! I'll start running through it now! Thank you, Judy!"

"Just make me proud," Judy called after her. Judy and I watched as Bianca ran off to speak to Mr. Dean.

"That was very nice of you," I said, placing an arm around my friend.

"I think your kindness is rubbing off on me," she laughed. "Am I becoming, *nice*?" she grimaced.

Giggling, I replied, "You've always been nice. You were the first person to befriend me when I arrived. Remember?"

"Well, that's true. But I had a feeling about you. I'm honestly just impressed that you've somehow transformed Bianca. I barely recognize her."

"I have that effect on people," I smiled.

"You really do have a knack for taming the untamable. Which I'll remind you is a great quality in a teacher," she said, raising her eyebrows.

"I said I'll think about it," I laughed.

"Please do. Don't forget that I'm the genius of the group," she teased.

"I would never," I jokingly huffed, hand to my chest.

"Wish me luck," Judy said standing up, headed for the infirmary.

"Good luck," I called after her. "See you at dinner!"

* * *

Rehearsals ran for the rest of the afternoon. I nailed my feature, pleased with myself and proud of the fact that I was able to pick up all the numbers so quickly after my hiatus. Bianca shone in Judy's solo, the girls fawning over her and offering their congratulations. She looked truly happy, which was a welcome change for Bianca. Things seemed to be falling into place.

Now Judy just needed a clean bill of health by the time we opened on Friday night, and all would be right in Rockland.

"Ladies, I want to remind you that tomorrow morning we'll be holding fittings first thing. You are to report here and see Miss Barker who will direct you where to go," Mr. Dean announced. "While you're in fittings I'll be managing the crew at the theater, getting the stage set for dress rehearsals which begin tomorrow afternoon. After we break for lunch, please report directly to the theater." In our excitement, we all began talking among ourselves, chattering about costumes and the show.

"Ladies!" Mr. Dean yelled, calling us back to attention. "Thank you," he clasped his hands together as if in prayer, bowing his head. "This show is going to be a hit!" he exclaimed. Whooping and clapping, the girls started over to their belongings, beginning to change shoes and packing their things, ready to return to the Inn.

"Lottie?" Mr. Dean called. I turned, heading back in his direction. "You know that Judy's solo should've been yours?" he asked rhetorically when I reached him.

Nodding my head I said, "Yes. I know she would've put me up for it first. But Bianca needed it more than I do."

"I was going to put you in for Judy, but because I don't think her injury is serious, I gave her the final say. Plus, I was certain she'd choose you, and not just because she's your friend. You've got something. You could become a big name after this, Lottie. I have friends from the city coming to see the show and they'll be recruiting talent. I'm talking Broadway. This is going to be big for all of you. This show could change your life."

"Wow," I replied, stunned to hear that he thought so highly of me. "I have to be honest; I'm surprised to hear you say that. I know you've given me a feature part, but I don't even have a solo."

"Truthfully, Charlotte, I brought you here as a favor to Billy. I couldn't in good conscience offer that to you when you arrived. As you said, you were a little rusty and you had all the numbers to learn. But after having seen how quickly you've caught on and excelled, I'm certain you could've handled it. You really do have a bright future," he praised.

"Thank you," I replied. "I don't know what to say."

"Don't say anything. Just dance your heart out on Friday. The rest will follow," he predicted, leaving me standing there dumbfounded.

Could I really become a big name? Broadway was every dancer's goal. Imagining my name in lights, I thought back to Judy's advice. The contributing factors had suddenly changed dramatically and my earlier decision to return to life as I knew it seemed less concrete. Each time I thought I'd figured things out, the variables suddenly changed on me, and I was right back to square one.

CHAPTER FORTY

Back at the Inn, I knocked on Judy's door, hoping to be met with good news. I waited a few moments before knocking again. No answer. "Must be out," I muttered to myself, turning, and heading for my own room. Rounding the corner, I nearly crashed smack into Judy. "Oh!" I cried, lurching backward in surprise.

"Sorry!" Judy called out, laughing as she realized it was me.

Hand to my heart, I chuckled, "You scared me. Why the rush? You came around that corner like a bat out of hell."

"I've got things to do, people to see," she replied cryptically.

"Okay, I'm sure you'll expand upon that later, but I was just looking for you. How did it go with the doctor?" I asked

"Well, I've just come back from speaking with Mr. Dean," she replied. "Do you want the good news or the bad?"

"Good."

"The good news is that it's only a light strain."

"Okay, so you'll be back in time for opening night?" I asked, hopeful.

"Possibly," she replied, crossing her fingers. "Dr. Cooper wants me to take it easy for the next couple of days and go back to see him on Thursday."

"Okay, so what's the bad news?"

"The bad news is I have to give up my solo," she explained. "But most likely only for the first few shows."

"That's not horrible. It could've been worse."

"No, but according to Mr. Dean, opening night is when the Broadway people will be scouting. So that was lousy news."

"I'm sorry, Judy," I hesitated.

"What is it, Lottie?" she asked.

"I feel bad telling you now," I explained.

"Tell me! Just because I had some not-so-great news doesn't mean that I can't be happy for you."

"Well, Mr. Dean pulled me aside after rehearsal to tell me he wanted to give me your part. He even said that I have a bright future and a real chance on Broadway," I told her.

"And you're surprised?" Judy asked, incredulously. "Lottie, why did you think I was going to give that part to you?"

"Because we're friends."

"No. I'm not that nice, remember?" she laughed. "It's because you have the most natural talent of any of us here. You don't give yourself enough credit."

"You really think so?" I asked. "Maybe at one time I did, but I'm so out of practice."

"I know it. It's taken you days to pick up numbers that we've been learning for weeks."

"Hmm…" I mumbled, considering what she'd said.

"Regretting giving it away to Bianca?" she asked. "I'll gladly take it back," Judy offered, grinning.

"No, it's not that," I started, smiling at her cheeky response. "In my mind, I suppose I'd given up on that kind of future. I thought I'd missed my chance on Broadway. You know, this was my big break. I'd dance in this show, and then I'd go back to my life."

"Your chance is still coming, honey," Judy asserted. "Maybe that little bird of yours was trying to deliver a different message. Maybe he was just doing regular bird things. Or, and this is my best advice, maybe you should just listen to yourself for a change."

Judy had a point. I was focused on interpreting signs that would make the tough choices for me. I still wasn't actively choosing anything myself. It was time that I broke that habit and really took charge of my life.

"What am I doing?" I asked, shaking my head. "Why can't I just make a decision on my own?"

"Because it's scary," she stated simply, shrugging her shoulders. "These are life-altering choices. But you either make them or they're made for you by default."

"True. That's how I wound up in the mess I'm in with Charlie in the first place."

"Charlotte," Judy began, "not all change is bad. You might be surprised to find that something better is waiting for you. And there are other options apart from the two that you've allowed yourself to see."

Retreating to my mind, I began to imagine all the different scenarios. How was I going to choose? Reading my thoughts, Judy said, "You don't need to decide anything right now. Just find your focus and knock those scouts' socks off. Take it as it comes. There's no use in driving yourself crazy before you know what your options are."

"Judy, how did you get to be so wise?" I asked.

"I was born this way," she replied. "Now," she started, clasping her hands together in excitement, "Do you want to hear the rest of my good news?"

"There's more? Do tell." Judy held up a shopping bag, dangling it before me. The label read "Bett's Boutique."

"I have a date," she announced, pausing to build anticipation, "with the good doctor," she finished triumphantly.

"Dr. Cooper? Well, I see that your afternoon wasn't wasted after all," I laughed nodding toward the package in her hand. "Good for you. What's in the bag?"

"Well, seeing as I wasn't wearing my nicest undergarments today for my examination, I decided to pick up something a little more flattering for the next time around. Betty runs the cutest little shop."

"Did you say, Betty?" I asked.

"Yes, why?"

"Petite, brown hair, blue eyes?"

"Yes."

"That's Chef Johnny's wife. She's also the girl he cheated on me with back in our school days," I explained. "She was the reason for my revenge plot. I haven't seen her since we were girls. I didn't know she had a shop. I'll have to pop in and say hello."

"So many interesting stories from your youth," she laughed. "Betty was the sweetest. I'm sure she'd love to see you, even after your evil plot. And you never know, you might want to pick up a little something for yourself," she added with a suggestive glance. Raising an eyebrow, I looked at Judy to explain further. "What?" she replied innocently. "A girl should always feel good about herself, man or no man."

CHAPTER FORTY-ONE

While Judy was busy getting ready for her big date, I decided to stop at the boutique. I had a little time to kill before dinner and thought maybe Judy was right. Why couldn't I buy something nice just for myself? I'd only ever bought lingerie for Charlie's benefit and that clearly didn't work out in my favor the last time around.

Rounding the corner onto Second Street, I spotted the storefront. It had a striped awning and the logo on the front window matched the shopping bag Judy had been carrying. I pulled open the front door, bells jingling to announce my arrival. The shop was darling. Betty had outfitted it to feel like a quaint cottage. Painted dressers with open drawers held lacy bras and panties. Closets were hung with corsets, chemises, and silk robes. There were pairs of accent chairs placed about the shop in coordinating striped and floral prints. In the center of the shop sat a tufted ottoman beneath a sparkling chandelier. I noted candles burning at the front counter, the warm scent of vanilla filling the boutique.

Browsing the shop, my eyes landed upon an emerald green silk chemise. I ran my fingers along the smooth silk. It had spaghetti straps, fine lace inset panels that formed a v-pattern beginning at the hip and along the neckline to show a peek of skin, and lace along the hem. It reminded me of the dress Judy let me borrow. The night I saw Walt again. That familiar warmth washed over me at the thought of him.

"Hello, may I help you with anything?" a voice called out behind me. Turning, I released the chemise, my eyes landing on Betty Wilson.

"Charlotte?" she asked.

"Betty! I was hoping I'd see you," I exclaimed. "My friend, Judy, was here earlier and was raving about your shop. It's lovely."

"Thank you," she replied. "Johnny said you were back in town for the show. I'm glad to see you."

"Likewise," I said. "I'm happy that there are no hard feelings."

"Of course not," she laughed. "We were just kids. Besides, Johnny deserved it. He should've been honest with both of us."

"Fair point," I agreed.

"So have you found anything you like?" she asked. "I saw you looking at the emerald chemise."

"Yes," I breathed. "It's absolutely beautiful."

Noting my wedding band she suggested with a knowing glance, "I'm sure your husband would love it."

"Actually, I was thinking of getting it just for me," I said.

"I love that," she smiled. "Nothing wrong with treating yourself. This piece is from Paris. I import a lot of my fine lingerie from France. You have great taste. Would you like to try it on?"

"Paris," I gushed. I'd always loved anything Parisian, anything French, even though I'd never been. Everything I'd ever seen or read about it always seemed so romantic. "Yes, I'd love to."

Betty shuffled through the rack until she found my size. She retrieved it, saying, "I have a matching robe, would you like to try that as well?"

"Please," I said. Might as well go all out.

"Here we are," she replied, pulling the matching green silk robe off the rod. "Right this way," she directed, heading toward a row of fitting rooms, each with a gold-framed full-length mirror, crystal sconces, and an upholstered chair. She hung the lingerie on the hook, stepping aside to allow me to enter.

"Thank you," I said, taking it all in. "You've really paid attention to detail. I love everything about your store."

"Thank you, Charlotte. It was important to me that women feel comfortable shopping here. I had a vision from the start."

"It's perfect," I said.

Smiling, Betty pulled the heavy velvet curtain closed to give me privacy. "Let me know if you need anything," she called.

"I will, thank you."

I undressed, draping my clothing over the chair. Inspecting myself in the mirror, I was impressed at the flattering lighting given off by the sconces. Betty really had thought of everything. Carefully removing the chemise from its fabric hanger, I slipped it over my head. The emerald silk draped my body perfectly, skimming my curves and highlighting my figure, the fine lace landing mid-thigh.

Turning to examine myself at every angle, I noted how the silk expertly fell, as though it was tailored for me. I had to have it. Pulling the robe off the hanger, I slipped my arms into the sleeves. The cool fabric felt amazing on my skin. Wrapping the robe tight, I cinched the sash, tying a bow at my waist. The robe was cut thoughtfully, stopping just short of the chemise to allow the lace to peek through. If I can't visit Paris, at least I can look like a French girl, I thought to myself. Next best thing. Running my hands over my hips, I threw a coquettish look at the mirror.

"How's it going in there?" Betty called from the opposite side of the curtain.

Fixing my face as though Betty could see me, I laughed, "Great, Betty! I absolutely love both pieces, I'll take them."

"Wonderful," she said. "Take your time. Once you're changed, we can sit and have a cup of tea if you have a few minutes."

"That sounds perfect. I'll be right out."

* * *

"Over here," Betty called, "The tea is just steeping. How do you take it?"

Walking over to the armchairs and side table where she waited, I said, "Just milk, thank you."

I sat down, draping the lingerie carefully across the back of my chair. "This is quite lovely, Betty," I said, my arm sweeping to encompass the whole of the boutique. "What a nice shopping experience."

"That was the idea," she said happily, pouring tea into each cup. "I'm so glad that it all came together." Handing me the cup and saucer, she sat back in her chair.

"Thank you," I replied, taking a sip. "This hits the spot. It's been a long day of rehearsals," I explained.

"I'm sure. Tell me, how is it to be back in town after all these years?"

"You know, I hadn't realized how much I missed this place. Being here now, I can really appreciate all it has to offer."

"I know it's quaint, but there's something to be said about small towns."

"There really is," I agreed. "I'm finding friendships here that I don't have at home."

"Massachusetts, right?"

"Yes. My town is probably three times the size of Rockland. You just don't get that tight-knit feel in such a large community as you do here."

"You could always come back," she suggested.

"I'd be lying if I said it hadn't crossed my mind," I confided.

"And your husband? Would he be willing to make the move?" she asked. Doubt clouded my features at the thought. "I'm sorry," Betty said, noticing my hesitation. "I didn't mean to pry."

"That's okay. It's not you, Betty. I'm just going through some... challenges... in my marriage right now if I'm being honest," I revealed. "There are so many things up in the air. I don't know what will happen once the show ends."

"Oh, Charlotte, I'm so sorry to hear that," she sympathized, placing a hand over mine. Her genuine kindness didn't go unnoticed. Her kind gesture opened the floodgates and suddenly I couldn't contain it anymore. The whole sordid story came flowing out of my mouth. I couldn't stop myself.

"Wow. I can see why you're struggling, honey. That's a lot to deal with," she said.

"I'm so sorry, Betty," I began. "I don't know why I told you all of that. I haven't even seen you in ages. I shouldn't have dumped all that on you."

"It's quite alright," she assured me. "Sometimes it helps to just get everything out and it looks like you really needed it. Listen, why don't you come by the house for dinner? Johnny is off on Monday nights, and we'd love to have you."

"That would be so nice, thank you. I could use a change of scenery."

"Why don't we say 7 o'clock?" she asked. "That'll give you time to go back to the Inn and freshen up."

"Perfect," I replied.

"Now let me ring you up for those," she said, gesturing toward the chemise and robe. "And I'm going to give you the Rockland resident discount," she said with a wink.

"Betty, you don't have to do that," I argued.

"I don't have to," she agreed. "I want to. Besides, if it wasn't for you, I might not have ended up with my Johnny. I owe you one."

Chuckling, I replied, "Well, when you put it that way, I suppose I can't refuse."

CHAPTER FORTY-TWO

Walking back to the Inn, I examined Rockland in a new light. I could see the girls and me stopping at the General Store to buy candies or all of us having a family dinner at the Inn. I imagined Judy stopping by for coffee and a chat while Penny played at our feet.

Betty had opened my eyes to yet another possibility. What if we relocated to Rockland? It was the perfect town for families. Everyone knew each other and watched out for one another. It was a wonderful place to grow up.

But Charlie would never leave the garage. It was his baby. Though it made sense for us to start over without Alice looming across the street, I wasn't sure he'd be open to it. Grimacing at the thought of her, I crossed First Street to get to the Inn.

And what about Broadway? This was my big chance at everything I'd ever dreamed of and had written off as out of reach. If I was offered a spot, would I take it? If I did, how long would I be away from my girls? Was that fair to them? Could Charlie and I make a fresh start? Would he even support me?

Climbing the front steps, so many questions raced through my mind as the entrance door opened and Judy emerged. Her red hair was set in waves around her face. She wore a demure navy sheath dress and had chosen a bright red lipstick in contrast to her buttoned-up look.

"You look great, Judy!" I cried. "Are we dressing the part?"

"He IS a doctor, Lottie. I have to be on my best behavior," she explained with a giggle. "I thought this look was more doctor's wife."

"Wife?" I said, eyebrows raised.

Chuckling, Judy said, "You never know. I've always thought of myself as doctor's wife material."

"As long as you can still be yourself."

"I'll never change for anyone. What you see is what you get. I'm glad to see you decided to take my advice," Judy said, gesturing to my Bett's Boutique shopping bag. "Now, what have you got there?"

Blushing, I replied, "I treated myself and bought a little something. And it looks amazing if I do say so myself."

Clapping, Judy exclaimed, "Confidence looks good on you, my friend! Keep this up. I like this Lottie," she gestured to the new, self-assured version of me. Smiling, I had to agree.

"Thanks. Betty actually invited me to dinner at hers tonight."

"Oh, I'm glad you got on well."

"We sat down for tea and a chat," I began, wincing, "and I ended up telling her everything."

"Everything?" Judy asked with a hint of concern.

"Everything."

"Okay, well what's done is done," Judy stated. "Can we trust her? She seems like a good person."

"Let's hope so. I felt comfortable enough to tell her in the first place, so my gut says yes."

Judy put a hand to her chin, lost in thought. "Maybe it will be good for you to get another perspective, from someone who's known you since you were young. She's more of a neutral party so she may see things differently from Billy and me."

"True. I guess I'll find out soon enough," I said. "Well, I'd better go freshen up. Enjoy your date, I want to hear all about it."

"I'll pop by your room afterward if it isn't too late. It all depends on where the night takes me," Judy replied with a sassy grin.

"With you, one never knows," I laughed, hugging my friend goodbye.

* * *

Knocking on the door of the Wilson home, I smoothed my skirt and stood up a little straighter. Betty opened the door, smiling. I handed her the bouquet of flowers I'd picked up on the way over. "Oh, thank you, Charlotte, these are lovely. Please, come in. Johnny's in the kitchen finishing up dinner," she explained.

"Thank you, it smells wonderful. That has a nice ring to it, 'my husband is in the kitchen,'" I joked.

Betty laughed, leading me inside. "It works for us. I haven't got a leg to stand on when it comes to cooking, especially next to this guy. I'll just put these in water," she said, arranging the flowers in a vase.

Johnny turned from the saucepan he had been attending to and gave Betty a sweet kiss on the cheek. "Lottie! Glad to see that you took us up on our offer."

"Yes, thank you. Now we can properly catch up," I said.

"Why don't you ladies have a drink and I'll bring dinner out as soon as I'm finished?" he suggested.

"Sounds perfect, honey," Betty agreed.

These two made a great match, working together easily and so obviously appreciative of one another. Watching them, I felt a pang of jealousy. My marriage didn't look like that.

"Lottie, what can I get you to drink?" Betty asked, interrupting my train of thought. "I have wine, I can make martinis or Tom Collins..."

"Wine would be great," I decided.

"Perfect, I have a white chilling. I'll be right back," she announced, leaving me alone in the dining room.

Looking around, I could see touches of the boutique reflected in the room. Running along the inside wall was a painted sideboard, like the dressers in her shop, with an antique gold-framed mirror hanging above. The dining chairs were covered in a pin-striped fabric complemented by floral curtains. A framed wedding photo sat beside a few candles burning on the sideboard, with another candle at the center of the dining table.

"Here you are," Betty offered, placing a wine glass on the table. She sat opposite me holding her glass mid-air. "Cheers," she said.

"Cheers," I replied, clinking my glass against hers. "This is really lovely, Betty. I can see so many touches of the boutique."

"Thank you, I really wanted to make the shop feel like an extension of home since I spend so much of my time there."

I took a sip of my wine, crisp notes of pear and vanilla awakening my taste buds. "This is great," I said, motioning to my glass.

"Johnny selected it specifically as a complement to the meal," she explained.

"I can't wait to see what he's made. My mouth is watering," I laughed. "Occupational hazard with so many rehearsals. I'm always famished!"

"I bet," Betty agreed. "I think it's great that you've come back home for the show. You always were the best dancer in town."

"Thanks, Betty," I replied sheepishly.

"I mean it. The rest of us girls were always in awe of you. I was certainly intimidated, especially when Johnny and I started speaking. At the time I thought you were an ex-girlfriend. If I'd known you two were still together, I wouldn't have dreamed of talking to him."

"Of me? I never knew that. I suppose I was a bit feisty back then," I chuckled. "Johnny got himself into some hot water over that, didn't he?"

"Well, you got him good. He's never looked at a blueberry the same," she joked, taking a sip of wine. "Did you keep up with dance after the move?"

"Not really. I went out dancing with friends for fun, but soon after I met Charlie, and my life went in a different direction."

"I hope you don't mind my asking," Betty hesitated, "but is that part of the reason for everything going on now? I know that if I didn't have the shop, I'd go crazy."

"I think it's part of it. Somewhere along the way I lost myself." Betty nodded, listening intently. "I've always wanted a family, especially after losing my dad, so I think I just placed all my focus on that," I continued. "As time went on, I started to feel restless. Don't get me wrong, I love my girls, I love being a mom. Some days I enjoy being a housewife, but I started to feel invisible. When Mr. Anderson called, I was over the moon, and it finally clicked."

"I can't imagine you being invisible. You were always the life of the party,"

Betty said.

"Not lately," I told her, swirling the wine in my glass. "Over the years I just started to fade into the background. Charlie was starting a business, so I supported him. The girls came along, and my life revolved around them."

"And now?" she asked. "How are you feeling since returning to dance?"

"I finally feel like myself again. Except this isn't reality."

"Well, maybe it's the first step in figuring out what's next," Betty offered.

As I pondered that thought, Johnny swept into the room carrying a platter of oven-roasted chicken and vegetables in one hand and a pan gravy in the other.

"Soups on, ladies," he announced, placing our dinner on to the table. "Let's eat!"

CHAPTER FORTY-THREE

Johnny served our dinner family-style, each of us helping ourselves. To complement the roast chicken and vegetables, he'd made an apple sausage stuffing, a green salad with pears and walnuts, and fresh-from-the-oven dinner rolls. Passing the dishes around the table, I thought of Charlie and the girls, all of us sitting around the dinner table.

"Roll?" Johnny asked, holding a basket before me.

"Thank you," I replied, reaching in to grab one. "Oh, they're still warm!"

"Is there any other way to serve a dinner roll, Lottie?" he asked, voice dripping with sarcasm.

"Johnny never cuts corners," Betty said with pride. "You'd think that after cooking all week at the Inn, he'd want a break."

"Are you telling me that you eat like this every night?" I asked in amazement.

"We do," Johnny assured me. "I love it. I wouldn't want it any other way." He and Betty caught each other's gaze, and I could see their mutual admiration. It was sweet. A pang of jealousy hit me. I wanted that again. "So, Lottie," Johnny began, carefully selecting each component on his plate to create the perfect bite, "Betty tells me you're thinking you'd like to come back to Rockland."

Betty, nearly choking on the food in her mouth, quickly swallowed saying, "Johnny that's not what I said." Turning her attention to me she added, "I mentioned our conversation and how you missed it here."

She shot Johnny a look that told him to zip it and he sheepishly replied, "Yes, right. That's what I meant."

Looking at the two of them, guilty looks creeping onto their faces, I knew that Betty had shared the full conversation. "It's okay that you shared our conversation with Johnny," I said, looking from one to the other. "I trust you both."

"Lottie, please know that we would never share that outside these walls," Betty reassured me.

"Really, we wouldn't," Johnny confirmed. "Betty was worried about you."

"You seemed so overwhelmed," Betty blurted out. "I'm just happy that you were comfortable enough to share everything with me after all these years. We just want to be here for you."

"I am and I appreciate it. To answer your question Johnny, I'm starting to think that I would like to come back to Rockland for good," I decided.

"That would be great, Lottie. We'd be glad to have you. I know Billy would be thrilled, he's so happy to have you back in his life," Johnny said.

"I need to talk to Charlie about it," I said. "We're obviously on shaky ground right now. I suppose I have the upper hand after the incident, but his garage is finally becoming profitable, so I don't know if he'd be willing to start over."

"Oh, he's got an auto body shop?" Betty asked.

"Charlie's Garage," I nodded. "Which is coincidentally located across the street from Baker's Brew. Alice's coffee shop."

"Oh," Betty said, "much too close for comfort. I can understand why a fresh start might be a good thing."

"You know, there's no garage in Rockland," Johnny added. "Just a few guys who know a little about cars. In fact, the only auto body shop around is probably 40 miles away. It could be a smart business move. Supply and demand."

"Hmm," I considered his suggestion. "I didn't realize. I'll have to see how he feels about it. For the moment, we decided that I would focus on the show, and we'd work things out afterward."

"That seems reasonable," Betty said. "Sometimes taking a little time to process things makes all the difference."

"I agree," I said.

"Lottie, Betty told me the rest… about what happened on the train," Johnny revealed, shooting an apologetic look in Betty's direction. Cheeks burning, I dropped my gaze to the table, unable to make eye contact as I waited to hear his take on the situation. "First, I want to say no judgment. You don't need to feel ashamed in front of us."

I looked up from the spot I'd been staring at. "I'm so embarrassed. That's not who I am."

"You're going through something. People make mistakes. Which brings me to my point. I'm sorry for being dishonest with you all those years ago. I should've been upfront about my feelings for Betty." He looked lovingly at his wife, and then back at me with a regretful expression. "You didn't deserve that," he said.

"I didn't. But we were kids, and I'm beginning to understand how you felt. You probably didn't deserve to walk around with blue hair for weeks, so I'm sorry too. But at the time, it made me feel better," I teased. "Everything worked out for the best. We can all agree to that." They nodded in agreement.

Johnny continued, "I also wanted to say that I know how it feels to be caught between two people you care about. I can only guess how difficult it must be once you add marriage and family into the equation."

"Don't forget infidelity," I added somewhat sarcastically.

"That too," he noted. "It's complicated, but when the time comes, you'll know what to do."

"Just follow your heart," Betty added, gazing at her husband.

We sat in silence for a few moments, each thoughtfully pondering my dilemma. It was nice to hear that they understood and to know that I wasn't alone in all of this.

"Can I say something else?" Betty asked, breaking the silence. Johnny and I looked up, waiting for her to continue. "At the very least, I think you should introduce Charlie to that blueberry filling," she smirked. "Don't lose your edge, Lottie."

I burst out laughing, nearly sending my wineglass careening across the table. Luckily, I caught the stem just in time. "You might be on to something, Betty. Maybe I just need to tap into the old me."

* * *

After clearing the table, Johnny returned with a chocolate cream pie and a fresh pot of decaf coffee. “Now that pie looks perfect for throwing,” I laughed, pointing at the decadent dessert.

“Watch out, Charlie!” Betty pantomimed throwing a pie and we dissolved in giggles.

“Ladies, my pie is not going to be part of your revenge plot. This is a masterpiece,” he stated with a British accent, reverently placing it down in the center of the table. Serving up three healthy slices, he passed them out to us.

“Cream and sugar?” Betty asked me, preparing the coffee.

“Yes, please,” I answered, anxious to dig into the slice sitting in front of me. It looked amazing, the golden crust flaky and the whipped cream forming perfect peaks atop the rich layer of chocolate filling.

Once everyone was served, we all tucked into our desserts. The pie was better than I’d imagined. Johnny’s crust was better than mine and I’m known for my pie crust. “Johnny, this is amazing,” I said. “What did you add to the crust?”

“Chef’s secret,” he said with a wink.

“Fine,” I huffed, “but expect that I’ll be taking a slice for the road.”

“I can do you one better,” he replied. “You can take the rest of the pie. I made two.”

“Well, I know what Judy and I will be having for our midnight snack,” I laughed.

“Judy’s great,” Betty added. “She seems like a lot of fun. We had a ball at the shop today.”

“She’s the best,” I agreed. “I’m lucky to have met her. She’s been a great friend.”

“She also has impeccable taste. She picked out some of the finest pieces in the shop,” Betty said, taking a sip of coffee before continuing. “You know, she actually reminds me a little of you when we were younger. Maybe with just a touch more attitude.”

"She's quite sassy," I agreed. "I never thought of that, but now that you say so, I think you're right. Maybe that's why I was drawn to her."

"Kindred spirits," Betty approved. "It seems to me that you ended up back in Rockland for a reason. Just think about what life would be like in Massachusetts right now if you'd never come."

"That's a good point," I said, imagining it. "I couldn't bear having to face Charlie every day, especially knowing that Alice is always just across the street. Or having to hold it together in front of my girls. The distance has at least given me room to think and work my feelings out."

"And it's opened up new opportunities," Betty added.

"And reunited you with old friends," Johnny chimed in.

"And brought new friends," I smiled. "Betty, I like your perspective. I'm glad we reconnected. I actually feel like I'm exactly where I'm supposed to be at the moment."

"Agreed," Betty said, placing a friendly hand over mine. "You have so many great options right in front of you and you're strong. I know that you can handle whatever challenges come along with whatever choice you make."

"She's right, Lottie," Johnny added. "Betty has never steered me wrong."

"Thank you," I said, smiling in gratitude. "Both of you, truly. I'm so happy that I came to dinner tonight. This has really helped."

"That's what friends are for," Johnny said, placing an arm around Betty's shoulders. She leaned over, resting her head on his shoulder. Sitting back in my chair, I drank the last sip of my coffee, enjoying the company of my old friends. I could really see myself here. I felt a sense of excitement just thinking about it. This trip was proving to be so much more than I'd anticipated.

CHAPTER FORTY-FOUR

On the off-chance Judy had already returned from her date, I knocked at her door. After a few moments, the door swung open. Judy stood before me in pajamas, all traces of makeup had been removed, and her hair was tied up in a scarf.

"I take it the date wasn't all you'd hoped it would be?" I surmised, taking in her appearance.

"Come in," she began, ushering me into her room. "He was a total drip. Only talked about his work. There's only so much interest I can hold for anatomy, Lottie. Unless I'm studying the male form up close and personal."

"Judy!" I exclaimed, laughing out loud. "You're wicked."

"I'll accept that," she said with a chuckle. "You'll never accuse me of being boring."

"True," I agreed. "Can I use your phone to call downstairs?" She gestured to me to help myself. Picking up the handset, I dialed the kitchen.

"Kitchen," Billy informally answered the call.

"It's me. She's here, so if you don't mind bringing it up?"

"I'll be right there. Lucky for you because I was going to dig in myself if I'd had to wait much longer," he admitted.

"See you in a minute," I replied hanging up. Directing my attention to Judy I explained, "Billy."

"Oh good! I like lounging around with the two of you."

"You'll really like what he's bringing," I hinted.

"I hope it's not cocktails," she moaned.

"No," I laughed. "Something better."

A few minutes later Billy called, "Knock, knock," from the hall. Judy answered the door, relieved when she saw the chocolate cream pie on the tray Billy carried.

"What did you think it was going to be?" I laughed. "Johnny sent me home with leftovers, so I thought I'd share."

"How was your dinner tonight?" Billy asked. "Johnny mentioned that Betty invited you to join." We all sat down cross-legged on Judy's bed, pie plates in hand. Billy had brought peppermint tea for each of us, the perfect counter to the rich chocolate dessert.

"I had a great time," I started. "I already told Judy, but I stopped into Betty's shop earlier and we got to talking. I told her everything."

"Did you?" he asked. "I'm surprised."

"It just came out. There's something about Betty. She's got such a calming way about her."

"I know what you mean. She's like a natural truth serum," he laughed. "You're so grown up, Lot. Who would've thought you'd spill your darkest secrets to Betty of all people?" he teased.

"Hilarious," I rolled my eyes. "We talked about all that. It was ages ago, and those two are perfect together," I said. "They actually helped me look at things differently."

"I told you," Judy chimed in. "Sometimes it helps to get a different perspective."

"It did. Betty pointed out some things that I hadn't thought of. Rockland being a blessing in more ways than the obvious, considering. Can you imagine what it would be like if I was still at home? If after finding Charlie and Alice like that, I had to face him and my girls every day?"

"That would be torture," Judy sympathized.

"Completely," Billy agreed.

I took a bite of my pie, savoring it, before dropping a bomb on my friends. "So," I said, pausing for effect. "I'm considering moving here. Permanently."

I was met with a moment of silence. Not the reaction I'd been expecting.

"Are you serious? That would be amazing!" Billy exclaimed, placing his plate down and hugging me. "Really? Are you pulling my leg?"

"I'm serious. I really like it here. I didn't realize how much until coming back. And I missed having real friends and that small town feel. Besides, I don't know if I can go back and look at anything the same. How could I be there knowing that Charlie and Alice were right across the street from one another every day? I would drive myself crazy."

"I love this idea!" Billy cried, clasping his hands together in delight. "It'd be like old times."

Judy emphatically put her plate down on the tray, as if taking a stand. "If you stay, I'm staying, too," Judy announced.

"What do you mean? What about Broadway?" I asked.

"I could still go to Broadway," she explained. "I'm saying I'd put down roots here. With my back as is it, it's not looking too promising right now, but someday."

"Would you really?" I asked, excitement creeping into my voice. "I have to admit that when I was imagining living here, you both were in my vision."

"Obviously," Judy deadpanned. "In all seriousness, I've had the best time here. Mostly thanks to you two. I've never had friends that I cared about more than myself," she laughed.

"Can you imagine?" Billy said. "The three of us taking on Rockland. I'll have my own bar where I'll serve my signature cocktails and your cookies. You two can open a dance studio together. Madame DuBarre must be ready to retire soon. It's perfect!"

It was perfect. Looking at my friends, I felt truly happy and excited for the future for the first time in a long time.

"To Rockland," I said, holding up my teacup for the others in cheers.

"To Rockland," they said in unison, as we delicately clinked our teacups in solidarity.

* * *

Back in my room, I got changed and ready to go to bed. Tomorrow's schedule was jam-packed with fittings and dress rehearsals, and I needed my beauty sleep. Climbing into bed, my mind raced at the prospect of moving back to

Rockland. I looked over at the clock on the bedside table noting that it was a bit late, but not much past the time that Charlie usually turned in for the night. Picking up the handset, I dialed my home number.

On the third ring, Charlie picked up, apprehensive. "Hello?"

"Charlie, it's me," I said.

"Lottie! Is everything okay?" he asked, concern lacing his words.

"Yes, I'm fine. I didn't mean to alarm you."

"It's pretty late," he replied.

"I know. I just needed to talk to you," I answered.

"Oh," he said, hopefully. "I'm glad you called."

"I've been thinking," I began. "Before I tell you, promise me that you'll really hear me out before you give an answer?"

"Okay," he agreed.

"Well, I've thought about coming back home after the show is over. I just don't see how I can ever look at anything the same or how I'll ever drive down Main Street again, to be honest." Charlie remained silent, listening intently. "I really love it here in Rockland. I didn't realize how much until coming back. I have real friends here. It's such a welcoming community, it would be a wonderful place for the girls to grow up," I continued. "I know that the garage is finally doing well, but I've asked around and the closest garage is 40 miles from here. You wouldn't have any competition. It could be a great business move," I suggested. "I'm also thinking that I'd like to open a dance studio. My friend, Judy, wants to stay, too. We could be partners and-"

"Whoa, Lottie, slow down," Charlie interrupted.

"It could be a fresh start for us," I blurted out.

"Are you saying you want to try to fix things?" he asked cautiously.

"I think I do," I said, not completely certain myself. "I'm still angry and hurt, but I suppose I can see why it happened. I think we owe it to ourselves and the girls to at least try."

"But a move, Lottie? We'd be back at square one. Can we handle that? Isn't it what got us here in the first place?"

"I don't know," I said simply. "But I don't see us moving forward if I come home." I could hear a long exhale from the other end of the line. I could picture Charlie lying on his back, staring at the ceiling, and running his fingers through his hair.

"I just don't know, Lot. Is it practical?" he asked. "And what about your mother? Are you going to leave her here with no family?"

"I thought she could come with us," I said. "She still has plenty of friends here. I know for a fact that she's kept in touch with Mrs. Hall. It might be good for her to come back and make peace with this place. Charlie, I don't know if this is the answer, but it feels right to me. Knowing what we do now, I don't think we'd make the same mistake twice."

"We hope," he said, not sold on the idea.

"And I'd have my friends and my own goals to focus on... and distance from everything that happened there to work on us." We remained on the line, silent except for the sounds of our breathing. I'd said my piece, feeling a sense of relief after having put my thoughts on the table with Charlie.

"Listen, it's late and I have to be up early since one of my guys is out. Let me think about it," he finally said, breaking the silence.

"Okay," I replied.

"It's nice to hear you excited. You sound happy. I've missed that."

"Me too. We should both get the bed, but please think about it?"

"I will. Night Lottie, I love you."

"You too," I said, unable to say the actual words. "Night." I replaced the handset on the receiver, flopping back against my pillow. I'd have to speak to my mother in the morning to introduce the idea. Feeling satisfied with my plan, I rolled over, quickly falling fast asleep.

CHAPTER FORTY-FIVE

The ringing alarm jarred me out of a deep sleep. I'd been dreaming, the conversation between Charlie and me obviously carrying over into my subconscious. In the dream, we lived in Rockland. We had a house that resembled Johnny and Betty's place. Charlie had his garage, and I had my studio. Mother had an apartment close by on Second Street. For all intents and purposes, we seemed happy.

I had walked the girls to school, stopping to say hello and have a chat with the other moms before dropping by the garage to bring Charlie a fresh coffee, this time without incident. I met Judy at our dance studio to run through a few routines before classes commenced.

The next thing I knew, I was standing on the bridge by myself. In the dream, it had been a cool, foggy autumn morning. I heard footsteps behind me and turned to see a male figure approaching through the mist. I sensed that it was Walt, a surge of warmth rushing over me, but strained to make out a face through the fog. It was too thick. I got a little closer and the face started to come into focus. And then I woke up.

Frustrated, I exhaled in a huff and rolled over to switch off the alarm. If only I could've made out the face. Curious about what it had all meant, I yearned to go back to sleep to find out what was next, but I was due for my fitting in an hour. I pulled myself out of bed, washing and dressing for the day before heading downstairs to meet the girls for breakfast.

* * *

Judy sat in her usual spot, talking animatedly with the girls, no doubt filling them in on her doctor's visit and the outlook for her solo. I joined the group, sitting in my regular seat next to Judy. "So, I told him I would see him Thursday and no sooner," Judy quipped. "There most definitely will not be a second date."

"Boo!" Jean cried out. "That's not the story I was hoping for Judy, especially from you," she teased. "How are we supposed to live vicariously through you with a date like that? Bor-ing," Jean yawned for emphasis.

"Listen, honey, it's not the date I was looking forward to either. I dropped a dime at Bett's Boutique only to end up alone in my jammies," she laughed.

"Look at the bright side, girls," Jean began, "It means that the good doctor is still on the market!" I noticed a few heads perk at the mention of Dr. Cooper. He was quite a handsome man, though he sounded a bit dry. Mary M.'s cheeks shone a bright pink, giving away her obvious interest.

"Mary," Judy called across the table noticing her flushed cheeks as well, "he's all yours!"

"Are you sure you wouldn't mind?" Mary asked timidly.

"Not at all. I've got a date with Jack tonight anyway. He's much more my speed," Judy replied, pouring herself a glass of orange juice.

"Fast?" I chimed in.

"Well, Lottie, you're awake after all," Judy chuckled. "And yes, why waste time getting to the good stuff?"

"You're too much," I said, shaking my head.

"Looks like that trip to Bett's might've been worthwhile after all," Jean joked.

"Time will tell," Judy answered with a grin. "Don't wait up for me tonight, ladies."

* * *

At the Community Center, Miss Barker, Mr. Dean's assistant, waited for us, clipboard in hand. There were various stations set up with makeshift dressing curtains, a seamstress waiting at each, with labeled costumes hanging on various racks. Miss Barker directed Judy and me over to the far corner of the room where a middle-aged woman sat, ready with pins.

"Hello," Judy held out a hand, "I'm Judy James and this is my friend Charlotte Abbott."

Taking our hands and shaking them, the woman replied, "I'm Ms. Madsen, pleased to make your acquaintance."

"Nice to meet you as well," I replied.

"Okay ladies, I have your costumes organized on separate racks. I'll have you both change into the first option and I'll pin them to make the necessary adjustments before the show," she said, staring at me curiously.

"Sure thing, we'll head back and change," Judy replied, quickly shuttling me behind the curtain.

Handing me an ice blue bodysuit with beaded fringe that reminded me of icicles, Judy whispered, "What was that about? Was she never taught that it's rude to stare?"

"Beats me," I replied. "She does seem a bit odd."

"You can say that again," Judy commented, pulling on her costume, and striking a pose.

"You look amazing," I said. "Like winter personified."

"You mean like Bianca?" she joked. "I'm only kidding, relax. You too, yours fits like a glove," she commented. "Maybe we won't need tailoring after all. Come on." I followed Judy out from behind the curtain, standing before Ms. Madsen.

"Judy, you're first," Ms. Madsen said, directing Judy to step up on the platform. "Hmm, this looks okay. I'll just take up the straps ever-so-slightly," she told us, pulling the straps tighter to give Judy's bust a boost.

"Yes, definitely," Judy said, admiring her reflection. "I'll take any help I can get in that department."

"Very well, why don't you go ahead and change into the next look," Ms. Madsen instructed. "Your turn," she said, turning to me. "You said it's Charlotte, correct?"

"Yes, but you can call me Lottie," I responded, stepping up onto the platform.

"Lottie, then," she repeated, inspecting the costume from every angle. "I can't see anything that needs to be altered. It looks like this one was tailor-made just for you."

"Thank you," I replied. "That makes this easy."

"Indeed," she agreed, looking more closely at my face, examining my features. I looked back at her with a quizzical expression.

"I'm sorry," she said, realizing I'd caught her staring once again. "You remind me of someone I used to know."

"Oh," I replied, nodding in understanding. "Are you from Rockland? I actually grew up here."

"No, not originally, but I live here now," she said. "Did you? I don't recall seeing you around town."

"Oh, yes, that's because I moved away when I was younger. I've just returned for the show."

Studying my face she asked, "By chance, are you related to the Dawsons?" just as Judy rounded the curtain.

"I am," I replied, intrigued to hear more. "Dawson is my maiden name."

"Oh my," she said, her face going white, a hand flying to cover her gaping mouth. "I believe I knew your father." Overhearing the conversation, Judy moved closer to me, demonstrating her allegiance, and looking from me to Ms. Madsen.

"John Dawson?" I asked, wondering who this woman was.

"Yes," she whispered, her gaze softening. "John," she said with admiration. Stepping off the platform, I approached Ms. Madsen, a chill running down my spine as I heard my mother's voice in my head. "I didn't want to tarnish your memory of him..."

"How did you know each other?" I asked cautiously.

"He was a friend," she said.

Swallowing, I replied, "And my mother? Did you know her?"

"We'd never formally met," she answered, carefully choosing her words.

Looking closely at Ms. Madsen, I took note of the unique locket she wore around her neck. It was gold with a blue enamel face inset with pearls and diamonds in the shape of a star or possibly a compass rose. Suddenly I had goosebumps, the hair on my arms standing on end, on high alert. I had seen that necklace before.

CHAPTER FORTY-SIX

"Ms. Madsen," I swallowed. "Have we already met?"

I watched as her hand immediately flew to her heart as she absentmindedly rubbed the locket between her thumb and index finger. Hesitantly, she replied, "I believe that we have… when you were a child."

"Honey, why don't you sit down a minute?" Judy suggested. "You look as though you've seen a ghost."

"I think I have," I whispered, taking a seat next to Ms. Madsen. "I've seen that necklace before. And she knows me."

"Oh boy," Judy muttered under her breath. "I'm going to let the two of you talk while I fetch you a glass of water, okay?"

I nodded in agreement. Ms. Madsen looked at me with a mixture of shame and sadness. The same look I'd gotten from Charlie. From the expression on her face, I was sure of the answer, but the question begged to be asked. Taking a deep breath to try to build up my courage, I forced out the words that had invaded my head, "Ms. Madsen, did you and my father have an affair?"

Her head dropped and her shoulders began to shake. Part of me felt almost sorry for her. When she regained her composure, she sat up to face me. "I don't know if I can explain properly," she began. "I loved your father with all my heart. I wouldn't call it an affair. That implies that it was fleeting. There was something between us that drew us together." I nodded, thinking of Walt.

"When I met him, I didn't know about you and your mother. At the time,

I lived a few towns over. John came into the shop where I worked to have a button sewn back onto his jacket as he was passing through." The mere mention of his name in this woman's mouth, now that I knew who she was, made me cringe.

"I remember that day like it was yesterday…" her voice trailed off, recalling the memory. When our hands touched as he handed me that button, I felt a charge. I hadn't ever felt that before, or since. I repaired the jacket as he waited. When I was finished, he asked if I'd like to join him for lunch and I accepted." Listening intently to her story, I couldn't help but compare it to my own. It was hauntingly similar.

"From then on, we'd meet whenever he was passing through. I fell for him. I'd count the days until I could see him again. Eventually, I learned of you and your mother, and it crushed me. I couldn't bear the thought of breaking up your family, so we ended things." She paused, trying to work out whether to share the rest of the story with me.

"Go on," I prompted.

"The last day I saw your father he gave me this locket," she began. "He brought you along with him and introduced me as an old friend."

In my mind's eye, the memory came back to me. I was standing on a sidewalk in front of a storefront. There were window boxes painted green holding brightly colored flowers, and a bench where my father sat with Ms. Madsen. I watched as a bumblebee buzzed among the flowers. I had to be no more than six years old.

"He told me that this signified the North Star," she explained holding the locket to display the design, "and that someday it would lead us back together," she continued. "You spotted the locket and asked if it was my birthday. John went along with the lark. You said that it was a beautiful present and told your father that we should have a cake to celebrate properly. Not one to disappoint his girl, he suggested that we walk over to the diner to share a slice of chocolate cake. And then we said goodbye. That's the last time I ever saw him," she said, a note of sorrow in her voice.

I sat there, digesting all of what I'd just been told. I didn't know whether to feel sorry for her, angry for my mother, or simply disappointed in my father. "I don't know what to say..."

"I'm sorry for any pain I caused your family. Truly," she said.

"Ms. Madsen, I never knew any of this until today," I replied. "My mother hinted at something regarding my father just recently, but never confirmed anything."

"Oh, dear," she said. "After the funeral, I would've thought she told you."

"No."

"You ask your mother," she said. "I never meant to upset her. I just needed to say a proper goodbye."

* * *

Judy returned with glasses of water for each of us. Looking from me to Ms. Madsen, she realized that she'd missed quite a story. "We should get a move on if we're going to stay on schedule," she announced. "Lottie, why don't we go and change?" Thankful for her take-charge demeanor, I followed Judy behind the curtain. Handing me the next costume, she motioned for me to change. "Are you okay?" she whispered, concerned.

"I don't know," I replied somewhat bewildered.

"What happened?"

"Long story short, that's my father's mistress," I said.

"Oh, boy," she said, drawing out her words for emphasis.

"Do you want to know the strangest part?" I asked.

"Of course, I do."

"I almost feel sorry for her. I'm not even angry outside of the fact that I feel for my mother. Their story sounds just like me and Walt."

"Oh, honey," she said, putting an arm around me. "Maybe I was wrong about the signs. If there was ever a sign, I'd say that this is it."

"Almost ready, girls?" Ms. Madsen interrupted over the curtain.

"Be right there," Judy hollered back before saying quietly to me, "If he was trying to send you a message, what do you think he's trying to say?"

Looking up at the ceiling and letting out a long exhale, I replied, "I can't say for certain, but I think he's telling me to follow my heart. He never got the chance to."

CHAPTER FORTY-SEVEN

Rushing us both out the door of the Community Center, Judy pulled me around the corner of the building. Checking to be sure none of the other girls were around, she asked, "Lottie, are you really okay?"

"I am," I nodded, strangely serene.

"Honey, that woman basically just dropped a bomb in your lap. It's okay, perfectly expected even, to be upset."

Leaning against the wall, I thought about everything Ms. Madsen had said. "You know, Judy, I've been beating myself up since I got here. I've been feeling so guilty about my feelings for Walt and that kiss. I've been constantly questioning whether I'm living up to the expectations my father set for me when he gave me that necklace. When all along, he was clearly not adhering to any of those principles himself. He was stepping out and even included me in it, probably to be sure nothing happened when they broke things off," I said. "All this time, I've been trying to live up to an ideal that isn't even real." Judy remained silent, letting me get my thoughts out as they came, working out my feelings as I spoke. "I guess what I'm saying," I continued, "is that none of us really knows what we're doing. We just do the best we can. We make mistakes. And we carry on."

"Wow," she began with a skeptical expression. "Okay, you're handling this much better than I expected."

"It's all starting to make sense to me," I said calmly. "There is no real right or wrong answer. It all depends on your perspective. I think the lesson is to follow your heart and you'll find your way. That was the significance of the locket."

"I like that sentiment," Judy agreed. "It's good advice, something a father would want to impart to his daughter."

"I think so," I said. "I need to talk to my mother. She mentioned something about not wanting to tarnish my father's memory when I told her about Walt. She had to have known. Ms. Madsen said something happened at the funeral but wouldn't say what. I don't remember anything, but I was so heartbroken at the time, I probably wouldn't have noticed even if I had been paying attention."

"Maybe you can give her a call during our lunch break," she suggested. "Though that may not be enough time from the sounds of it."

"I think I'll try her after rehearsals. I have a feeling that it's going to be a long conversation."

* * *

Opening the door to the theater, I was met with a strong sense of nostalgia. The building had undergone some improvements since I'd last been, but the architecture remained the same. I was still awestruck by the deco details incorporated throughout, from the ceilings to the moldings, sconces, and even the handrails. I attended so many productions here with my parents when I was young. Every year we'd go to see the holiday show. It was our Christmas tradition. I looked forward to us all getting dressed up in our Sunday best to watch the dancers entertain us in their fancy costumes, the jaunty music putting everyone in the holiday spirit.

Inhaling deeply, I took a moment to relax my shoulders away from my ears. I was here. I had finally made it and it was my turn to create that magic. I headed backstage, bumping into Mr. Dean. He was harried, rushing to request the finishing touches on the sets.

"Lottie! Let the girls know I'll be there in five," he called after me, out of breath and heading in the opposite direction. "We're going a little out of order today since some of the costumes are still being altered. We'll start with your feature."

"Okay, will do!"

Backstage was a chaotic scene. Dancers at one end warming up. Seamstresses hurriedly making alterations. Set designers moving looming scenes on wheels to their proper locations in sequential order. In the middle of it all stood Miss Barker with her clipboard, cool as a cucumber as always, overseeing it all. Jogging over to join the troupe, I said, "Hi girls! I just bumped into Mr. Dean. He'll be ready for us in five. We're starting with the third number."

"Thanks, Lottie," Nancy replied. Trying to hype everyone up, she turned to the group exclaiming, "Okay, ladies, let's get ready to show Mr. Dean what we're made of!" The girls cheered and whistled, kicking their legs sky high in response. We were nearing the culmination of our hard work and the troupe's excitement was palpable.

* * *

Stepping out onto the stage dressed in the ice-blue ensemble I first wore when Ms. Madsen shared her story, I shook my head, in an attempt to physically remove that thought from my mind. Regaining focus, I got into position for the third number, my feature. Lights trained on us, music building, the curtains opened, and I got my first taste of what it was like to perform on a big stage. Even without an audience, I felt a rush.

The music swelled, signaling the start of the routine and I flowed through the moves as if on autopilot. No thinking was required. My body knew what to do. It was a welcome reprieve from the past few days of living in my head. Sailing through the routine, we ended in formation. The endorphins running through me, I couldn't help but grin. I could never understand the need to remind dancers to smile. How could one help it?

The applause from Mr. Dean, Miss Barker, the seamstresses, and various crew members echoed throughout the empty theater. "Well done, ladies!!" Mr. Dean shouted. "Beautiful! Please head backstage to change for the next number, and let's keep this momentum going!" As we shuffled backstage, my heart swelled with pride. I'd made it. I'd found my way.

* * *

The rest of the afternoon flew by. We ran through each number, quickly changing into the accompanying costumes while the sets were changed and then rushing back to our positions on stage. It was a race against the clock. My favorite was the final costume, a deep crimson velvet short dress with white fur trim. It was a little on the nose but fitting as the closing number was an upbeat take on the famous final scene in White Christmas, complete with a large, decorated tree center stage just like in the film. The fast pace of the music was infectious, making it easy to forget one's troubles and revel in the holiday spirit, exactly what I needed. With my mind laser-focused on the show, I was present in this moment only. There was no room for anything else, and all my worries fell away.

CHAPTER FORTY-EIGHT

"That was amazing!" Judy exclaimed, breathless from excitement. "I really wanted to give it my all. I had to keep reminding myself to take it easy, my solo could be just days away," she said, holding up her crossed fingers.

"Exactly. Let your body heal," I agreed. "I have no doubt that you'll be back at 100% in no time." Both of us practically skipped down the steps of the theater, giddy with excitement. We headed down Main Street, back to the Inn.

"So, was it everything you'd always dreamed of?" she asked. "Your feature was flawless by the way. Between you and me though, Kay better step it up before Friday."

"Judy!" I cried, though I had noticed that Kay's movements were a bit stiff. "I think she just gets too much in her head and loses the ease of the transitions. And yes, it was amazing," I gushed. "I can't imagine how it'll be with a packed house."

"Infinitely better," Judy decided. "I really love the closing number. It's so, merry."

"Positively merry," I agreed. "It's my absolute favorite. Everything about it; the music, the choreography, the costumes. White Christmas is my number one holiday film and Vera-Ellen's my idol."

"You're just living out a fantasy, aren't you?" Judy laughed.

"I believe I am," I confessed. "You know, when we were out there, I felt so content. I wasn't thinking about Ms. Madsen or my father or Charlie or Walt. It was just me truly enjoying myself."

"I know what you mean," she concurred. "Everything fades away and you're just in the moment."

"Exactly," I said. "And that's what I need more of in my life. More time to just be me."

"Well," Judy began, "linking an arm through mine. We can do that every day once we open our studio," she hinted, suggesting that the decision had already been made. "I honestly think it will do wonders, for both of us."

"Agreed," I said noting the hopeful expression on Judy's face. "I need to stop seeking happiness from other people and taking a backseat to everyone else's wants and needs. This is what I want and I'm going to make it happen," I declared.

"That a girl!" Judy cried. "I like this take-charge side of you."

"So do I," I agreed. "She's been M.I.A. for far too long." Arm in arm, we continued on our way, making plans for the future. It was starting to look like blue skies up ahead.

* * *

Closing the door to my room, I sailed over to the bed, flopping down onto the coverlet on my back. Stretching my arms wide, I laughed out loud, excited by my prospects in Rockland. I never could've expected any of this when I picked up the phone the day that Mr. Garrett called. I rolled over, looking at the clock. Picking up the handset, I dialed home. It's now or never, Lottie, I thought to myself.

"Abbott Residence," my mother's voice sang over the line.

"Hi Mom, it's me."

"Charlotte! I'm happy to hear from you. How is everything?" she asked cautiously.

"It's great, I just got back from dress rehearsal, and it was amazing to be onstage. I can't wait for Friday. With an audience, it'll be unbelievable."

"Oh honey, I'm so glad that it's working out for you. You've waited so long for this," she began. "I've been thinking about our last conversation, and I wanted to tell you I'm sorry. I never should've moved us away when you were so close to being in the show all those years ago. I really regret that."

"Wow, thanks for saying that, Mom. It's okay. I really think it was supposed to happen this way."

"How so?" she asked.

"Well, I actually wanted to talk to you about something. Do you have a few minutes? Where are the girls?"

"Sure, dear. The girls are outside with Charlie. He's been coming home a little earlier to spend time with them while I fix dinner," she explained.

"Oh! That's nice. I'm surprised. He's never really done that before," I said.

"Truthfully, I think he's had a change of heart since *the incident*," she whispered.

"Hmm, interesting."

"It is."

Pausing for a moment to build up my courage, I finally spoke, "At fittings today the seamstress and I got to talking. She looked at me as though she knew me. And I found out that she knew Dad." The silence on the other end of the line was deafening. "Mom?"

Clearing her throat, my mother murmured, "Virginia."

"Ms. Madsen?" I countered.

After a long pause and audible sigh, my mother said, "One and the same. And what did she have to say?"

"I know about the affair," I blurted out.

"You've always known," she answered. "You were just so young. I first found out about it from you. You and your father came home one day, and you told me all about the nice lady. How you'd had a birthday party and he'd given her a beautiful blue locket with a star made of pearls."

"I don't remember telling you," I said, searching my memory. "But Ms. Madsen did tell me about that day. I must've buried it somewhere deep down. I recognized her necklace."

"That doesn't surprise me. It's very distinct. I'd had my suspicions of course, but until that day I wasn't certain. I knew that your father's heart belonged to someone else. I could feel it. He loved me, but not as he loved her."

"I'm sorry, Mom. I didn't want to upset you, but I needed to hear your side of the story."

"It's okay. I've struggled with whether to tell you, especially after hearing that you'd be returning to Rockland."

"What did you do when you found out?" I asked.

"I didn't do anything. I was afraid to confront the truth. It was eating me up inside, knowing that it had been happening right under my nose. I looked for comfort elsewhere."

"What?" I asked, shocked. "Do you mean what I think you mean?"

"Yes," she said plainly. "I met someone who was smitten with me. His compliments and undivided attention filled me up in a way your father had neglected over the years. It was short-lived. I felt such guilt even though I'd been wronged first. It's never sat well with me."

"Oh," I replied, not sure of what to say while making the obvious comparisons.

"That's why I was cautioning you against getting involved with Walt. I know all too well that these things don't tend to end well for either party."

"I see," I said, finally understanding her standpoint. "What happened?"

"Well, your father stopped making out-of-town trips for work after you told me about the necklace, so I gathered that Virginia was out of the picture. I ended my dalliance. I couldn't live with the sneaking around."

"So, neither of you told the other?"

"We never did. Some things are better left unsaid," she explained. "We both had to live with our choices. Eventually, as years passed, we grew close again. It wasn't the same as it had once been, so much had happened, but we were partners and respected one another."

"I can't believe it. I always thought of you two as the model of marriage."

"We're all just people, Charlotte. We make mistakes."

CHAPTER FORTY-NINE

Talking candidly with my mother, I realized how little I knew of my parents. The people I recalled were only a piece of the picture. They'd protected me from seeing the rest of it to preserve my happiness. I was starting to see that my struggles weren't so unique after all.

"Ms. Madsen mentioned something about the funeral," I revealed. "She thought I'd already known but said I should ask you to tell me."

"Ah yes, the funeral," she began. "I think I'll sit down for this. That day, at the cemetery, the priest had just finished the service. We brought tulips to place on the coffin."

"Dad's favorite," I interrupted.

"Always," she replied, wistfully. "You and Billy had placed your flowers and went off for a walk. You were devastated and wanted to get away from it all. No child should ever have to experience that loss. As the widow, I was expected to stay until all the mourners had offered their condolences. Mrs. Hall had stuck around to support me. After everyone had gone, a woman approached."

"Ms. Madsen," I inferred.

"She was dressed in black, wearing a matching headscarf and large sunglasses. Dressed as she was, I didn't recognize her as a friend or acquaintance from town. I watched as she knelt, placing two red roses on top of our tulips. She stood, turning in my direction, and against that backdrop of black shone a blue enamel locket with a pearl star inset."

"Yikes," I said, my words laced with worry.

"As soon as I laid eyes on that pendant, everything I'd been holding in for years, the jealousy, the betrayal, the guilt, the anger, came spewing out of me. I was a lunatic. There's no other way to put it. Thankfully, Mrs. Hall took charge of the situation and escorted Virginia to her car. She was consoling me when you and Billy returned, having heard the commotion. I assumed you thought I was just overcome with emotions given the day."

"I do remember you crying and carrying on," I said thinking back to that day, her body shaking inconsolably as Mrs. Hall rubbed her back with Billy and me standing to the side, helpless. "Why didn't you ever tell me?"

"Because it wasn't your problem, Charlotte. It was between me and your father. It had nothing to do with you. He was gone, so what good would it have done to tell you? You'd always been daddy's girl and I wasn't going to sully that. Seeing Virginia brought all those feelings back. I was stuck in the past. I couldn't move on, and I didn't want to keep dragging you down with me. That's when I made the decision to move out here with Aunt Jane."

"I had no idea."

"Well, you wouldn't. You were a teenager. You had your own life and interests and friends. And dance."

"It's funny how as a child you don't realize that your parents have a life outside of you."

"Sometimes that's a good thing," she said.

"I have to agree. I don't know how I would've reacted back then had I known all of that."

"You're a married woman now," she said. "You understand the nuances of relationships. When you're young, things look black and white."

"I'm sorry you went through all of that. I wish I could've been there for you."

"I came through it. Your aunt was a help and Mrs. Hall has always been a wonderful friend to me."

"I'm glad you kept in touch," I began. "In fact, there's something else I wanted to talk to you about, but now I'm hesitant to bring it up."

"Goodness, what else could there possibly be? Is this about Walt?" she asked, a hint of suspicion in her voice.

"No, not that. It's just that being back in Rockland has made me realize how much I missed it here. I have Billy and now Judy, and of course, Mrs. Hall, and Johnny and Betty."

"I'm glad to hear that Johnny's forgiven you," she chuckled.

"He has. I had dinner at his house, and we all got on splendidly," I smiled, remembering. "My point is, I'd like to move back here. Permanently. And I'd like for you to come with us."

"Oh, I don't know honey. I haven't been back there in years."

"I know, but maybe it would be good for you. You could finally make peace with everything that happened here," I suggested, hopeful.

"It's something to consider," she replied tentatively. "Have you spoken with Charlie about this? What about the garage?"

"I have. It would be a smart business move for him. He's thinking about it."

"Interesting. I suppose I can understand the desire for a fresh start given recent events," she said. "And Walt? Is he out of the picture for good?"

Hesitating, I finally answered, "I haven't seen him. I've decided to focus on myself for a change. I really think the girls would love it here. Rockland is a wonderful place to grow up. And I haven't told you the best part. My friend Judy and I want to open a dance studio. The girls could be with me while I teach. When they're not in school, that is."

"You know, I think that sounds perfect for you, Charlotte. And it's a reasonable plan. A promising move for all of you. I do hope Charlie agrees. You'd be a marvelous teacher. It sounds like things are starting to move in a positive direction. Maybe going back to Rockland was the best thing for you and your marriage after all."

"I really think so," I agreed. "Please say you'll come."

"It's a lot to think about."

"I know. Maybe you'll get some clarity when you come to see the show," I proposed.

At that moment, the slam of the screen door and the patter of little feet vibrated through the handset. Excited cries rang out when the girls learned I was on the line. "There are some excited little girls here who'd like to speak to you," she announced, handing the phone to the girls. Smiling, I listened as they both talked animatedly into the receiver, not able to get a word in edgewise myself, pure happiness filling my heart.

CHAPTER FIFTY

Readying myself for an evening out, I slipped into my new chemise, admiring my reflection in the full-length mirror. Somehow, it camouflaged all my flaws while highlighting my assets. I shrugged on the robe, executing a spin to let it fan out around me à la Marilyn. Hearing a knock at the door, I pulled the robe tight, cinching the sash.

"Ah, and what do we have here," Judy announced, pushing her way into the room. "I'm glad to see that you took my advice," she said examining me from all angles. "Very nice choice, Lottie."

"Why, thank you," I replied.

"Now let's see what's underneath that robe," she pressed. "It's just us girls." Removing the robe, I did a twirl before striking a pose. "You did good," Judy nodded her approval. "This is a knockout. Paris?"

"That's what Betty told me. Imported."

"Well, you deserve it. Tell me you don't feel amazing."

Laughing I replied, "I feel amazing, Judy. You were right."

"Naturally," she joked. "Now, how do I look?" she asked, checking her reflection. She looked stunning as always. Judy wore an off-the-shoulder wrap-top dress with a billowy skirt in a deep red hue. She had paired it with gold pumps and a matching clutch. Her hair was pulled back in a loose chignon.

"Perfection," I said. "Jack won't be able to keep his hands off you."

"That's what I was going for," she giggled. "I came to ask if I could borrow a pair of earrings? I need something simple and classic to complete this look, and you know that I don't really do simple."

"You've come to the right place," I said, reaching for my jewelry case and pulling out a pair of gold starburst stud earrings.

"These are perfect!" Judy cried, snatching them from my palm. "You don't mind, do you?" she asked.

"Of course not! They're all yours," I said, smiling.

As she put them on, Judy asked, "Did you get a chance to speak with your mother?"

"I did," I replied. "There was a lot more to the story. I'll have to fill you in later. You don't want to keep Jack waiting," I reminded her.

"Oh, you're right," she said checking the clock. "Will you meet us at the hall afterward?"

"You can count on it," I replied.

"Fabulous, see you then," she called, closing the door behind her.

* * *

Moments later, there was another knock at the door. I rushed over, pulling it open as I scolded, "You're going to be late Judy, what did you for-," stopping mid-sentence once I realized it wasn't Judy after all. I was standing face-to-face with Walt. We stood frozen for a moment, before I regained my senses and choked out, "Hi."

"Hi, yourself," he said, eyebrows raised, taking in my attire. Standing there in only my chemise, I peeked into the empty hallway before yanking him into the room, quickly closing the door behind us before anyone saw. We were suddenly alone, inches apart, me scantily clad in the new lingerie that was supposed to be just for me.

"I wasn't expecting you," I said, looking up at him. When we made eye contact, the tension between us grew and the room suddenly felt 10 degrees warmer.

"I came to apologize," he said, hands forced into his pockets. "For the other night. I shouldn't have let myself get carried away."

"Oh," I said, my gaze resting on his mouth as I was instantly transported back in time to that moment. That kiss. A wave of heat rushed through me just remembering it.

"Lottie, I'm not sure I'll be able to say what I came to say with you dressed like that," he said, greedy eyes traveling over every inch of me.

"What?" I replied, distracted by my wandering thoughts. Staring at each other, our eyes communicated everything we were both thinking. Our matched gaze unwavering and the tension between us building, we began to move toward each other. Like two magnets, our attraction was an invisible force snapping us together. Our bodies met, charged energy flowing through us.

Without conscious thought, I reached up, sliding my hands over Walt's neck, running my fingers through his thick hair before pulling his head down, holding his face mere inches from mine. Our gazes affixed, neither of us moved. We had reached the breaking point. I knew this thing between us couldn't work outside of this room. There was no place for this relationship in my life and I needed to end things, but at that moment everything about him felt so right, so good. My need outweighed any rational thought. I wanted to feel him. My body demanded it. I silently willed him to understand, my eyes pleading with him to make a move. He understood.

In the next instant, his hands slid down over the smooth silk covering my backside and past the lace trim to my bare skin, his breath catching as he made contact. Lifting me up, my legs reflexively wrapped themselves around his body as my pulse started to race. Leaning into me and pinning my back against the wall, his hands gripping my bare bottom and his body pressed into mine, our mouths fervently met. Fireworks bursting inside me, I gripped his back, my nails digging in, pulling him even closer, wanting to feel every part of him against me. This feeling was like nothing I'd ever experienced. Pure desire. I couldn't get enough of him. I wanted more. I wanted everything he had to give.

His mouth on mine, his tongue teasing, he pressed his body deeper against me. I felt every inch of him tense as a rush of warmth flowed between my legs. A moan escaped my lips as he groaned my name. A few layers of fabric were the only things keeping me from feeling all of him and I wanted nothing more than to get them out of my way, to rip off his clothes so there was no barrier between us. Reaching down in search of his belt buckle, my fingers couldn't move fast enough. As I pulled at the leather strap, the shrill ring of the telephone shattered the spell we were under, quickly snapping us both back to reality. Heart pounding, I hastily untangled myself, rushing over to answer the call. Nearly tripping over my own feet as I grabbed my robe, I threw it over my shoulders.

"Hello?" I called into the handset, breathless and a little too loud.

"Lottie? Is everything okay?" Billy's concerned voice came through the line. "You sound like you've just run a marathon."

"Yes, Billy. I'm good! Everything is great!" I assured him, over-selling myself.

"Okay," he said tentatively, sensing that something was up, and I wasn't going to share, "I have some fabulous news. You're not going to believe it! I'm going to pop in before my shift."

Half-listening, I replayed the last few minutes in my mind and felt my cheeks redden. What was I doing?! I was losing it. If Billy hadn't called. *Oh God.* I don't think I would've stopped. What was happening to me? I wasn't this person. An overwhelming sense of guilt washed over me. I needed to end things before I did something I couldn't take back.

"Hello? Is that okay?" Billy asked.

"Great, thanks! Sounds good, Billy!" I exclaimed, ending the call, and rushing to place the handset back on the cradle. Looking back at Walt, I forced a sheepish smile. He leaned back against the wall, running his fingers through his thick hair just as I had done moments earlier. "That was Billy," I explained.

"I heard," he nodded.

"Listen, Walt-" I began, as he said, "Lottie, I think-"

"Ladies, first," he said, ever the gentleman.

"I'd actually prefer it if you went first," I said, procrastinating. This was it. I knew we had to end this before it was too late, but a part of me wanted to prolong things. It felt good to feel good. Pulling the robe closed as tightly as I could, I covered myself up as much as possible with the skimpy fabric. "You came all the way out here unexpectedly; whatever you wanted to say must be important."

"May I?" he asked, gesturing toward the armchair.

"Of course," I agreed, sitting down on the edge of the bed, tugging the silk down to cover my bare thighs.

"Lottie," he said, taking a deep breath, "I know I'm probably going to regret this, I'm not even fully sure as I'm saying it now, but we've got stop, before we can't," he hung his head, wringing his hands. "Don't get me wrong, if it were up to me, I'd be with you in a second, obviously. But it's not up to me. You have so many other people to consider. And I can't be responsible for breaking up a family. I won't do that to you or your girls," he said, raking his fingers through his hair in frustration and defeat.

I nodded my agreement, a wave of nausea rolling through me.

"I hope that your husband realizes how lucky he is," he went on. "I'd take his place in an instant if it wasn't already filled."

"I know," I whispered, sadness filling me. Even though I'd already made my decision, hearing him say it out loud didn't hurt any less. "I've been thinking the same thing. I owe it to myself and my family, and to you, to at least try to work through things. We don't work outside of this bubble we've created. Once we go out into the real world, the pieces don't fit together. There's a part of me that wishes things could be different, but I just don't see how. I'm so glad to have known you, but I can't trust myself with you."

"I know," he sighed, leaning back further into the chair.

"If Billy hadn't called when he did..."

"I know," he repeated. We sat in silence for a minute, mourning what could have been. Clearing his throat, Walt said, "I'm here until the weekend, I'm helping my aunt square away a few things and fixing some repairs my uncle never got to. I'd still like to see you dance before I go if it's alright with you."

Forcing a smile, I replied, "Of course it's alright. I think it's the perfect send-off. You can see what I'm really made of."

"I already know," he answered, gazing at me with genuine sincerity. "You're everything."

Gazing back at him, it took all I had to remain seated on the bed as he walked out of the room. His words would be forever etched on my heart. I wanted nothing more than to run to him, to be with him, to feel his hands on my body, his mouth on me. But I'd made my decision.

CHAPTER FIFTY-ONE

Closing the door softly behind Walt, hot tears began to fall onto my cheeks. I had just said goodbye to the man who might've been the love of my life. Sitting down in the armchair still warm from Walt's body, I sank back into it, trying to soak up some comfort. A tapping at the window grabbed my attention. Turning my head, I saw the same bluebird sitting on the sill, looking at me through the glass. He almost looked sorry for me. "What do you want?" I said aloud, watching him hop along the sill before flying off.

"Knock, knock, it's me," Billy called from the hallway. I got up and slowly opened the door, allowing Billy to enter. Taking one look at my swollen eyes and splotchy face, he rushed inside, placing his usual tray down on the bed.

"Is this about Walt?" he asked knowingly. Nodding in response, I remained silent. "I saw him pass through the lobby, and he didn't look good" he explained. "What happened, Lottie?"

Sniffling, I wiped my eyes in a futile attempt to stop them from leaking. Billy handed me a tissue, patiently waiting as I blew my nose before tossing it in the trashcan. He put an arm around me, shuttling me over to the bed where we sat down. Gathering my thoughts, I took a deep breath, retelling the whole story before collapsing onto my friend, sobbing. He rubbed my back, allowing me to let it all out until I had no more tears to cry.

"I'm sorry," I whimpered, wiping my eyes, "now I've ruined your shirt."

Looking down at the tear-soaked spots dotting his shirt, Billy replied, "Lottie, you know that I always have another shirt on hand. I'm worried about you; the shirt can be replaced."

"Oh Billy, what if I've made the wrong choice?" I cried, voicing my fear.

"Lottie, look at me," he said. "I've known you since we were kids and I know that there's no way you could've kept that up. The guilt alone would've eaten you alive. It sounds like Walt was doing what's best for you, which shows that he truly understands and cares for you. He put you before himself."

"I know," I sniffled.

"It's like they say, 'If you love something, set it free.'"

"If it comes back, it's yours," I added.

"If not, it was never meant to be," he finished, pushing a stray strand of hair off my face. "Look, you need to sort things out with Charlie first," he continued. "See what happens. Maybe you and Charlie work things out and live happily ever after. Maybe not and you find out you and Walt were meant to be. You still have your whole life ahead of you. Your story isn't over yet, but you have to live it to find out what happens." Forcing a half-smile, I nodded in agreement. "You can't skip ahead."

"For now, put all that out of your mind because I have a real fairy tale moment for you," Billy began, pulling the tray closer. Handing me a champagne flute, he continued, "And the main character in this story is you, Charlotte. Forget about the men in your life for a minute and think about what you really want," he paused for effect. "Because I spoke with Madame DuBarre. I ran into her at the market," he said, searching my face for any hint of interest.

At the mention of her name, I perked up, "And?" I asked.

"And..." he said, plucking a set of keys off the tray, dangling them before me, "she would love nothing more than to pass her studio on to you!" he exclaimed.

"Billy!" I cried in disbelief, forgetting my troubles for the moment. "That's spectacular news! I can't wait to tell Judy! You have to come with me to the hall tonight, we'll tell her together!" Clinking our glasses together, we toasted the wonderful news, quickly draining our glasses in our excitement. It was all coming together.

Squeezing me tight, Billy released me and said, "Congrats, Lottie. You deserve this. It's your time to shine."

"Thank you," I grinned. "Now tell me what was said."

"Well, I simply mentioned your thoughts about returning home and she was delighted to hear it. You know you were always one of her favorites. Anyway, she said she's been struggling with planning her retirement because she'd yet to find a suitable person to take over the studio space."

"It's just perfect, Billy! I really can't believe it. It's all coming together so perfectly."

"You're like the prodigal son, or daughter, without all the negativity," he laughed. "You're back where you belong."

"I am," I agreed, smiling down at the set of keys I held in my palm. The literal keys to my future.

* * *

"Now that that's settled, what's going on here," Billy gestured to my attire.

Aware that I was still wearing the lingerie set, I began, "Judy stopped into Bett's Boutique earlier this week. She was raving about the shop and adamant that I pop in to buy something just for me," I explained. "To feel good about myself."

"Okay, empowering. I like that," he nodded. "And did you happen to know that Walt was stopping by today?"

"No!" I cried. "I only answered the door because I thought it was Judy."

"That must've been quite a shock for you both," Billy said, eyebrows raised.

"Yes, you could say that," I agreed. "Thank goodness you called when you did. Otherwise, there's no telling what could've happened," I blushed.

"I think we both know the answer to that," Billy insinuated. "Looks like I've saved you twice today. I'm your knight in shining armor," he proclaimed.

My gaze softening, I replied, "Thank you, Billy. You've been a better friend to me than I have to you. I'm sorry for abandoning you for all those years. I should've kept in touch."

"It's forgotten. I'm just happy to have you in my life again," he assured me.

"Let's focus on the future. You can make it up to me with dance lessons. I want to impress Bobby."

"Consider it done," I replied, switching gears. "You know, before Walt showed up, I spoke to my mother."

"About moving back?" he asked.

"Well, that, and some other things," I began, filling him in on the fitting with Ms. Madsen and my conversation with my mother.

"What a day!" he declared. "Who knew your mother had it in her, she's always been so... buttoned up."

"Apparently not always," I joked.

"It just goes to show that everyone goes through things in relationships. Even your picture-perfect parents," he said.

"I'm starting to see that life is a just series of complicated events."

"You can say that again, sister," Billy agreed. "You just have to make the best of it."

"That's exactly what I plan to do," I declared.

CHAPTER FIFTY-TWO

Practically flying up the steps to the Rockland Dance Hall, I pulled the door open so hard that it swung back fully on the hinges, nearly knocking Billy over. "Gee, Charlotte, a little excited?" he teased. "You almost flattened me."

"Sorry, Billy!" I called over my shoulder. "I just can't wait any longer to tell Judy the news!"

"Slow down, girl. You're going to hurt yourself, or someone else, namely me," he hollered sarcastically over the big band music. Walking into the hall, we scanned the dance floor for Judy and Jack. Spotting her red dress, I headed toward the tables flanking the dance floor. Judy saw us approaching and gave an apathetic wave. Billy and I shot puzzled looks at one another, and shrugging our shoulders made our way through the waves of dancing couples.

"Hi!" I yelled, breathlessly. "Quite a crowd for a Tuesday night, isn't it?"

"It's pretty hopping," she replied, deflated. "Everyone's on holiday for the opening."

Sitting down, I patted the chair next to me, motioning for Billy to take a seat. "Why the long face?" I asked Judy. "Where's Jack?"

"He went home," she pouted.

"Bad date?" Billy asked.

"Not at all," Judy replied over the music. "It was a great date. It was going so well at first."

"What happened?" I asked.

"I'm not sure," Judy began. "We stopped back at the Inn so I could grab my gloves. We'd planned to take a walk over to the bridge later this evening," she hinted suggestively. "But by the time I came back downstairs, he said that he'd better call it a night. 'A friend needed him,'" she gestured, a look of suspicion on her face. Looking from Billy to me and noting the knowing expressions we wore, she asked, "What? You think he's seeing someone else, don't you? I knew it was too good to be true."

"Walt," Billy and I said in unison.

Confusion washing over her, Judy cried, "You think he's seeing Walt?!"

"No!" Billy burst out laughing, with me following suit.

"I was going to say," she answered. "I didn't get that feeling from either of them. No offense, Billy," she added as an aside.

"None taken," he replied. "Those two, definitely not. Shame though."

Rolling my eyes at Billy, I explained to Judy, "Walt was at the Inn earlier. He came to see me right after you left. In fact, I answered the door assuming it was you. In my lingerie," I added pointedly.

Judy's eyes lighting up upon hearing that titillating tidbit, she leaned forward saying, "Ooh, tell me more..." After realizing that Walt was nowhere to be seen she asked, "Did you turn him down, Lottie?"

"It's complicated," I began.

"Oh boy," she grinned. "Like I said, tell me more."

"Things would've gotten a lot more heated than they already were if Billy hadn't called and interrupted us," I started.

Looking at Billy, Judy shook her finger, jokingly reprimanding him, "Shame on you, Billy."

With a laugh, Billy replied, "I'm actually the hero in this scenario. You'll see,"

Raising an eyebrow and turning her attention back to me, Judy instructed, "Go on."

"Walt came to apologize, and to end things," I began, telling the story for the second time. Once I got to the end I said, "So it's likely that Jack ran into Walt as he was leaving. I'm sorry, Judy. Your date was ruined because of me," I revealed, crinkling my nose.

"Don't worry about it, Lottie. It seems that I just left him wanting more,"

Judy replied confidently. "Now that I know that there's no one else, I'm just dandy," she smiled mischievously, eyes twinkling.

"You'll be better than dandy when you hear the rest," Billy teased. "Lottie? Care to finish the story?"

"Yes," I started, "we owe a huge thanks to Billy here because," I paused, pulling the set of keys from my handbag, and jingling them in front of Judy's nose, "we have a studio!" I squealed.

Snatching the keys from my fingers, Judy jumped up from her seat, bouncing over to Billy, and throwing her arms around his neck. Planting a kiss on his cheek, she cried, "I always knew you were a keeper!"

Lapping up the attention, Billy shouted, "That's what they all say!"

Turning to me, Judy shook the keys like she'd just won the grand prize on a game show and hollered, "It's really happening?!"

"It's really happening!" I repeated, grinning from ear to ear.

"Sure is, ladies!" Billy yelled. "Now let's dance!" And with that, the three of us headed out onto the dance floor, not a care in the world to bring us down.

* * *

"I have an idea!" Judy shouted over the music, flailing her arms and legs to the beat.

"What is it?" I hollered back, matching her moves.

Eyes gleaming with excitement, she suggested, "Let's go check out our studio!"

"Billy, do you think it would be alright with Madame DuBarre?" I asked, leaning in so he could hear me.

Nodding, he replied, "That's why she gave me the keys. Let's do it!" Giddy with the prospect of seeing our future business, Judy and I sashayed all the way to the front door of the hall, Billy trailing behind us chuckling. Exiting the building onto Main Street, the cool, quiet night was a welcome contrast to the sweltering, raucous atmosphere of the dance hall.

Wiping her brow, Judy announced, "Wow, quite balmy in there, wasn't it?"

"Agreed," I said, pushing stray strands of damp hair off my face. "You don't notice it while you're having fun. This night air feels amazing though."

"Indeed," Billy agreed. "Now, off to take a peek into your future..." he crooned in a deep voice, hands floating around an imaginary crystal ball.

"You're a regular mystic, Billy," Judy quipped, smacking him on the shoulder.

"I am. I did make this happen," he pretended to be humble. "Granting wishes, making dreams come true."

"Actually," I chimed in, putting an arm around Judy, "We made this happen. But to be fair, you were instrumental in getting the ball rolling, so we thank you," I said, landing a kiss on Billy's cheek.

"Happy to be at your service, ladies. So long as you don't forget my free lessons," he joked. We walked the rest of the way in companionable silence, rounding the corner to the studio entrance on First Street. The looming brick building sat on the corner, frontages on Main and First flanked with oversized arched windows. Filling the studio with natural light during the day, the windows and high ceilings contributed to the open, airy feel. I couldn't have designed a better studio space myself.

Stopping at the door, I paused, looking up at the window lettering that read "Madame DuBarre's School of Dance." Pride swelling within me, it registered that I had come full circle. Once a student at this very studio, I would soon be imparting my knowledge and skills to aspiring young dancers, perhaps even discovering the next Vera-Ellen myself. Smiling, I pulled the keys from my bag, a wave of anticipation and excitement rolling over me.

"Do the honors, Lottie," Judy prodded, with Billy looking on in delight.

"Here goes nothing!" I exclaimed, turning the key in the lock, and opening the door to my future.

CHAPTER FIFTY-THREE

Flipping on the switch and flooding the space with light, Judy and I squealed gleefully. The studio was exactly as I remembered it. A perfect clean slate with soft white walls, gleaming hardwood floors, and a mirrored back wall, a barre running the full length.

"Lottie! It's better than I imagined!" Judy exclaimed, arms raised as she walked the length of the room, turning to take in the full expanse of open space.

"This is where it all started," I said, running my fingertips along the barre. "This is where I first discovered my love of dance." Thinking back to my first dance class, I recalled a quite young Charlotte poised at the very spot I was currently standing, practicing pliés, determined to perfect the technique even on the inaugural day.

"I never told you this, Lottie, but I watched your classes sometimes from the Shake Shop," Billy admitted, blushing as he pointed to the soda fountain across the street. "I'd sit at the window with a coke or a malt pretending to read the comics my father pushed on me to 'be like the other boys.' I never liked them, so I'd watch you dance instead. You always stood out among the rest. I've always known you had something special," he revealed. Turning to Judy, he smiled, nodding in my direction, "This one was always in the studio. She was relentless about getting everything just right."

"Sounds like we're two peas in a pod, honey," Judy said to me. "I did the same thing."

"When you love something, it's not work, and I truly loved it from the very first class," I shrugged. "I never knew that Billy but thank you for supporting and believing in me all this time," I smiled appreciatively.

"You made it easy. You're a true talent," he replied. "I feel the same way about my cocktails. Why work when you can potentially make money at something you genuinely enjoy?"

"That's my motto," Judy called from the barre, stretching, "I'll be damned if I ever work a day in my life!"

Laughing at her candor, I headed for the stairwell, calling, "Come on, let's check out the studio upstairs!"

"Another studio? Why didn't you say so?" Judy replied, nipping at my heels.

* * *

Climbing the stairs two at a time, Judy and I raced to the top like children dashing to claim a swing at the playground. Reaching the last step, neck and neck, we both dove onto the landing, collapsing into a fit of giggles. Billy, stepping over us, flicked on the lights, shaking his head in disbelief as he entered the studio first. "Well, look at that," Billy teased, "I win."

Picking ourselves up and straightening our skirts, we entered the second studio space behind him. It was identical to the first, the only difference being a more impressive view of downtown Rockland. Walking over to the windows, I hoisted myself up onto the ledge. Seated on the bricks, I could see all the way down Main Street, the streetlights illuminating the people on the sidewalks hurrying to get out of the cold. The marquee from the dance hall shone blue in the distance. The theater created a red and gold beacon in the opposite direction, soon to read "Rockland Holiday Show 1956."

Looking out over my hometown, I was struck by how little had changed over the years. The important things had remained constant here, untouched by the expansion transforming other parts of New England. Some of the shops had been replaced by new owners with new wares, yet the General Store had stood the test of time, a tribute to the past. The Shake Shop with its jukebox gave a new generation of teens a place to hang out, starting to find their independence. The dance hall, theater, and community center were still supporting and contributing to the arts. The Inn continued to give travelers a comfy place to call home while they enjoyed the offerings of the area. Rockland had somehow retained its small-town charm while also evolving to meet modern needs. It really was a hidden gem.

"Penny for your thoughts?" Judy asked, hopping up onto the ledge to sit next to me. "Oh! How beautiful," she sighed looking out at the town below.

"Isn't it?" I said, squeezing her hand.

Never one to be left out, Billy approached, putting an arm around each of us. "Look at how far we've come in such a short time, ladies" he mused. "Promise me you're both here to stay," he said, looking from Judy to me. Both of us nodding, it was understood that we were committed to putting down roots in Rockland. Pleased with our response and ever the dramatic, Billy proclaimed, "To the Three Musketeers! All for one and one for all!"

"United we stand!" I chimed in, raising my free arm skyward.

"Divided we fall!" We finished in unison, smiles lighting up our faces. With a hand from Billy, Judy and I jumped down from the ledge, the three of us closing the studio. Heading back out into the cold, we huddled together, warmed by the bond of friendship and the promise of a happy future together in Rockland.

CHAPTER FIFTY-FOUR

"Is it true, Lottie?" someone called from behind me.

Turning toward the direction of the voice, I saw Bianca hurrying down the hallway toward me, wearing a hopeful expression. "Is what true?" I asked, puzzled.

"Is it true that you're taking over the DuBarre School of Dance?" she blurted out breathlessly.

"Gee, news certainly travels fast around here," I replied. "But yes, that's the plan. Just as soon as I get my husband on board. Why do you ask?"

"I've just seen Madame downstairs. I overheard her talking to Mrs. Hall about the studio. She'd like to sit with you for breakfast, so I offered to fetch you."

"Oh, then I should hurry down. Thanks, Bianca," I smiled.

"Lottie, wait, I wanted to ask something else," she began, hesitant.

"Go on then," I prodded.

"Do you think there's anything I might do to help out at the studio? I mean, as a job?"

"A job? I thought you were headed for Broadway?" I questioned, somewhat shocked by her request.

"I am. I mean, I'd like to, someday. The thing is," she said, twirling a strand of hair around her finger, "I like Rockland. It's starting to feel like home. And you and Judy and the other girls are beginning to feel like family. I'm not sure I want to give that up," she explained. "Besides, I've realized that I still have a lot to learn, and I'd like for you to be my mentor," she added expectantly. "I think you could prepare me for Broadway."

"Wow, Bianca, that's very mature of you, though I don't know that you need any help in that department. Your performances have been flawless," I started, considering her proposition. "For now, I'll say this. Nothing has formally been decided yet, though it's moving in a positive direction. I can't agree to anything just now, but if things work out as I hope they will, I'll do my very best to help you reach your full potential."

Throwing her arms around my neck, Bianca squealed, "Thank you, Lottie! You're the best!"

Laughing, I warned, "Don't get too excited, we don't want to jinx it."

Removing her arms and regaining her composure, she replied calmly, "Of course, just keep me posted."

"Will do," I said, heading for the lobby as I called over my shoulder, "and you better be ready to work, a mentorship with me doesn't come for free!"

"I'm ready for whatever you want to throw at me. I can take it!" she hollered back.

"Don't I know it," I muttered to myself with a chuckle.

* * *

Walking into the lobby, I spotted Mrs. Hall speaking with Madame DuBarre. She waved me over, eyes twinkling. "Here she is now," Mrs. Hall announced my arrival.

"Hello, Charlotte," Madame DuBarre greeted me, smiling as she took both my hands in hers. "I'm so happy to see you again."

"You too, Madame. It's been too long." She was as poised as ever, with perfect posture and the same graceful way about her that I'd always admired. She was quiet and kind, yet still commanded attention.

"Too long, indeed," she agreed. "Shall we?" she asked, making a sweeping motion toward the dining room.

"Yes, let's," I replied, following her to a table for two. Once seated, Madame placed her napkin neatly across her lap, crossing her feet at the ankles. I followed suit.

"Well, I have to say that I was so happy when Billy approached me about the studio," she began. "I've spent my best years there, but I'm ready to retire. Maybe do a bit of traveling. I can't let it go to just anyone, so I've been dragging my heels." Nodding my understanding, I waited for her to continue.

"Among all my students over the years, you always stood out in my mind, you know. Such a precocious young child when you began. And so very determined. I remember many nights where I'd have to call your father to come and get you, just so I could close up," she chuckled. "You've always had a natural talent and the drive to take you places. After speaking with Mr. Dean, I'm aware that you took a hiatus, but have picked up right where you left off. I just have one question before we move forward with this proposition. Tell me, Charlotte, why did you stop dancing?" she asked, searching my face for clues.

Not anticipating her line of questioning, I sat in stunned silence for a moment. I wasn't expecting her to come out and ask me directly. I thought we were just exchanging pleasantries as a formality, but she wanted to get down to the heart of things. It was just assumed that it was the natural progression of things; get married, have children, focus on supporting the home and family. But deep down, I knew that there was more to it than that.

Clearing my throat, I said, "Madame, thank you for the kind words. It means a lot to hear that, especially coming from you. If I'm being honest, I don't think I've ever said this out loud," I said, my voice catching. "The truth is, I lost a piece of myself when my father died. I lost interest in everything. I was devastated; I turned my back on everything that had once given me joy. Once we left town, there was a part of me that resented moving from Rockland, away from any real chance of starring in the Holiday Show or a future in dance, away from my friends and everything I'd always known. I closed that chapter of my life and left it all behind me."

"I eventually began to dance again socially. By then, my attention had already moved away from honing my craft. I focused only on creating a family, on replacing what I'd lost. I concentrated on being the perfect, supportive wife to my husband and loving mother to my children. And I was. I was so good at it that I completely lost sight of who I am," I said, a single tear rolling down my cheek. I quickly wiped it away before revealing, "And I regret it deeply."

"Oh, Charlotte, I don't mean to upset you," Madame said. "I just need to be certain that this is what you want, that it will fulfill you."

"I was fortunate enough to be given this second chance. Most people can't say that. Coming back to Rockland has put everything into perspective for me. You know, Madame, all my life I've dreamt of dancing on Broadway. I've imagined my name on the marquee, I could see myself center stage, spotlight trained on me, the sound of applause filling me with purpose. I'm realizing that maybe that's not my dream anymore. Don't get me wrong, I love to dance, and I will do it until the day I die. I just no longer need that outside recognition or attention. I have my family, good friends, and if you'll allow it, a career that allows me to spend my days doing what I love, maybe even helping someone else reach their dreams of dancing on Broadway."

Madame DuBarre gave a satisfied smile and replied, "That's exactly what I needed to hear, Charlotte. I'll have the paperwork drawn up. And don't give up on Broadway just yet. You never know where life might take you." Patting my hand with her age-spotted one, she said, "Now that that's settled, let's enjoy our breakfast. Tell me all about your family. What are the little ones' names?" she asked.

"I have two girls," I began, "Kathy, I call her Kitty Kat, and Penelope, my little Penny." I filled Madame DuBarre in on most of what had happened over the years, editing out the more recent salacious parts. She listened intently before thoughtfully sharing her story with me. We sat, chatting over croissants and tea, founder and successor, forever bonded by our love of dance.

CHAPTER FIFTY-FIVE

As Madame and I finished up our breakfast, Judy strolled in dressed for rehearsals, hair coiffed and makeup expertly applied. Waving her over, I called, "Judy! Over here!"

Judy approached, with an inquisitive look on her face. "Good morning," she said, nodding in Madame's direction.

"Madame DuBarre, meet Judy James, my good friend, and future partner," I introduced the two women.

"Madame! How lovely to meet you," Judy gushed as soon as she heard the name, taking Madame's hand in hers. "Lottie and I are simply ecstatic about the opportunity you've given us!"

"Judy James, it's wonderful to meet you as well," she replied, approvingly. "I can see that you two have the enthusiasm to succeed and I trust that you'll take great care of the studios."

"We certainly will," I assured her.

Rising to stand, Madame smiled, "I look forward to doing business with you both. It's time for me to pass the baton to the next generation as it were. Judy, why don't you sit," she suggested, patting her now empty seat. "I'm sure you and your partner have much to discuss. I'll be in touch once the papers are drawn up."

"Thank you," Judy replied, taking a seat.

"It's my pleasure. It does my heart good to know that the school will remain in capable hands," she said.

"Thank you, Madame. For everything. I owe you so much," I said.

"Charlotte, I appreciate that, but I only gave you the tools you needed.

You've had the desire and natural ability all along, and that's not something I can cultivate. I'm happy to see that you're finally claiming your place in this world. It's where you belong." Pride swelling in me, I choked out a thank you. "I'll see you both on opening night," she said with a wink. "If I don't see you before, good luck, blow them away." Watching Madame DuBarre exit the dining room, I leaned back into my chair letting out a long exhale.

"You okay?" Judy asked, concerned.

"I am," I said. "She just caught me off guard and made me realize something that I suppose I've known all along."

"And what's that?"

"After my father died, I sort of gave up on myself. I put all my energy into creating a picture-perfect family and lost sight of who I am."

"I can see that. You were young, Lottie. That seems like a natural reaction to such a traumatic loss."

"I suppose. I'm just so lucky to have gotten this second chance. I'm finally being true to myself, and it feels like everything I ever wanted is within reach."

Smiling, Judy replied, "I'm glad. Because if there's anyone who deserves to have it all, it's you."

* * *

Onstage, we ran through all the numbers, tightening up our lines and making full use of the expanse of space. There was much more room to move on stage as compared to the community center. Hitting our marks here required more focus.

"Lottie, Kay, I want to run through your feature again in the third number," Mr. Dean called. "From the break from the kick line, please," he instructed the orchestra. Taking our respective places at opposite ends of the kick line, Kay and I readied ourselves to begin. I had a nagging feeling that Mr. Dean wasn't happy with the feature. Hopefully, Kay would get out of her head and really push the limits on this take.

"Come on, Kay," I whispered.

"And 5, 6, 7, 8," Mr. Dean yelled from his seat in the auditorium, watching our movements intently. "Pas de bourrée, pas de bourrée, and fan, and fan!" he commanded. "Cut the music!" We halted all movement, frozen in place and awaiting his next instruction. As I feared, the feature wasn't up to snuff. Looking over, I saw Kay hanging her head in defeat.

"Kay!" Mr. Dean shouted. Kay's head snapped up at attention. "Do you want this feature?" he demanded.

"Yes," she responded timidly.

"Not convincing! Try again!"

"Yes!" she shouted.

"That's more like it! I want the two of you backstage running through it while the rest of us move on to the next number. Lottie! You want to be a dance instructor? Here's your first chance. I trust that you can get her fan kick where it needs to be?" he challenged.

Nodding, I called, "I can!"

"Okay, go on then! There's no time to waste. We're getting down to the wire ladies, and my show will be nothing less than perfect!"

* * *

Kay and I hurried backstage, making no haste in following Mr. Dean's orders. As we rounded the curtain, Kay burst into tears. "Kay," I soothed, rubbing her back to try to calm her, "it'll be okay. He's just stressed."

Wiping her tears away, she replied with a sniffle, "I'm so sorry, Lottie. I know that I've been dragging the feature down."

"Listen, I'm confident that I can help you. But I need for you to listen to me, and do exactly as I say," I told her.

"Okay," she agreed. "I'll do my best."

"That's all I ask," I said. "Now, first things first. Get out of your head. You know the steps?"

"I do."

"Okay, then stop counting them off in your head as you perform."

"How did you-"

"I can see it. Your eyes give you away. You look up every time you run through it in your mind," I explained. "I want you to look directly at me. Run through the entire feature and keep your gaze here," I instructed, pointing at my eyes. "I'm going to mirror your movements so you can see it in front of you. Ready?" She nodded in agreement.

Standing opposite Kay, I called out, "And 5, 6, 7, 8!" We began with the pas de bourrée, transitioning into the fan kicks. I could see that she was leaning slightly into the kick, barring herself from full extension. "Eyes on me!" I shouted as soon as her eyes began to drift skyward. She immediately returned her gaze, mirroring my moves. We ran through the steps over and over until she was performing them with ease.

"Now, I want you to try it on your own this time," I said noting her tentative expression. "Kay, you've just done it multiple times. You don't need me. You've got this."

Kay ran through the steps, keeping me in her focus the entire time. When she was finished, she cried triumphantly, "Lottie, I did it!"

"Of course, you did. You only needed that muscle memory to take over. Your body knows the steps. That was great!" I praised. "We need to look at one other thing before we go back out there."

"My kicks?" she assumed.

"Your fan kicks," I concurred. "Do one for me now and pay attention to your body positioning." Kay executed a kick, still leaning forward ever so slightly. "Okay, now watch me and see if you can pinpoint the difference. I want you to be aware so that you're able to make adjustments on your own. Notice my posture," I hinted. I moved into a tombé, turning while maintaining my posture as I kicked my right leg up to the left corner and fanning it all the way down.

"I'm not keeping my back straight," she decided.

"Exactly," I smiled.

"I have a bad habit of slouching," she admitted, gesturing to her ample bosom, "courtesy of these."

"Well, all I can say about that is, be proud of your assets and stand tall. So many girls would kill for curves like yours. Let's try it again. Stand tall, shoulders back, long neck, chin raised." Kay followed my instructions, and the kick was improved.

"Much better," I told her. "Now, I'm seeing that you're starting your kick too early and you're losing the fan shape. I want you to begin the kick like this," I demonstrated, kicking my leg high, "starting high in the opposite corner and then fanning it all the way to the other corner and down. Your turn." Kay stood up tall and tried to perform as I'd asked.

"Still a tad too early. I'm going to put my hand here," I held my arm out, my hand suspended on her left side. "I want you to aim to start your kick here, okay?" Nodding, Kay rolled her head from side to side and took a deep breath. "You've got this," I assured her. Her gaze trained on my hand, Kay turned and kicked, forcing her toes toward the mark, and fanning her leg down to the ground.

"Perfect!" I cried. "Let's do a few more." Each time she executed the kick flawlessly. "Now, I'm going to remove my hand. Just imagine something there. Whatever you like, as a target."

"My ex-boyfriend's face?" she suggested with a chuckle.

"As long as that puts a smile on yours, it's fine by me," I laughed. With a look of determination on her face, Kay performed her fan kick beautifully. Grinning, she ran over and hugged me.

"Thank you, Lottie. I never thought I could do it."

"You have to believe in yourself, Kay. You're here for a reason. But if you're struggling, I'm always happy to help," I said.

"Thank you. You're a wonderful teacher. I think you've found your calling," she said.

"I think you're right," I replied, grinning.

CHAPTER FIFTY-SIX

As Kay and I rejoined the troupe onstage, we were met with hopeful glances from our fellow dancers. Judy and I made eye contact across the stage. I could see the question in her mind. Nodding confidently in her direction, she smiled back at me knowingly.

"Welcome back, ladies," Mr. Dean called to the pair of us. "Let's see what you've accomplished. Places everyone!"

We hurried to our positions flanking the stage. Leaning forward to catch Kay's attention, I winked, mouthing to her, "You've got this." She winked back, straightening her posture, and lifting her chin, ready to prove herself.

"And 5, 6, 7, 8!" Mr. Dean yelled over the swelling music. One by one, pairs of girls glided out onto the stage as if it were made of ice. Forming a line, we linked arms to create a chain, kicking our legs sky high. Gradually, Kay and I began to turn our bodies away from the audience, pulling the line with us, until we met downstage. Linking arms, we completed a circle, rotating as we kicked. Once Kay and I faced the audience once again, reaching center stage after completing one and a half revolutions, we broke away from the circle, fanning out to stage right and left, respectively. Each pair followed suit until once again forming a kick line.

After eight more counts, our feature began. Training my eyes on the imagined audience, I flowed through the steps, the pas de bourrée, followed by tombé into the fan kicks. Praying that my impromptu lesson with Kay was worthwhile, we moved into the chassé, both of us weaving through the kick line from opposite ends of the stage until we met in the middle, linking arms and seamlessly falling into formation as the entire line rotated a half-turn, our backs to the audience.

Beginning at stage right and continuing one by one down the line, each girl fanned her right arm to meet her left, breaking the link. Once the last link was broken at stage left, each girl consecutively fanned her right arm back upstage, immediately followed by her left to form a V-shape with her arms while twisting to face the audience, a domino effect. With the entire troupe facing forward, every other girl took a step forward, the balance taking a step back. We fanned our arms out in unison, half of us rotating up, the other down, jazz hands exaggerating the movement, to end the number in a zigzag shape in perfect time with the music. The number was meant to mimic the feel of ice dancing and it hit the mark.

Remaining in position, stage smiles on our faces, we waited. I searched Mr. Dean's face for a sense of how we'd performed. He stood, motionless and expressionless for a moment before breaking into a grin. "Bravo!!" he shouted, clapping enthusiastically. "That was perfection everyone! Kay, simply amazing! Lottie, I have every faith that your school will be a smashing success!" he praised. "Let's all take five to switch the sets! Keep up this energy, you're all absolutely stunning up there!!" Relaxing from our positions, everyone began to shuffle backstage, spirits high. Judy ran over, putting an arm around me.

"Girl, I hate to say it, but I told you so," she teased, one eyebrow raised.

"You did," I agreed, beaming, as we walked offstage together. "And I can never thank you enough."

* * *

The rest of the afternoon went smoothly. Mr. Dean's praise buoyed everyone's spirits inspiring all of us to push ourselves to our best performance. As a troupe, we were determined to put on the greatest holiday show Rockland had ever seen.

"And let's call it for today ladies!" Mr. Dean shouted from his seat in the auditorium. "I am beyond pleased with your work today. I'm confident that Friday's opening will be spectacular! As such, I'm going to alter the schedule slightly for tomorrow. We'll push our start time back two hours to allow you all a little extra rest. That will also give seamstresses time to make final alterations. We'll meet here tomorrow at 10 a.m. for a final dress run-through," he informed us. "Thank you!" The news was met with a few whoops and high-fives. I couldn't remember the last time I was able to sleep in. It sounded so decadent. "Judy! Lottie!" Mr. Dean called. "Can you two hang back for a moment?"

"Sure thing!" she called for both of us, as we headed down to the auditorium floor.

"Great work today," he began. "Lottie, I have to admit you impressed me with Kay. I was worried I was going to have to replace her in the feature."

"Thank you. She just needed a little technical direction. I have a few tricks," I replied.

Nodding, he continued, "I've spoken to Madame DuBarre, and I've given her my impression on you two running her studio. Of course, I've given you both glowing reviews."

"We appreciate that, thank you," I said.

"You've earned it," he said simply. "I want to share a few thoughts. I know that you're eager to get your school up and running." We nodded in agreement. "Judy, with your injury I'm hesitant to put you back in for your solo on opening night. Let's see what the doctor has to say first, but I caution you to rush back in too quickly. Further aggravating your back could slow things down for you in terms of opening the studio." Concern clouding her features, Judy nodded.

"I mentioned to you both that representatives from Broadway would be here Friday night," he continued. "Both friends of mine, a writer/director and a choreographer. Lottie," he said turning to me, "I know you have a family and Broadway is no longer a long-term dream for you, but I want you to think very carefully before rejecting it if you're given an offer. Appearing in just one show could be a great thing for the studio. Think about the draw for prospective students. And before you argue, it's only a few months out of your whole life."

"Hmm," I said, pondering his point, "you make a good argument. I'll admit,

I hadn't thought about it like that."

"It would be great advertising for the studio," Judy agreed.

"Just keep an open mind, Lottie," Mr. Dean said. "You have a great support system in Rockland."

"I will. Thank you for the advice. It's certainly something to think about," I replied, wheels already turning as I tried to work out the details in my head.

CHAPTER FIFTY-SEVEN

Back at the Inn, I drew a hot bath, sprinkling in a handful of rose-scented bath salts from a glass jar on the counter. The bathroom filled with steam, a heady floral scent permeating the mist. Slipping out of my rehearsal clothing, I stepped into the clawfoot tub, sinking back until my head rested on the edge. Taking a deep breath, I relaxed into the water, letting all the tension melt from my overworked muscles.

My mind, on the other hand, was racing. Mr. Dean's comments had struck a chord. He made perfect sense from a business standpoint. Any dancer would love direction from a Broadway veteran. If I got an offer, I'd be a fool to turn it down. But if I was being truthful, that wasn't the real reason I'd do it. There was still a tiny part of me, as much as I deigned to admit it, that held on to my childhood dream.

I could see myself excelling as a dance instructor, something I'd never considered before Judy suggested it. It was a good fit for my lifestyle, and I was good with people. After helping Kay with the feature, I knew that teaching would give me a sense of fulfillment and purpose which I'd been sorely lacking these past few years. I would truly be happy to spend my days at the studio with Judy by my side. But the idea of a stint on Broadway, however brief, was exhilarating.

Sighing, I ducked down under the water, swaying my head from side to side, my hair fanning around me. Pushing off the foot of the bathtub, I sat up, wiping the water from my eyes. "Slow down, Charlotte," I muttered to myself. "First things first."

Grabbing a towel, I stepped out onto the mat, quickly drying myself off. I pulled a second towel from the rack, twisting it around my head and tucking in the loose end to secure it in place. Tugging the plush white bathrobe from the hook, I slipped into it and headed into the bedroom. Flopping back onto the bed, I grabbed the telephone handset. With a quick glance at the clock, I rang the garage.

"Charlie's," one of the guys answered.

"Is Charlie still in? It's his wife calling," I explained.

"Pretty sure he's in his office, ma'am. Let me get him for you."

"Thank you," I replied, waiting for Charlie to pick up. The racket from the shop suddenly ceased as my husband came on the line.

"Lottie?" he said.

"Hi. I just thought I'd check in seeing as we haven't talked any more about Rockland," I began.

Clearing his throat, Charlie said, "I'm working on it. I've been crunching the numbers and I may have a plan. I just need a few more days to figure some things out," he paused. "You're sure this is what you want?"

A smile forming at the corners of my mouth, I silently threw my hand up in triumph. "I'm sure. Judy and I have already secured a studio! It's official!"

I was met with silence on the other end of the line.

"Charlie?"

"Yeah."

"You're not saying anything."

"I would've thought you'd ask first."

"An amazing opportunity fell in my lap, and I couldn't say no. Nothing's been signed yet. It's not official in that sense. But I have made my mind up."

"I can see that."

"I thought you'd be happy for me."

"I am. It just feels like I'm not part of the discussion."

"We already had the discussion. I was clear on my stance, and you just said you're working it out," I explained. "I need this. If we're going to have a chance, I need this for myself. This is me asking."

After a moment passed, he answered, "Okay."

"Okay," I sighed my relief.

"Is there anything else I need to know?" he asked.

Not wanting to press my luck, I said, "No, I don't think so." I'd have to limit myself to one step at a time. The Broadway conversation could wait. It wasn't even a sure thing at this point. No sense in bringing it up yet.

"Well, in that case, we'll see you Saturday. The girls can't wait to see you onstage."

"I can't wait to hug them. I've really missed my girls."

"We miss you too," he said. "I'm sorry we can't make it for opening night."

"That's okay. Saturday works just as well."

"Love you."

"Love you," I parroted back, replacing the handset on the receiver. A feeling of unease settled over me. Saying I love you to Charlie had become so forced. It used to be so natural, automatic. I never gave it a second thought. The words just flowed after his name like they belonged there. Now it felt like a forced effort.

He was my husband, the father of my children, and I did love him. But that love felt so different. So much had changed between us. It was hard to make sense of it all. Would this move make a difference? Would we find the love we used to know, or would it be forever changed by our actions?

My mind drifted back to the morning I went to see Charlie, flashing through the scene at the shop window as if it was on film. Immediately following it was the image of Walt and me pressed up against the wall in my room. I glanced over to the very spot, my heart racing just thinking about it. Pushing it all from my mind, I got up, pulling out a dress for dinner.

* * *

Sitting down in my usual spot, I looked around the table. The girls were talking animatedly, excited about the opening. "Did you see Mr. Dean's face?" Jean cried. "I don't think he's ever grinned before." Laughter erupted around the table.

"To be fair, I saw him smile one other time," Linda said.

Laughing, Jean responded, "Exactly! One other time. You've proven my point, Linda."

"All jokes aside," Barbara began, "Mr. Dean is a great choreographer. Look how far we've come in a matter of weeks."

"She's right," Mary M. piped up.

"If he walked around smiling like the Cheshire Cat during rehearsals, would we push ourselves to be better?" Bianca added.

"Exactly right, Bianca," Barbara agreed. "It's all part of the job."

"Mr. Dean has done a wonderful job," Kay began, looking in my direction, "but I'd like to give someone else the credit she deserves." I felt a flush creeping up onto my cheeks.

"Lottie, I can't thank you enough for your help today," Kay began. "If it wasn't for you, I would've lost the feature."

"Happy to help," I replied. "You had it in you all along, you just needed a little nudge."

"I wish I'd had an instructor like you growing up. You have such a unique way of teaching technique. I think the studio will be a great success."

"Thank you," I said. "Judy and I are excited at the prospect."

"Speaking of the studio," Jean began, "Word is you and Judy are hiring." A confused Judy looked at me for confirmation. I caught Bianca's eye before she quickly glanced down at her water glass, busying herself with wiping off the condensation.

"We're only in the planning stages," I revealed. "Judy and I have a lot to discuss and work out first."

"But it may be a possibility," Judy jumped in.

"Well, keep us posted," Jean replied. "This little town is growing on me."

"If we do decide that we need help, we'd definitely look here first," I said, gesturing to the group.

"And who knows where we all might end up after Friday," Linda said, hopefully. "Some of us may be headed for Broadway."

"That's a definite possibility," Judy agreed, her pointed glance aimed right at me.

CHAPTER FIFTY-EIGHT

Billy appeared from the kitchen, placing platters of roast pork and sweet potatoes at either end of our table. To accompany the main, there was homemade applesauce tinted a lovely pink from the apple skins, and garlicky green beans. "Bon appétit, ladies," he announced to the table, lingering behind Judy and me. Bending down within our earshot he whispered, "I have a little surprise for you two."

"I don't know about Lottie, but I just love surprises," Judy gushed.

"Meet me in the lobby after my shift. We're going to my place tonight," he declared.

Suspicious, I replied, "Interesting, what have you got in store for us?"

"That's for me to know and you to find out," he said, bopping me on the nose.

Shaking my head, I laughed. "We'll see you then, right Judy?"

"Right," she agreed.

Billy returned to the kitchen, busing meals to his other tables as we joined the rest of the girls devouring the fabulous dinner Johnny had prepared. As usual, the flavors were spot on, and everything was cooked to perfection. "I don't know about you girls, but I'm really going to miss Chef Johnny's cooking. This is delish!" Jean exclaimed. Contented mutters were heard around the table, our mouths full.

Swallowing, I said, "Having someone cook dinner every night, gourmet dinners at that, has been such a bonus of this trip. We've certainly been spoiled."

"But we deserve it!" Judy cried.

"I'll second that," Kay agreed.

"Girls, raise your glasses," Barbara said. "To the Rockland troupe of 1956, may we always follow our passions and never stop dancing!"

"Cheers!" we exclaimed, clinking our glasses, and toasting to ourselves and the possibilities that awaited us.

* * *

"What do you think this is all about?" Judy asked as we sat in the lobby waiting for Billy.

"I haven't got a clue. You never know with Billy," I said.

"Speak of the devil," Judy nodded toward the dining room.

"Ladies," Billy said coyly, enjoying keeping his secret from us. "Follow me." Exiting the Inn, Billy led us down Main Street, turning left when we reached Third. Stopping at a navy-blue door, Billy held it open for us to enter. Climbing a flight of stairs to the first landing, he pulled a set of keys from his pocket, unlocking the door. Ushering us inside, he fumbled for the light switch. As he flipped it, light flooding the room, a few voices yelled, "Surprise!"

My eyes adjusting to the brightness, I saw Mr. Dean, Johnny, and Betty standing in the living room holding glasses of champagne. Before them on the coffee table was a beautiful cake, with the word "Congrats" scrawled across the top, two dainty ceramic dancer figurines placed above it. Grinning, Billy pushed us into the living room, handing us each a glass of champagne.

"I know that this is a little premature, but with the show opening it had to be tonight," Billy said turning to me. "I know you, Lottie, once you finally make up your mind, there's no going back."

"You may have a point," I chuckled.

"So, let's drink to your new venture, to old friends, new friends, and to our success as business owners! Cheers!"

"Cheers!" We cried, toasting with our glasses.

"We're so happy that you've decided to stay, Lottie," Betty said. "You, too

Judy. I think you'll really love living here. Rockland is lucky to have you both taking over Madame's."

"Thank you," Judy answered. "You can be sure that sales at your shop are certain to go up."

Laughing, Betty said, "Another bonus!"

"I, for one, am looking forward to the caliber of dancers your studio will bring for my next show," Mr. Dean said. "Recruiting will be a cinch."

"Happy to oblige," I said taking a sip of champagne. "Billy, back to that toast. Are you a business owner? What haven't you told me?"

"Not yet, but I have plans. I figure putting it out into the universe can't hurt," he replied.

"The power of positive thinking," Judy added.

"Exactly," Billy replied. "Now let's cut into this fabulous cake. Did you notice the dancers? I made sure to find a brunette and a redhead."

"You never miss a detail," I smiled. Johnny served six slices of his cake, passing out the plates as he described the dessert to us. He had chosen white cake with raspberry filling and lemon icing. It was light and flavorful, pairing wonderfully with the champagne.

Looking around at the group, friends chatting and laughing with one another, I was filled with happiness. These people wanted the best for me, they celebrated my successes and were there for support when I needed it. Overcome with emotion, my eyes began welling up. Catching my gaze, Judy cried, "Oh honey, what is it?"

Shaking my head, I smiled. "I'm just so happy," I choked out.

Putting an arm around my shoulders, Billy gave me a squeeze. "Me too."

"Thanks," I said.

"Come here, I have something to show you," Billy said, pulling me away from the group and toward his study. Entering the space, I noticed the modern gray sofa along the back wall, a buttery leather accent chair with wood detailing sat beside it. Built-in bookshelves in dark wood held his collection of titles. Modern art sprinkled the walls, which were painted a muted mustard, giving the room a warm, cozy feeling.

"Billy, I have to say that you've done well for yourself. Your place is impeccably furnished," I said.

"Did you expect anything less?"

"Well, no. But after seeing it for myself, I'm impressed."

"Thank you," he replied, pulling a book from the shelf. "Have a seat," he gestured toward the sofa. Sitting down next to me, he placed the book on his lap. "Recognize this?"

The white cover read "Rockland High School 1942" in maroon lettering. Grabbing it, I cried, "Our sophomore yearbook!"

"I dug it out of an old box of things the other day," he explained. "I want to show you something." Handing it back to him, I watched as Billy flipped through the pages until he came to the superlatives for our class. Pointing with his index finger, he ran down the page stopping at my photo. "Here," he said, holding it before me. "Read this."

"Charlotte Dawson," I read aloud. "Most likely to be spotted on Broadway."

"Um-hmm," he concurred. Looking at the young girl on the page, I noted the hopeful expression, a whole life ahead and dreams to be pursued. A jumble of feelings washed over me. I felt a pang of sadness, realizing how quickly time had passed and how much had changed over the years, but also a sense of accomplishment. I might have taken a detour, but I was finally in reach of those dreams, even if it was later than I had expected.

"I get it," I said.

"Do you?" Billy asked, head cocked to one side.

"I do."

"No matter how much you try to convince yourself otherwise, I know that she's still in there," Billy said, pointing at my heart. "Bobby told me about your chances for Broadway. They look good, so don't sell yourself short. We're all here for you and we're happy to pitch in any way we can." A tear sliding down my cheek, I thanked my oldest friend, squeezing him tight. "And when you make it," he added, "I want good seats."

CHAPTER FIFTY-NINE

Judy and I walked back to the Inn, our ceramic doppelgangers in hand. We'd find a spot for them in the new studio, good luck charms from our friends. Looking over at me, Judy asked, "You okay, honey? You seemed pretty emotional back there."

Nodding, I replied, "I'm fine. I guess it just hit me how much I've missed having good friends around me. I have friends back home, but it's just not the same. I've never shared personal secrets with them like I do with you and Billy."

"I know what you mean," she agreed. "It's difficult to find your people as an adult."

"Exactly," I replied. "More so once you have children. There's even less time to cultivate relationships outside your own household."

"I can imagine. In any event, I'm glad that we found each other. I knew I liked you the moment I saw you. And I don't say that about many people."

"Ditto." Turning onto Main Street, the wind whipped past, a gust nearly blowing us backward. Huddling together for warmth and imagined strength against the elements, we pushed past the shop windows decorated for the holidays. A small gift shop called The Perfect Present had various miniature Christmas trees in their window display. Glancing at the trees as we walked past, an ornament caught my eye. Stopping, I pulled Judy to the side. "Look at that dynamic duo," I said, pointing to a glass ornament near the top of the largest of the trees.

Following my direction, Judy cried, "It's us!" There on the tree suspended by a silver ribbon were two dancers joined together at the arms, frozen mid-kick. One brunette, the other a redhead. They wore blue and silver costumes like the leotards from our opening number. The same costume I wore when I met Ms. Madsen. "There's no denying it," Judy declared. "That is definitely a sign."

"You read my mind."

"I know," she laughed. "That's why I said it."

"And why you're one of my people," I smiled, playfully shoving my friend. "Come on, let's get back, it's freezing out here."

"Agreed," she said, lightly pushing me back before we hustled off. "That ornament gives me an idea."

"What's that?"

"Have you thought about a name for the studio? I just assumed we'd make it our own."

"I actually have been thinking about that. It doesn't make much sense to keep the name, and I like the idea of making it special to us. I just haven't come up with anything."

"I hadn't either, until just now."

"Well, what is it?" I asked.

"What about Studio Duo?"

"Studio Duo," I repeated.

"You know, just like the ornament, like us. A duo. We are pretty dynamic," she said fanning her hands.

"Studio Duo Dance Academy. I like it," I declared.

"It sounds very professional," she said.

"Also meaningful," I replied.

"And it's about friendship, which is how this crazy idea came about in the first place," she concurred.

"I love it!" I cried as we both started jumping up and down on the sidewalk, unable to contain our excitement. Both realizing what a spectacle we were making of ourselves, we abruptly stopped. Laughing at our outburst, we trudged on to the Inn making plans for Studio Duo along the way.

* * *

The next morning, I awoke with a spring in my step. Deciding on a name for the studio made it all seem more real and I was anxious to move forward. After a quick breakfast, I grabbed my things and headed into town. I had a little time to kill since our rehearsals had been pushed back. Strolling down Main Street, I headed back to The Perfect Present to purchase the ornament we'd seen the night before. It was the perfect gift for Judy. Reaching the shop, I peered through the glass at the window display. The ornament was gone.

Walking over to the entrance, I pulled open the shop door, holiday music drifting through the air. Stepping inside, I approached the counter looking for a salesperson. No one was to be found. Shrugging, I walked over to the display, scanning the little trees. No sign of the dancers.

My gaze landed on a little bunny. "Bun-bun," I whispered, plucking the ornament from the tree. Holding it in my palm, I smiled. Kathy would love it. I had a tradition of getting each of my girls a unique ornament each year at Christmastime. Every ornament held a special meaning, and they loved telling the story behind each one as we hung them on the tree. Now for Penny...

A sparkling snowflake was tucked into the smallest tree. I pulled it off the branch, my heart warming as I recalled the last time we baked my famous chocolate chip cookies. I'd taken the sifter full of flour to create snowfall in our kitchen. Penny was delighted. My heart ached a little as I looked at the ornaments, missing my girls. These were perfect for Saturday. Little gifts to let them know I'd been thinking of them.

"Hello," a voice called out. "May I help you with anything?"

Looking up, I saw a woman bustling over. She was tiny with a head of fluffy white hair and kind blue eyes, crow's feet giving away her penchant for smiling. She reminded me of my grandmother. "Hello," I smiled. "Yes, I found a couple of ornaments that I'd like to purchase," I replied, holding up the ornaments I'd selected for the girls. "I actually stopped in because I saw an ornament in your window display last night that I'd like as well. It was a pair of dancers."

"Oh yes, that one was lovely," she replied. "Someone purchased that earlier this morning."

"I see. I noticed that it was missing from its spot. Do you have another anywhere in the shop?"

"Oh dear," she frowned. "I don't. One of a kind. I don't get duplicates. I believe that each ornament has a special meaning."

"You know, it's funny, I always say that same thing," I agreed. "Do you happen to remember if a redhead purchased it?" I asked, thinking Judy had beat me to the punch.

"No, no, I don't think so," she said. "I'd remember such a defining trait."

"Hmm," I said, looking over the trees one last time. Peeking out of the branches was a blue Ford pickup ornament. It looked just like Charlie's truck. Hesitating a moment, I removed it from the branches. "In that case, I'll take these three."

"Lovely, dear," she replied, heading over to the counter. "I'll just get a few gift boxes to keep these safe," she said, disappearing behind a curtain. As I waited, my mind drifted back to the dancers. I wondered who would have purchased the ornament if not Judy. Someone in the show maybe? The costumes were so much like ours, any of the girls would've spotted that. My eyes drifted to one last tree seated at the far end of the counter. Hanging on the lowest branch was a little glass bluebird.

Taking it off the tree, my mind drifted to Walt and our conversations about signs. Even though nothing more could happen between us, meeting him opened my eyes to all the possibilities available to me. I wanted him to know how much I treasured the short amount of time we'd spent together and that it mattered to me. Tomorrow night I'd see him for the last time and give him the ornament. It was a nice memento to remember me by. Reappearing from behind the curtain, the shopkeeper emerged with her hands full. "I see you found my bluebird," she nodded to the ornament still in my hand. "Special meaning?"

"Yes," I answered. "For a friend."

"It's one of my favorites," she said, dropping four gift boxes on the counter as if she'd already known I'd need another. Removing the tags, she wrapped the gifts in white tissue paper before gently placing each in a box, closing the lids over top. Completing our transaction, she held out a tissue paper-topped gift bag, asking, "Care for a candy cane, dear?"

"Sure, thank you. I haven't had a candy cane in ages."

"I think I'll have one with you. Reminds me of the magic of Christmas," she said.

"Certainly," I agreed, accepting a miniature cane.

With a twinkle in her eyes, she said, "I hope you find something special under the tree this year."

Unwrapping the candy, I replied, "I hope St. Nick is good to you, too. Have a nice day." Her eyes crinkling in the corners, she waved the little candy cane in farewell as I exited the store.

CHAPTER SIXTY

Walking out of The Perfect Present, I felt a strange sense of kismet. The shopkeeper seemed to know something I didn't. Maybe Judy had come in for the ornament and cautioned her not to say anything. It sounded plausible. And how had she known I would purchase four items, instead of the three I'd intended? Unless she'd simply counted wrong.

Even though I hadn't gotten the ornament I'd come for, I'd found three perfect little gifts for the girls and Charlie. Imagining how it would go with all of us together on Saturday, I wondered if the girls would pick up on anything different between their father and me. Hopefully, my present would break the ice between us a bit, a nice opener to their visit.

The bluebird ornament was my closure. Walt and I could've been something great in another time or place. Meeting like we did, it was almost like we were suspended in time where we could just be. But reality ruined the magic of us. He'd understand. Climbing the front steps of the Inn, I crossed through the lobby, meeting Judy on the stairs. Noting my shopping bag, she read, "The Perfect Present. Ah, you went back for the ornament."

Tilting my head with a knowing look at my friend, I replied, "I'm sure you already know that it was gone."

Confused, Judy said, "How would I know?"

"You didn't purchase it this morning?"

"No, I haven't been out yet. I've only just had breakfast and I'm heading out to see the doctor for my follow-up."

"Hmm, I was sure it was you," I replied.

"You mean to say that someone else beat us to it?"

"I do."

"That's our ornament!" she cried in disappointment.

"I know. According to the shopkeeper, it was the only one."

"Boo, that's a letdown. It was the inspiration for our name."

"To be fair, we're the inspiration."

"True. Oh well, what's done is done I suppose."

"Exactly."

"Well, I'm off. I'll fill you in on the appointment at rehearsal. Wish me luck," she called, hustling off.

"Good luck!" I called after her, climbing the stairs. Unlocking the door, I entered my room. Dropping the gift bag on the armchair, I grabbed my tote and headed back out to rehearsals.

* * *

At the theater, we gathered backstage, Miss Barker with her trusty clipboard, checking off various items on her list. Milling about until Mr. Dean's arrival, a nervous excitement permeated the air. We stretched, warming up our muscles before we'd run through the numbers for the last time. It was our final rehearsal before the show opened.

Out of the corner of my eye, I saw Ms. Madsen approach Miss Barker, a comfortable familiarity between them. Miss Barker was usually all business. She seemed to be a very serious young woman. I wondered what their relationship was. Maybe just a friendly bond from years of collaboration on the show? With such an obvious difference in age and personality, they seemed like an odd match as friends. I watched as they inspected all the costumes hanging on multiple racks, separated by cards with each dancer's name marking her section. Nodding her approval, Miss Barker made another check mark on her list.

"Ladies, gather round," Miss Barker announced. "Mr. Dean will be here momentarily for the last run-through. Alterations are complete. You each have a section marked with your name. It's alphabetical, so it will be easy to locate your section. Have a great rehearsal!" Feeling a tap on my shoulder, I turned around to face Miss Barker.

"Charlotte, I wanted to let you know that Mr. Dean took the liberty of securing a table at The Rockland Grille for brunch Saturday morning. Mr. Dean spoke about you to the Broadway people, and they'd like a meeting," she said discreetly.

"Wow," I breathed, somewhat shocked. "They haven't seen me dance yet."

"They trust his judgment. Count yourself very lucky."

"I do. Thank you," I replied.

Softening, she said, "Don't worry. Of all the girls I've seen come through here, Charlotte, you have what it takes."

"I don't know what to say," I began, flabbergasted by her commendation. "I'll definitely be there."

"Wonderful, I'll confirm it," she smiled.

Approaching us wearing a quizzical expression, Jean said, "I don't mean to interrupt, but has anyone ever told you that you two look like sisters?" Taken aback by her comment, I shook my head, watching as Miss Barker did the same. Ms. Madsen, who was within earshot, quickly turned back to the rack of costumes before her, busying herself with rechecking seams. "You really do. You've got the same high cheekbones, the same button nose, eyes are a different color, but the shape is the same, similar build," Jean continued.

"You think so?" I questioned Jean.

Miss Barker appeared to be sizing me up, making comparisons herself. "I suppose there is a resemblance," she agreed.

"I guess you're right, I can see it now," I added. "I've always wanted a sister."

"Me, too," Miss Barker said, loosening up a bit. "Honorary sisters, then?"

"Sure," I laughed, catching Ms. Madsen's stare. Making eye contact with me, she quickly rushed off as I replied, "I'll take it."

* * *

"And that's a wrap on rehearsal ladies!" Mr. Dean yelled from the auditorium. "Bravo! Tomorrow night will be dazzling. Get some rest and I'll see you back here tomorrow afternoon to warm up." Shuffling backstage, nerves and excitement fueling our exhausted bodies, we chatted about Friday night's show. It was the talk of the town. The event of the season had finally arrived, and all our hard work would be showcased on stage.

"Judy!" I called, sidling up to my friend. "How'd the appointment go?"

"It was fine. As expected, he wants me to remain in the chorus line for the first week."

"I'm sorry," I said. "I know that you were hoping for a miracle."

"I was," she revealed. "But I know that this is the smartest course of action in the long run. Comes with the territory," she shrugged.

"Listen, I don't mean to rain on your parade, but Miss Barker told me that Mr. Dean set up a brunch Saturday morning for me to meet the Broadway people," I explained.

"Lottie! That's amazing!"

"I know. I just hope they're not let down tomorrow night."

"Give yourself some credit. Mr. Dean knows what he's doing and I'm confident that you'll be better than they're expecting."

"Don't worry, I'm fully capable of holding down the fort. If you get an offer, you'd better not hesitate to take it."

"Thanks, Judy."

"That's what friends are for," she replied. "Besides, I'm planning on taking my turn next year," she winked.

"You've got it," I agreed, grabbing my tote. "Hey, do you think Miss Barker and I look alike?"

Looking from me to Miss Barker, Judy said, "Well, now that you mention it, yes. I don't know why I didn't see it sooner." As Mr. Dean approached, she continued, "You know, you could pass for sisters."

"Who could pass for sisters?" Mr. Dean asked.

"Lottie and Miss Barker," Judy answered.

"It's funny you say that because I was thinking the same thing a few days ago. If she could dance, I would've written in the 'Sisters' number for the two of you," he joked.

"That's one of my favorites," I laughed.

"Judy," he said, turning his attention to her, "I spoke to Dr. Cooper. We're in agreement that you allow yourself to heal fully and return to your solo for the second week of shows."

Nodding in agreement, she said, "While I have to admit I'm disappointed, I know that it's the smart move."

"Good. And Lottie, Miss Barker let you know about brunch?"

"Yes, thanks for setting that up. I'm looking forward to it."

"Don't thank me just yet. You'll have to prove yourself tomorrow night. Keep your focus and I'm more than confident you will," he replied. "Okay," he said, clasping his hands, "I think that was everything. I'll see you both tomorrow afternoon," he said, turning to leave.

"Mr. Dean?" I called, stopping him. Something was nagging at me about Ms. Madsen's odd behavior.

"Yes?"

"One more thing. It's sort of an unrelated question, but does Miss Barker know Ms. Madsen, the seamstress, outside of working together on these productions?" I asked as casually as I could muster.

Cocking his head to the side, he replied, "Of course. Ms. Madsen is her mother."

CHAPTER SIXTY-ONE

"What is it, Lottie?" Judy cried as I dragged her out onto the street and around to the side of the building to our usual spot for discussing anything scandalous. Looking around to be sure we were alone, I pulled Judy closer so I could whisper my hypothesis.

"What if Miss Barker really is my sister?" I murmured.

"What? Why on Earth would you think that?"

"Think about it Judy, we look alike, my father had an affair with her mother, the timing is about right. Ms. Madsen looked awfully skittish when Jean started talking about our similarities. As soon as she heard the word 'sister' she took off."

Raising an eyebrow and pursing her lips, Judy considered my points. "I suppose it could be true. Still seems a little far-fetched though."

"Does it?" I asked. "My mother knew of the affair. I wonder if she knew about Miss Barker. I don't even know her first name. What if that was the reason she flew off the handle at the funeral? Maybe she's known all along?"

"It's possible," Judy shrugged. "But if that was the case, don't you think she'd be more concerned about your return to Rockland? Wouldn't she have told you when you talked?"

"I don't know," I paused, deep in thought. "I need to talk to her. And to Ms. Madsen."

"I agree. But Lottie, don't let this consume you. The show is tomorrow night and there's a lot riding on it."

"I know, Judy. But I need to find out the truth."

* * *

Running up the stairs to my room, I unlocked the door, tossing my bag on the floor. I dialed the house, praying my mother would answer. Holding the handset to my ear, I listened impatiently to the trill of each ring. Having counted five rings, I replaced the handset back on the cradle, frustration consuming me. I went back down to the lobby, heading for the front desk. There was no one to be seen. "Figures," I muttered.

"What figures?" a voice called from behind the desk.

"Mrs. Hall? Is that you?"

"It is," she said, popping up from behind the desk. "I was just getting organized. Can I help you with something Charlotte?"

"You can," I said, studying Mrs. Hall's face. "There's a seamstress who worked on my costumes for the show, a Ms. Madsen. Does she have a shop in town?"

At the mention of her name, Mrs. Hall flinched. "Do you need a repair?" she asked measuredly. "I hope you haven't had a problem with any of your costumes for tomorrow night."

"No, no, nothing like that. Just a personal item."

"I see," Mrs. Hall nodded, her expression blank. "She does have a shop on Fourth. Ginny's Tailoring and Alterations."

"Thank you," I called, already headed for the door as Mrs. Hall looked on, wearing a look of concern. Skipping down the steps, I turned onto Main Street. Looking at my watch, I figured I probably only had a few minutes until the shop closed for the day. Hustling down the sidewalk, I was on a mission to get some answers. Rushing past the various storefronts, I couldn't recall a single thing in any of the window displays I walked by. I was focused solely on my destination.

What was I going to say to Ms. Madsen when I got there? I couldn't very well just come out and ask if Miss Barker was my sister, could I? Would she even tell me the truth if I did? Rounding the corner onto Fourth, my mind preoccupied with what I was going to say, I ran straight into another pedestrian. Right into a man's chest. "Oh!" I cried, almost bouncing backward on impact, my handbag flopping down onto the sidewalk. "I'm so sorry!"

"Lottie?" a familiar voice said.

"Walt! What are you?" I shivered, surprised to see him, and ignoring the tingle that ran up my spine. "I'm so sorry. I wasn't paying attention."

"I can see that," he said, a look of amusement on his face as he handed me my bag. "We've got to stop meeting like this," he joked. "Are you okay?"

"Yes," I laughed nervously, smoothing my skirt. "I just have something I need to do, and I'm running out of time."

"Well don't let me stop you," he said with a smile.

"I'm sorry to rush off," I called over my shoulder. "Will you be at the show tomorrow night?"

"Wouldn't miss it for the world," he called back.

* * *

Spotting the royal blue awning halfway down the block, the same blue as the locket, I hurried down Fourth hoping I'd made it in time. As I approached the door, noting the compass rose-shaped logo above the name of the shop, I noticed that the sign had been flipped to read "closed."

Darn. I was so close. Sitting down on the bench out front to catch my breath, I slumped against the backrest. One more day wouldn't make much difference, I thought, trying to convince myself enough to believe it. As I was about to get up to head back to the Inn, I heard the shop door close and then the sounds of a key fumbling in the lock. Looking up, I recognized Ms. Madsen, her back to me. I hadn't missed her after all. Turning to leave, she stopped when she noticed me sitting on the bench. "Charlotte," she said. "I had a feeling I'd be seeing you."

"You did?"

"I did. If I'm not mistaken, you have a question to ask," she predicted.

"I do," I replied, taking a deep breath.

"Well, go on then," she said, taking a seat next to me on the bench. "Ask away."

"Ms. Madsen," I began, my eyes searching hers for the truth.

"Call me Ginny," she interrupted, her eyes softening.

"Ginny," I paused, taking another breath to steel myself for her reply. "Is Miss Barker my sister?" I finally blurted out.

Her eyes softened and she gave a knowing half-smile before replying, "Yes, she is." Looking at Ginny, so many thoughts ran through my mind. It was a jumble of questions. I didn't know where to begin. I had a sister. "Charlotte, I know that this must come as quite a shock. When I met you, I wanted to tell you," she explained. "But Vivvie doesn't know. My daughter." Nodding, I remained silent, waiting for her to continue. "I knew it was only a matter of time before people began to notice the resemblance between you and Viv. I saw it straight away at the fittings of course," she said.

"Did my father know?"

"No. I never told him. It was very early on when we ended things. The day we said goodbye I wasn't even certain, but I had an inkling. I met someone soon after, James Barker, so I just let him believe he was the father. Over time, I almost believed it myself. He was the only father Vivvie ever knew. He died in the war before I ever worked up the nerve to tell him the truth. But he was every bit a father to Vivian."

"Wow," I replied, still stunned that my guess was correct. "Were you ever planning to tell Miss Barker, er, Vivian?"

Fiddling with the set of keys in her hand, Ginny said, "You know, I had planned to tell her when she was old enough to understand. But with James gone, she'd already had such a loss. I didn't want to put her through that twice. Over the years, it became harder and harder to broach the subject."

"I can understand that," I said.

"I suppose now I'll have to. She'll want to know that she has a sister," she glanced at me, hopeful.

"I'm sure she will," I agreed. "I can't believe I've had a sister all along and never knew it. If I'd never come to Rockland, I might've never known."

"It seems as though you were meant to return," she began. "And for more than dancing. Madame DuBarre tells me you'll be staying."

"Yes, Judy and I are taking over the studio. I'm inclined to agree with you.

I left behind so much more than I ever understood. I never expected any of this when I agreed to do the show," I told her. "Did my mother know?"

"I'm not certain. We ran into each other once when I was about 6 months along. We didn't speak, but we made eye contact. I was with James at the time, but I wouldn't be surprised if she had her suspicions. In fact, I've always wondered if that was the reason for her reaction at the funeral."

"Hmm," I responded, thinking back to my conversation with my mother. I wondered if there was more to her story than she'd let on.

"Charlotte, I'd appreciate it if you'd let me tell Vivian. I think this news should come from me," she said.

"I agree. I won't say anything until I'm certain you've spoken with her," I promised.

"Thank you. Your father was a man of his word. I wouldn't expect anything less from his daughter."

CHAPTER SIXTY-TWO

Walking back to the Inn lost in thought, I slowed to a snail's pace. There was so much to digest. Since embarking on this trip, my life had literally been turned upside down in all manners of speaking. Before Mr. Anderson's phone call, life had been quite simple, mundane if I was being honest. And now it was anything but. Everything I thought I knew was somehow being twisted into something else. A simple phone call had changed the entire trajectory of my life.

Ambling along Main Street, I watched the other people going about the day. Some smiling, others frowning, some preoccupied and simply going through the motions. I wondered what their stories were. What were their ambitions, their secrets? I was realizing just how much happens right under our noses every day without our noticing a thing. How much is really hidden under the surface? How much of what we think we know is even true?

Arriving at the Inn, I climbed the steps, sitting down in one of the rocking chairs on the porch. It was cold outside, but I didn't notice. After rocking a few moments, Mrs. Hall came out carrying blankets and a tray. She placed the tray on the side table. It held two mugs of tea. Shaking out one of the plush blankets, she draped it over me. Sitting down, she covered herself with the other. "I see you've gone to see Virginia," she noted my drained expression, handing me a mug of tea.

"I have," I replied.

Taking a sip, she said carefully, "Charlotte, I think you should talk to your mother."

Turning slowly to look at Mrs. Hall, searching her face, I asked, "You knew?"

"No, not exactly," Mrs. Hall responded, rocking gently. "I've always thought it a possibility. After your father's funeral, I was almost certain. But I never said a word to your mom. I figured if she wanted to talk about it, she would."

"I suppose," I said, taking a long sip of tea. "I just can't work out how so much happened right in front of me and I'm just now figuring it out."

"You were just a girl. You were focused on your life, your friends, your dreams. When we're children we seem to forget that our parents have lives outside of their roles as mom and dad," she explained. "I'm sure your girls don't know the intricacies of your marriage."

My mind immediately flashing through images of the past few weeks, I nodded emphatically. "There are things they don't need to know," I said.

"Right," Mrs. Hall agreed. "And we keep things in order to protect the people we love."

"That's true," I said, realizing I was doing the same. I hadn't told Charlie about Walt. And I wasn't sure I planned to.

Seemingly reading my mind, Mrs. Hall said, "Charlotte, it's okay to keep some things to yourself."

"Do you think?" I asked, skeptical.

"In my opinion, some things are best left unsaid."

I nodded, considering her statement. "Thank you, I needed to hear that."

"Of course," she said, patting my hand. "Now this will all be here tomorrow and the next day. Right now, you need to focus on the show. You've waited too long to let some ancient secrets affect your performance."

"You're right," I forced a smile. "For now, The Rockland Holiday Show is the only thing on my mind. Everything else will have to wait."

"Good girl," she replied as we rocked in tandem in the crisp air, huddled up in our blankets, watching the pedestrians hustle past to get out of the cold.

* * *

Back in my room, I dialed home once more. Twirling the cord around my finger, I said a silent prayer that someone would answer. “Hello?” Charlie’s voice came on the line.

“Hi, it’s me,” I said.

“Hey, Lot, I’m glad you called. I was hoping to wish you luck for tomorrow night,” he said. “Not that you need it.”

“Thanks. I’m feeling a bit nervous,” I admitted, though not only about the show.

“I’m sure you’re not alone. You’ll be great.”

“Is my mom there? I really need to talk to her,” I blurted out.

Concerned, he replied, “Is everything okay?”

“I’m fine. I’ve just had some news from our past in Rockland that is quite shocking. It directly affects her, so I need to speak to her first, but I promise to fill you in on Saturday.”

“I don’t know if I like the sound of that,” he said.

“Really, Charlie, everyone will be fine.”

“Okay,” he said. “I trust you.”

Flinching at his choice of words, I replied, “Can you ask her to come to the phone? And make sure she has some privacy, please?”

“You got it. Good luck tomorrow, you’re going to be great, and I’ll see you soon. The girls just want to say a quick hello before June picks up.”

“Okay, thanks.”

“Mommy?” Penny’s little voice rang through the earpiece.

“Hi, Sweetie! I miss you and I can’t wait to see you soon!” I exclaimed.

“I wanted to tell you to break your legs,” she said sweetly. Stifling a laugh, I listened to Kathy correcting her before picking up the handset.

“She means to say break *a* leg, Mom,” Kathy stated. “I told her what it means.”

“Good luck, Mommy!” Penny called out in the background.

“Thank you both,” I chuckled. “I can’t wait to hug you girls on Saturday!”

“Us too, Mom,” Kathy agreed. “And I’m excited to see you up on a stage!”

“You’ll love the show, honey. Wait until you see the costumes.”

“We’re going to wear new dresses that Grandma got us,” Kathy declared.

"She wants to talk to you, so I have to go now."

"Okay, I love you, and tell your sister the same," I said.

"Love you, too," she said into the handset before yelling, "Penny, Mom said love you."

"Love you, Mommy!" Penny yelled. I could hear Kathy place the phone down, the handset clattering on the table. Charlie was rounding up the girls and suddenly it was quiet. The sounds of home pulled at my heartstrings. Waiting for my mother to pick up, I drummed my fingers on the bedside table, anxious about the bomb I was about to drop on her.

"Charlotte?" my mother's voice came on the line.

"Hi, Mom."

"Charlie said you needed to speak to me privately. Is everything okay?"

"It is. I just got some information today and I couldn't sit on it until I see you."

"Okay, what is it?" she asked, nervousness tingeing her words.

Pausing to gather my thoughts, I took a deep breath and announced, "Mom, I have a sister." There was nothing but silence on the other end of the line. It was so quiet I could almost hear my heartbeat.

"Mom? Are you there?"

"I'm here, Charlotte," she replied.

"Did you know?"

"No, not for certain."

"Did Dad know?"

"Not to my knowledge."

"So, you never talked about it?"

"Never." I could hear her inhaling a deep breath, exhaling slowly before she spoke. "First, let me say that I wanted to talk to you about this in person. That's why I didn't bring it up when we talked about your father the last time. I thought it would be too much of a shock after everything else you'd learned."

"I can understand that," I replied.

"I ran into Virginia once when she was pregnant. She was with a man, but by the looks of her belly, she was pretty far along. Far enough along that it was possible Dad could be the father. I never spoke to her, but something in the way she looked at me when we made eye contact, well, it looked like guilt. I never breathed a word of it to your father. Mostly because I was afraid of what might happen if I did."

"I see."

"Lottie, you have to understand. Even after everything that happened, I still loved your father. I didn't want to lose him. He was your hero. You hung onto his every word and followed him wherever he went. I couldn't let anything ruin that for you. So, I kept my mouth shut."

"A few years later, Mrs. Hall and I were out holiday shopping. We had been looking at the ornaments on display at a little shop in town when I spotted Virginia walking by with a little girl. I quickly ducked out of sight so she wouldn't see me. The little girl though…" she hesitated, "she was the spitting image of you at that age. It was like looking at another little Charlotte."

"Mrs. Hall saw them, too. She'd seen my reaction, of course, and I'm fairly certain put two and two together. She never questioned me. Maybe she didn't want to upset me, I don't know. And then at your father's funeral, when I recognized the locket and saw that Virginia had placed two red roses on his casket, deep down I knew. I couldn't bear the thought of seeing them or of you finding out about the affair. So, I moved us away."

"I'm sorry, Mom. It must've been really hard for you," I choked out, trying to put myself in her shoes.

"It was. It was just too much. I should've told you before you went to Rockland, but I didn't want to keep you from your dream a second time. I couldn't do that to you again. And I knew you'd never go back if you knew the truth."

"I really wish you'd told me," I said.

"There's a part of me that regrets it, but I was doing what I thought was best at the time. And you needed to take this trip for yourself."

"I know."

Clearing her throat, she said, "I realize that I've spent all these years running. And I'm tired. If you'll still have me, I think I'd like to go back to

Rockland. Turns out the past caught up with me here anyway."

"Are you sure? I was certain you'd never consider it given the news."

"I'm sure. So much time has passed. I'm ready to move on."

"Me too." I agreed. "We'll do it together."

CHAPTER SIXTY-THREE

Rushing downstairs to dinner, I pushed all thoughts of Ginny and Vivian from my head. I was getting good at compartmentalizing all the dramas in my life. It was crunch time and I needed to focus. Tomorrow night's performance would determine whether I got an offer from a Broadway production. Everything I ever wanted was right in front of me, I just had to reach out and grab it.

Walking into the dining room, my heart sank. Our table had expanded for the evening. Seated at the head was Mr. Dean and next to him was Miss Barker. So much for putting things out of my mind. Standing up a little taller, I plastered a smile on my face and sat down in my regular seat. Reading my mind, Judy looked at me wide-eyed, tilting her head ever-so-slightly in the direction of Miss Barker. Without a word, I confirmed her thoughts with a nod. Her hand automatically flew to her mouth, shocked by the truth. Picking up my water glass, I brought it in front of my mouth, whispering, "She doesn't know," before taking a sip.

Shaking her head, Judy muttered, "You can't make this stuff up."

Interrupting our sidebar, Mr. Dean loudly cleared his throat as Billy arrived with a tray of champagne glasses. He moved around the table passing them out. Handing me a glass, he regarded me with a quizzical expression, instantly understanding that something was up.

"Later," I mouthed. With a silent nod, he left the table, heading back to the kitchen.

"I'd like to propose a toast," Mr. Dean announced, looking around the table at each of us. "To the ladies of The Rockland Holiday Show 1956," he said, lifting his glass, "here's to limitless possibilities and living your dream. Let's knock 'em dead tomorrow! Cheers!"

"Cheers!" we cried in response, our glasses clinking.

When the celebratory din died down, he continued, "I wanted to share a meal with all of you before we open tomorrow. Over the course of our time together, I know I've been tough, but it was only to get each of you to reach your full potential. You should all be proud of the progress you've made." Catching my eye he said, "You have bright futures ahead of you, so tomorrow I want you to dance like you know it."

"I also wanted to take a moment to thank Miss Barker for all of her hard work," he said, turning to face her. "Without you, and everything you organize and manage behind the scenes, this show couldn't go on. I'm sure I speak for everyone here when I say that we're all grateful."

Blushing, Miss Barker said a quiet thank you, seeming to shrink away with all eyes on her. There's a difference between us. I loved to be center stage, whereas Vivian preferred to stay out of the spotlight. I wondered what other similarities and differences we had. I still couldn't believe that I'd had a sister all this time.

At that moment, Billy returned with little crocks of soup for our starter. "Here we have a classic chicken noodle soup," he said, placing them down in front of each of us, a dinner roll on the side to accompany the appetizer. "Chef thought you all might like something comforting tonight."

"He hit the nail on the head with that one," Jean quipped. Nervous laughter erupted around the table at Jean's brusque, yet entirely accurate comment.

Raising a hand to get Billy's attention I said, "Do you mind bringing some oyster crackers? I can't eat chicken noodle soup without them. Tradition."

"Not a problem," he replied before addressing the table. "Anyone else?"

"Please," Vivian called from the other end of the table. "I'm the same way. Bread doesn't do it for me."

"Okay, two crackers. I'll be back in a jiffy," Billy replied. Turning to look at me, Judy raised an eyebrow, seeming to point out our commonality.

"It's soup," I replied, rolling my eyes good-naturedly.

Billy returned with the crackers, dropping them with Vivian and me.

Tearing open the packet, I poured them into the crock. Picking up my soup spoon I scooped up some of the broth, drinking it down. Johnny's recipe was spot on as usual. I could've eaten a bowl of this for dinner and been perfectly satisfied. I continued to eat just the broth, saving the noodles, vegetables, and crackers for last.

"Hey!" Jean called out. "I noticed something else about you two," she cried, "looking from me to Vivian. "You weirdos eat your soup the same way." Looking down at my bowl, I blushed, knowing it was an eccentricity of mine. "Never in my life have I seen anyone eat just the broth first," Jean teased. "And here you two go. Maybe you really are long-lost sisters," she joked, unaware of just how right she was.

Nearly choking on her soup, Judy coughed, explaining, "Went down the wrong tube."

"That's funny," Miss Barker mused, "I've always eaten soup this way. I know it's a bit strange. I'll admit I've never seen anyone else do it."

"Same here," I smiled. "Since I was a kid."

"Me too. Saving the best for last, right Charlotte?" she asked.

"Always," I agreed.

* * *

"What's going on?" Billy hissed, pulling me inside the kitchen as I passed by. Looking around at the kitchen and wait staff, I shook my head. "Come on, Charlotte. I know you. I know when something is up," he said looking me over and gesturing the length of my body. "And something is definitely up."

"Come up to my room when you're done. I can't talk here."

"Top secret, hmm?" he replied, lifting an eyebrow as he mouthed, "Walt?"

"Nope. Even bigger."

"What could be bigger than that?"

"Take my word for it, it's bigger."

"Fine. I can't believe you're going to make me work under these conditions. The suspense alone is going to kill me."

"You'll be fine," I assured him. "See you in a bit. And no cocktails. I need to be ready for tomorrow."

"I'll bring tea, something relaxing," he said.

"I may need a tranquilizer on the side for that to work," I sarcastically replied, heading for the door.

"We can always ask Judy to bring her muscle relaxers," Billy called after me, laughing.

* * *

A rhythmic knock on the door notified me of Billy's arrival. "Guess who?" he said as I opened the door.

"My two favorite people," I smiled, stepping aside to allow my friends to enter. Billy carried his usual tray, this time with peppermint tea and an Andes mint for each of us. Sitting cross-legged on the bed, he set the tray in the middle.

"Spill it, girl," he jokingly demanded. "It's a wonder I made it through my shift."

Picking up a cup of tea and taking a sip, I gently placed it down on the saucer. Looking at Billy, I calmly said, "I have a sister."

Nearly spitting out his tea, Billy replied, "I'm sorry, what?"

"You heard me. I have a sister. It's Miss Barker. Vivian."

Setting his teacup down on the saucer with a clink, he said, "Are you sure?"

"I'm sure," I said, taking another sip and telling him what had happened after rehearsal. "I spoke to Ms. Madsen today. She told me the whole story. I also talked to my mother who confirmed it."

"She knew?" he asked, his eyes growing wide.

"Well, not for certain. But there were enough clues that she gathered what had happened. At the funeral, she put it all together. And consequently, moved us away."

"Yikes," Judy piped up. "Not the best news to receive the day before our opening."

"I know. But not knowing would've driven me crazy. It's better this way," I said.

"This is wild," Billy proclaimed. "Who *were* your parents? And I always thought they were the picture of a perfect marriage."

"My thoughts exactly," I agreed. "Vivian doesn't know yet, so you two cannot breathe a word of this to anyone. Especially to Bobby," I said, looking pointedly at Billy.

Holding up three fingers, he replied, "Scout's honor."

CHAPTER SIXTY-FOUR

Opening my eyes, I recognized a familiar song at the window. Stretching, I smiled as I opened the curtain. There on the windowsill was the little bluebird singing and hopping to his heart's content. With all the craziness in my life, I counted this as a good omen for tonight's inaugural show. Nodding at him, I watched as he appeared to nod back at me before flying off into the distance.

I padded into the bathroom, washing my face, and getting dressed. Applying my facial cream, I was careful to pat it on around my eyes, so as not to stretch the delicate skin. Looking more closely I could see the faintest of lines beginning to crop up. Running the brush through my hair, I heard a soft knock at the door. Glancing at the clock, I saw that it was only 9:30 a.m. Not expecting visitors, I cautiously opened the door to find a somewhat disheveled Vivian on the other side of the threshold. "Hi Charlotte," she began timidly. "Can I come in?"

"Of course," I said, welcoming her, certain I knew the reason for her visit. "I was just getting ready, don't mind the mess," I gestured to my unmade bed. Nodding, she sat down in the armchair. I took a seat opposite her on the bed.

"I spoke with my mother last night after dinner," she said, nervously twiddling her fingers. "She told me everything."

"Are you okay?" I asked, concerned. "I'm sorry I didn't say anything. You needed to hear it from your mom first."

"It's not your fault. She should've told me years ago. On one hand, I understand why she didn't, but on the other, I just can't believe she kept this secret for my entire life," Vivian replied. "I'm not sure how I feel yet. Everything I knew was a lie. I have a father I never met and never will. I have a sister who I'm just meeting as an adult. I don't know where to begin."

"Believe me, I know how you feel. I was just as shocked as you. I thought I knew my parents," I whispered.

"Me too."

"So where do we go from here?" I asked. Shrugging, she sat back in the chair. "Well, sister," I began with a half-smile, "why don't we start with breakfast?"

* * *

"Good morning, ladies," Billy greeted us when we reached the dining room. "Table for two?" he suggested.

"That would be perfect, thanks Billy," I replied. Understanding the delicate situation we were in, he sat us in a private little corner, away from the rest of the troupe.

"He knows?" Vivian asked.

"He does. Billy and I have been friends since we were kids. He knew something was up as soon as he saw me at dinner last night," I explained. "I hope you don't mind."

"No, it's okay. People will find out soon enough. It's nice that he thought to give us some privacy to talk."

"He's a thoughtful guy," I assured her. "You can trust him to keep this to himself."

"As much as this situation is strange and awkward, I'm glad that you're sticking around. It'll give us a chance to get to know each other."

"I agree. I never thought I'd find anything more here than a spot in this year's show. Turns out I had a whole life waiting for me. We have a lot of catching up to do."

"We certainly do. I'd love to hear more about our father if you don't mind sharing with me," she said.

"Of course," I began, "he was my most favorite person. The kind of guy who could talk to anyone about anything, and he was truly interested to hear it. He was genuine and people could feel that."

Smiling, Vivian said, "He sounds nice. I wish I'd gotten the chance to meet him."

"You would've loved him. I miss him every day."

"Here you are," Billy said, placing a Belgian waffle with fresh berries and whipped cream in front of each of us.

"This looks amazing," I said, practically drooling.

"Agreed. Suddenly I'm feeling a little light-headed," Vivian said.

"Stress will do that to you," Billy said. "Eat up and enjoy." We tucked into our breakfast, chatting about our favorite things, sharing childhood stories and anecdotes. I was mid-bite when I noticed Vivian chuckling to herself on the other side of the table.

"What?" I asked, having swallowed my mouthful.

"Look," she pointed at our plates, almost identical. "You eat the edges first, too."

"Saving the best for last, naturally," I winked.

"It's actually kind of neat to see that we have the same idiosyncrasies. Like we've been connected all along."

"It really is. What other weird habits do you have?" I asked with a laugh.

"I'm sure time will tell," she said lifting her coffee and holding it out for me to cheers. "To sisters," she said.

"Sisters," I said, clinking my teacup against her coffee mug.

* * *

Returning to my room, I felt a strange sense of calm. Breakfast was nice. It had been easy to talk to Vivian despite the circumstances. I was excited to spend more time with her and to introduce her to Charlie and the girls. My girls had an auntie. They'd be ecstatic.

I had surprised myself with how well I'd taken the news. Even though it had been shocking to uncover these secrets, it felt like the pieces of a puzzle were being revealed and shifted into place.

I wondered how my mother would react to meeting Viv. It would be interesting, to say the least. I hoped she could put aside all the hurt and betrayal caused by my father's indiscretions and accept her into our lives.

Gathering my things, I packed extra hairpins, my cosmetics case, a tube of red lipstick, and my favorite fragrance in my tote. Reaching for the gift bag from The Perfect Present, I pulled out the gift box containing the bluebird ornament for Walt. I'd give it to him at the show, finally closing that chapter. Opening the box, I ran my finger along the smooth blue glass, remembering, before gently placing it inside my tote.

A sadness washed over me at the thought of what could've been. In another time and place, Walt and I would've been so happy together. I could feel it in my gut. But we both needed to return to our lives. He was heading back to Massachusetts, and I would be rebuilding my life here in Rockland. I had chosen my own path with a new career, a sister, great friends, and my family by my side. And that was enough.

CHAPTER SIXTY-FIVE

Adrenaline coursing through my veins, I entered the theater. In a few hours, I would be onstage, living my dream. Like it was yesterday, I remembered sitting in the audience as a kid, imagining I was up there with the dancers. "Can you believe it?" Judy said, walking up behind me. "It's finally here."

"I know," I breathed. "I almost can't. I'd ask you to pinch me to make sure I'm not dreaming, but I think you'd actually do it."

"I would," Judy laughed, holding up her thumb and index fingers, pretending. "So how did your breakfast go?"

"Billy told you?" I asked. She nodded. "It was nice. A little awkward at first, but once we got to chatting, it was easy."

"Like sisters?"

"Exactly."

"Good, I'm glad it's all working out," she said, shuttling me forward. "Now let's get backstage to warm up. You've got to get ready for Broadway."

* * *

The rest of the afternoon passed in a blur. Warm-ups went off without a hitch. We were more than prepared for the show. There was nothing to do but wait for the curtain call. In the dressing room, we did last-minute touch-ups to our hair and makeup, nervous energy filling the room. Looking up at my reflection I saw Mr. Dean approaching. "Charlotte," he said, a comforting hand on my shoulder, "are you ready?"

Looking back at him, I nodded, "I've never been more ready for anything."

"Great," he replied. "Show them what you've got." Patting my shoulder, he moved on down the line of girls, giving each of us a little pep talk. I smoothed on a layer of red lipstick, blotting off the excess on a tissue. Next, I brushed a little rouge on my cheeks and slicked on another coat of mascara. Satisfied, I sprayed my hair one last time, being careful to slick the fly-aways back. I was ready.

Dressed for the first number, I stood up in front of the mirror, inspecting the icy white costume. Setting the tone for the show, it was covered with silver sparkles reminiscent of snowflakes, telling the audience that winter had arrived. All the dancing I'd done since I'd been in Rockland had done me good. The costume fit me like a glove.

While the rest of the girls finished getting ready, I tiptoed out into the hallway and went backstage. I could hear the chatter of ushers and people finding their seats in the theater. Peeking out from behind the curtain, I saw the bustle of the crowd, the seats filling up quickly. Excitement filled the auditorium as the wait for curtain call filled me with anticipation.

My eyes landed on none other than Walt, seated alone to the far right of the auditorium. Seeing him there filled my heart with happiness. Just knowing someone was out there for me was comforting, but knowing it was Walt made my heart burst and break at the same time. Blinking back the happy tears threatening to fall, I took a breath to regain my composure. Seeming to sense he was being watched, Walt's gaze swept over to where I was standing. Through a sliver of the curtain, our eyes locked, and a tingle ran through me. Smiling, he held a hand over his heart. I did the same, bowing my head, before disappearing behind the curtain. Pushing the overwhelming feeling of sorrow aside, I made the decision to focus on opening night excitement only. Slapping a smile on my face, I returned to the dressing room. Sitting down next to Judy, she looked at me with skepticism clouding her features. "What?"

"What do you mean, what? I didn't say anything," I replied.

Narrowing her eyes, she said, "You didn't have to. I know a fake smile when I see one."

Sighing, I said, "Walt's out there. I just saw him."

"And? You knew he was coming tonight."

"I know," I muttered under my breath, careful not to let any of the girls overhear me. "He just gets me. There's still a little part of me that wonders about what might've been."

Placing a hand over mine, Judy squeezed it. "I know, honey. Maybe it's better this way though. Imagination is usually better than reality."

"True," I agreed with a shrug. "I just need to get through this show, say my goodbyes, and move forward."

"Exactly. Out of sight, out of mind."

"Right."

"It will all work out," she assured me. Changing the subject, she added, "I wish Jack had been able to make it tonight, but he had to go out of town for a few days."

"He'll be back in time for your solo?" I asked.

"Yes, at which point I plan to dazzle him. Onstage and off," she said suggestively, wiggling her eyebrows.

Laughing, I teased, "Judy, I wouldn't expect anything less from you, and I'm sure by now he won't either."

Swatting at me, she pushed her chair back and stood up, holding out a hand to me. "Come on, we have a crowd to entertain."

Allowing her to pull me to standing, I said, "Let's show them what to expect from Studio Duo."

"Only the best, of course," she replied as we headed backstage together, ready for our debut appearance.

CHAPTER SIXTY-SIX

As the bright house lights dimmed once, then twice, signaling that the show was about to begin, the noisy din of the auditorium quieted to hushed whispers. Taking our places, the faint beginning sounds of the opening number broke the silence, the melody slowly building until the curtains opened, spotlights illuminating our positions on stage.

One by one we came to life with the music, at first moving slowly, gently mimicking the first flurries of snow. Changing from a warm white to a blue cast, the lighting established the feel of a winter night, stars twinkling above. As the music gained momentum, our movements followed, creating the impression of a snowstorm, our bodies swirling about, twisting in a perceived wind. Suddenly, the music diminished, taking on a lighter quality, the quiet calm after a storm as we glided off stage to an explosion of applause.

Rushing to our costume racks, we hurriedly changed for the next number, an upbeat interpretation of the joy of playing in the first snow. I shrugged into the emerald green velvet jacket and gloves assigned to me. It was becoming my signature color. Next to me, Judy slipped into her ruby red version. Giving me a wink, we headed back to the stage.

All the girls wore the same jacket in various jewel tones. The set had been changed to recreate a city street; awnings blanketed with snow. We tapped in formation from either side of the stage, pedestrians going about our business when the lighting appeared to send flurries down over the city.

Breaking from the group, Bianca, in a sapphire jacket, took center stage, lifting her arms and beginning to spin on one leg, her other pumping at each revolution to gain momentum until she stopped on a dime. Appearing to scoop up the imagined snow, she pantomimed throwing snowballs at the passersby. Each of us joining in, jauntily echoing her movements until playfully chasing her offstage.

Once again, the burst of claps and whoops from the audience followed us backstage. Calling out our congratulations to a beaming Bianca on her solo, we changed into the icy blue costumes. Steeling myself for my feature performance with Kay, I said a quick silent prayer to my father, always my biggest fan. Catching Kay's eye, I gave a quick thumbs-up as she nodded back. This was it. It was my time to shine.

Gliding onstage as if it were made of ice, we joined together, first forming a line and seamlessly morphing into a large circle. Rotating as we kicked, Kay and I finally broke away as the line straightened itself, creating the backdrop for our feature.

Flowing through the movements effortlessly, I was invigorated, grinning from ear to ear. When it came time to perform the fan kicks, I executed each one to perfection. Flawless. I could feel pride swelling inside me as I began to weave through the kick line. Rotating and flowing through the movements like dominoes in a row, our ice dance came to a halt, each of us hitting our final position on the last beat of the music.

Beaming at the audience and panting to catch my breath without breaking my position, a blast of applause erupted from the auditorium. My heart swelled, the moment I'd been waiting for all these years was more amazing than I'd imagined. Despite the lights trained on us, I caught sight of the first person to stand, clapping emphatically, eyes focused only on me. It was Walt.

* * *

The rest of the show went beautifully. The performances were impeccable, the sets and costumes supported the story of each number, and the audience was captivated throughout. Changing into our costumes for the closing number, the excitement and camaraderie of the troupe were palpable. We'd come together and created something amazing. I was so happy to be a part of it. Smoothing the skirt on my crimson dress and fluffing the fur trim, I sailed over to Judy. "Look at us," she said. "A couple of Mrs. Clauses."

"More than a couple," I replied, nodding toward the rest of the girls.

Lining up, I could see a massive Christmas tree commanding attention at center stage. It was just like in the movie. One by one, we sailed onstage, twirling around the tree, the centerpiece of the final number. Forming a circle around it, we joined hands leaning in and back out creating snowflake shapes, until breaking apart. Spinning off in different directions, we landed at our respective marks in arabesque.

At that moment, the audience went wild. Moving into the next position, I spotted a surprise appearance by Mr. Dean, aptly dressed as St. Nick, complete with a velvet sack loaded with gifts. He performed a scissor step with the sack on his back, weaving through us as though we'd always rehearsed this way.

I'd always wondered why we were so static for that section in the number, but he'd obviously had this planned all along. Keeping it a surprise made our reactions much more authentic as he passed each of us a wrapped gift before we gathered at the tree to sing the final bars of White Christmas together as the audience joined in.

The merriment was infectious. Singing, smiling faces filled the theater. With our arms around each other, we swayed to the tune, the crowd following suit. When the music ended, the theater was filled with a cacophony of applause and laughter, whoops and hollers. The audience rose to its feet in a standing ovation as The Rockland Dance Troupe 1956 took a collective bow to thunderous praise, followed by an encore.

CHAPTER SIXTY-SEVEN

Backstage was chaos. The most wonderful chaos I've ever experienced. All around me people were embracing, laughing, hollering. Dancers, seamstresses, set designers, lighting people, and anyone who'd contributed to the show was celebrating. We were a success.

A loud whistle sounded, breaking through the revelry. Mr. Dean stepped forward, still dressed as Santa Claus, yelling, "Everyone! Excuse me!" Waiting for us to quiet down, he continued, "I want to take a quick moment to thank all of you. Without your hard work, this show would never have happened. I couldn't have asked for a better group of people. You were amazing! Tonight was amazing! I've reserved a section at the dance hall. Everyone's invited. Let's celebrate, you all deserve it! Bravo!"

A celebratory cheer rang out among the crowd as people began to disperse. Judy ran up to me, crushing me in a hug. "You were perfection!" she cried.

"Thanks, Judy," I replied, grinning. "It felt amazing."

"I bet. I can't wait until I can reprise my solo," she said. "I have to admit that Bianca's performance was exquisite. I almost feel bad taking the role away from her."

"Only a little longer," I assured her. "Besides, she knows it's coming. She's a natural. That girl has a fabulous career ahead of her. She'll have plenty of opportunities."

"I know, I keep telling myself that. Let's go grab our things." Walking back to the dressing area, I felt as though I was walking on air. I wondered what the Broadway people would have to say. Could I go if they made an offer?

What would Charlie say to that? Grabbing my tote, I decided I'd deal with that tomorrow.

Double checking that all my things were in the bag, I got the sense that someone was looking at me. Turning toward the doorway, I saw Walt standing with his hands in his pockets. I held up a finger to indicate that I'd just be a second. He nodded in response.

"Judy," I whispered, nodding toward the door. "I'm going to say goodbye. We'll be over by the Christmas tree. I don't know if I can do this," I confessed. "If I'm not back in five minutes send a rescue party."

"You got it," she replied. "Stay strong."

"Thanks," I said, heading for the door.

Reaching Walt, I suggested, "Let's go somewhere we can talk." Nodding, he followed me. Onstage with the curtains drawn, I led Walt over to the tree. He looked at me with a knowing smile. "What is it?" I asked.

"I was going to suggest we visit this tree," he said, bending down to retrieve a gift box hidden beneath the boughs. Handing it to me, he said, "For you."

"Thank you," I replied. "But how did you get it back here?"

"I've got connections," he winked. Rummaging through my bag, I handed Walt a matching gift box. Chuckling, he replied, "Great minds."

"Looks like it," I agreed.

"You were amazing tonight, Lottie. I couldn't take my eyes off you," he said.

Blushing and glancing at the floor, I murmured a thank you. "After my feature, I saw you. You were the first person to stand," I said, meeting his gaze.

Looking at Walt, I could feel the magnetism between us. I wanted nothing more than to jump into his arms, to feel his soft lips on mine just one more time, but I stayed cemented in place. Willing my body to remain strong, I changed the subject. "Go on," I said. "Open it." Removing the lid, Walt pulled out the glass bluebird. It looked so tiny and delicate in his strong hands.

"Thank you, Lottie."

"To remember me by," I replied.

"I couldn't forget you if I tried," he whispered before clearing his throat. "Your turn." Taking the lid off the box, I moved the tissue paper aside, gasping at what I found inside. Pulling the ornament out of the box, I was overcome with emotion.

"How did you know?"

"What do you mean?" he asked.

"Judy and I saw this very ornament at The Perfect Present. I went back to buy it and it was gone. The shopkeeper said something to me about finding something special under the tree. It was like she knew."

"I was walking past, and it reminded me of the two of you. I thought you'd like to have it, a memento of your time in Rockland," he explained. "Come to think of it, the woman at the counter acted as though she knew me, too. She made a passing comment, something about making the talented brunette very happy. I figured she was confusing me with someone else and I didn't have the heart to correct her."

"Interesting."

"Sounds a little like one of your signs," he said.

"It does. Walt, I wish…" I began.

"Lottie, don't. I already know," he interrupted, saving me from going any further. "You'll be going back home soon. I'm staying here…"

"Walt!" Judy called, sailing over to us. "Lovely to see you."

"You too, Judy. Great show."

"It was, wasn't it? And this one," she said gesturing to me, "she's going places."

"She sure is," he agreed, smiling at me.

"Walt, what were you saying about staying?" I asked.

"Oh, I…"

"Here she is!" I heard Billy announce loudly from behind us, a warning cue. Turning in his direction, he approached us with my husband. My eyes widened in shock, my heart sinking to my stomach, I forced the corners of my mouth to turn up. Judy immediately wrapped an arm around Walt's waist, pulling him closer to her.

"Charlie!" I exclaimed.

"Surprise!" he said, handing me a bouquet of flowers and grabbing me in a hug. "I couldn't miss your opening night. You were spectacular!" Releasing me, a confused look crossed his face. "Walt?"

"Charlie?" Realizing that my husband and Walt were already acquainted, I stood frozen, silent.

"You two know each other then?" Judy asked.

"Yep," Charlie quipped, clapping a hand over Walt's shoulder. "He's my best employee. I wasn't expecting to see you here."

"Walt's great friends with my beau, Jack," Judy jumped in. "He had to be out of town, so Walt came to the show tonight in his place."

"That's really good of you, Walt. I always knew you were a stand-up guy," Charlie said, completely missing the defeated look on Walt's face. "Since we're all here, I might as well tell you the news now."

"News?" I choked out, forcing a smile. Walt looked from me to Charlie, trapped. Judy smiled at everyone, trying to keep the mood light. Billy, for the first time ever, had nothing to say.

"I did it, Lot," Charlie announced, giddy. "I sold the garage! I sign on the dotted line on Monday. I wanted to tell you myself in person. Your mom and the girls will be here tomorrow to celebrate with us. I found a great location here in Rockland, and Walt has agreed to stay on with me. We're moving to Rockland just like you wanted."

Nodding my head, pasting a smile on my face, and ignoring the wave of nausea washing over me, I dug deep to try to inflect some positivity into my voice, "Wow. That's amazing news. And Walt is staying on with you..."

Tilting his head to the side, Charlie said, "I thought you'd be more excited, honey."

"Oh! I am excited! I'm just... surprised... that it all came together so quickly," I stumbled over my words.

"I'll admit, I was surprised myself," he agreed. "It was almost too easy, but it's going to be great!"

"Great!" Billy cried a little too loudly. Adjusting his volume, he continued, "Looks like congratulations are in order!"

"Indeed! Congrats" Judy exclaimed. "And congrats to Charlotte and me for our new dance studio!"

"Dance studio? Here? "Wow, that's great," Walt said, caught off guard. "Congratulations."

"Congrats again, ladies!" Billy exclaimed. "Lots of exciting news!"

Pulling me in close and giving me a squeeze, Charlie looked so satisfied, proud of himself that he'd fixed the problem. Catching Walt's gaze, he and I exchanged identical looks of concern. We would both remain in Rockland, both tied to Charlie and still inexplicably tied to each other.

CHAPTER SIXTY-EIGHT

"We should get going if we're going to meet everyone over at the dance hall," Judy declared. "You coming, Lottie?"

Looking from her to Billy to Walt and then to Charlie, I shook my head. "No, I don't think so, Judy. It's been a whirlwind, and I have that brunch in the morning. It's probably best that I head back early."

Nodding her understanding, she replied, "No worries, honey. You have a big day tomorrow."

"Bobby will completely understand," Billy assured me. "Knowing him, he'll only stay for thirty minutes before calling it a night."

"Lot, are you sure you don't want to go for a little while?" Charlie asked. "You've been waiting for this moment for years. I think you should celebrate."

"He's right, you know," Billy chimed.

"Okay, we'll pop in for a little while," I agreed.

"Walt, you've got to come along with us," Charlie said. "You're a big reason I'm even here tonight. I couldn't imagine getting the new garage up and running without your help."

"I guess I could come for a bit," Walt shrugged, unsure.

Threading her arm through his, Judy announced, "Well, let's go then!" escorting Walt offstage and out of the theater.

* * *

Walking to the dance hall, my mind was wrought with questions. What a cruel twist of fate. Just when I thought everything was falling into place, a bomb was detonated on my plans, obliterating them. "What's this about brunch tomorrow?" Charlie asked.

"Oh, I wanted to talk to you about that," I began cautiously. "I wasn't sure it would happen, but there's a possibility I could be offered a spot in a Broadway show."

"Broadway? As in New York City?" his voice raising a few octaves with each question.

"That's the one."

"Lottie, I just uprooted my entire business to be here for you and you're already planning on leaving?" he accused, stopping in the middle of the sidewalk.

"It's not like that, Charlie. It would just be a few months and it would be a great draw for the studio," I explained. "I just want to hear them out. Nothing has even happened yet."

"How do I know that? This was supposed to be a few weeks! *And we're moving here!* What about the girls? And us? Do we even factor into your decisions anymore?" he said, shaking his head in disgust and turning away from me.

Placing my hands squarely on my hips I shot back, "Charlie, I can't believe you'd even ask that question. Our family is always a factor. At the very least, I'm taking the meeting. We can talk more about it tomorrow."

After a few moments of silence Charlie asked, "Why didn't you tell me sooner?"

"Because I knew you'd react like this" I said flatly. "I'm doing something for myself for a change and I'm not going to give that up. I do know that I want to have a life here in Rockland. My family and friends will be here."

Considering my response, Charlie sighed. "I hope you're right."

"What does that mean?"

"You know what it means."

"Wow," I said sarcastically. "I've chosen you and the girls," *in more ways than you know,* "but I'm also choosing myself."

We walked the rest of the way in silence.

* * *

Arriving at the hall, Billy held the door open for us all to go inside. Big band music permeated the air, and the crowd was more hyped up than usual. I spotted a large group from the production, waving in their general direction. "Lottie and I are going to run to the ladies' room," Judy announced, pulling me away from the men. "We'll meet you over in our section."

Watching over my shoulder as Charlie, Billy, and Walt headed over to a group of tables, I turned to Judy wide-eyed. "I know!" she hollered over the music. "Come on!" Leading me up the stairs, she managed to find a single restroom tucked away in a back corner. Flipping the light switch, she pulled me inside, locking the door after us. "Are you okay?" she asked.

Shrugging, I replied, "Not really, no."

"I can't believe it. How did you not know that Walt works for Charlie?"

"I guess I never mentioned Charlie's business specifically. I just said he was a business owner. And Walt never told me where he worked."

"How wild."

"Tell me about it. Now that I think of it, I vaguely recall Charlie mentioning a new employee named Walt once, when I was first offered my spot in the show. I was so preoccupied that I wasn't really paying attention and obviously never made the connection."

"And Walt did tell me something about fixing up cars with his uncle when he was younger," I continued, "but I just figured it was a hobby. How could I be so oblivious?"

Looking at her reflection, Judy applied a fresh coat of lipstick, pouting her lips in front of the mirror. "Maybe you didn't want to see it?" she suggested.

"Maybe. What am I going to do, Judy?" I asked, putting my head in my hands.

"I don't know, honey," she replied, placing a supportive hand on my shoulder. "This is a toughie. All I can say is Broadway is looking even better now."

"Not exactly. I told Charlie about it on the way over. Long story short, he's not happy. He doesn't trust that I'll come back. I have no idea where that leaves us."

"Oh, I'm so sorry honey. Maybe he'll have a change of heart. Give him some time."

"True. And Walt. I feel terrible that he's even in this position in the first place. I wonder if he'll actually stay."

"I mean, this whole situation has got to be torture for him. And you. All I can say is that you need to follow your heart and stay true to yourself. Everything else will fall into place."

"I hope you're right, Judy."

"When have I ever been wrong?" she laughed. "Besides, we'll always have each other no matter what."

"Thank goodness for that. If there's a chance that Charlie decides not to sell, I'm sure Alice will be waiting in the wings," I muttered, "ready to swoop in at the first sign of weakness."

"There will always be an Alice no matter where you live. Charlie seemed proud of you tonight, and excited about starting fresh here. It sounds to me like he's afraid of losing you. He just doesn't know how to tell you how he feels," she said, matter of fact, linking her arm through mine. "Come on. We just had an amazing opening night and for now, we celebrate! You can deal with the rest tomorrow."

* * *

Returning to the group, I spotted Walt seated at a table with Billy. Charlie was nowhere to be seen. As we approached, Billy quickly explained, "He just went to the restroom. Come on, Judy, this is my favorite song!"

They took off, leaving me alone with Walt. "I'm sorry," I blurted out loudly to be heard over the music. "I had no idea."

"Me either."

"I'm afraid I might've ruined your opportunity to stay in Rockland, Walt."

"How so?" he asked, confused.

"Well, there's a good chance I'm going to be offered a spot in a Broadway production."

"Wow, Lottie. Well deserved. Congratulations!"

"Thanks. Charlie doesn't feel quite so enthusiastic. I'm not sure that he's actually going to move the garage here if I go."

Walt raked his hands through his hair, sighing loudly and choosing his words carefully. "I'll be honest with you; I was shocked when Charlie walked in. When I put it all together, it felt like a bad joke. You know how I feel about you, and whether I'm here or somewhere else, that won't change. Probably ever. It is what it is. I'll be alright, so don't worry about me," he paused, steeling himself to continue. "There's a part of me that doesn't want to tell you this, but it's the right thing to do, so here goes. Having worked with Charlie, I know how much he loves you. He tells the guys at the garage all the time how lucky he is. How he'd be nowhere without you. Maybe he's not saying it to you, and he should, but he's saying it because he feels it. He's moving his business for you. Not because he feels guilty, but because you're his life. He's not the guy you described to me. Yeah, he made a mistake, but so did we. He deserves a second chance."

My heart ached as I listened to him, partly because I loved hearing that his feelings for me would never change and partly because he had so selflessly reaffirmed my faith in my husband. I nodded, "You're a good man, Walt."

After that, we sat in silence. There was nothing left to say.

CHAPTER SIXTY-NINE

Back in the room, I lay in bed staring at the ceiling. I had never considered the possibility that Charlie was afraid of losing me. Or that he still loved me as much as Walt seemed to think. Why would he cheat if he cared so much? Did he want to get caught? Was he trying to beat me to the punch? Was he trying to feel good in the moment to forget? I could certainly understand that tactic.

I'd made Charlie out to be the bad guy, but maybe I was partly responsible. I could've told him I was unhappy, but I didn't. I let my resentment fester until I'd turned him into a monster in my head. And maybe I didn't hide my real feelings as well as I thought. Maybe he'd known all along. What was I going to do if they offered me a role on Broadway? Could I be happy saying no to something I'd dreamed about since I put on my first pair of tap shoes?

"Lot? You still awake?" Charlie asked, rolling over to face me.

"Yeah. Can't sleep."

"Me either."

"I'm worried about us," I admitted.

"Me too."

We lay in silence, neither of us willing to move the conversation forward any further. Neither of us knowing how to fix us.

"Hey, what was the news you were going to tell me?" Charlie asked, effectively changing the subject.

"Huh?"

"Remember, you called your mother about it? Top secret."

"Oh right! I can't believe I forgot to tell you. I've been so preoccupied with everything else. The thing is, I found out that I have a sister," I revealed.

"What?" Charlie replied, incredulously. "You're serious?"

"I know, it sounds crazy. I found out that my father had an affair when I was a young girl. She works on the production. Her mother was my seamstress. We look a lot alike. One of the girls noticed it."

"Wow. That's crazy. What's she like? Did your mom know?"

"Her name's Vivian. She's great! We have some funny quirks in common and in other ways we're complete opposites. Mom suspected but didn't know for certain. I don't think she wanted to face the truth."

"Wow. And you're sure she's okay with moving back?"

"She said as much."

"Well, a lot of time has passed so I'm sure that helps."

"I hope so," I paused, reminded of his dalliance with Alice, as I'm sure he was. My mind wandering to my entanglements with Walt, I felt a twinge of guilt. We were both treading lightly, staying at surface level.

"Time and distance make a difference," he said, seemingly trying to convince the both of us. "I'm sure of it, Lot."

"Yeah," I agreed half-heartedly, wondering if that was enough.

* * *

After a less-than-restful night's sleep, I got up and pulled my favorite dress from the wardrobe. Navy blue with white polka dots, always a classic. Charlie, grabbing a shirt from the wardrobe, pulled another hanger, holding it before me. "What's this?" he asked, eyebrows raised, a smile pulling at the corners of his mouth.

Snatching the emerald lingerie set from his hands, I blushed thinking of the last time I'd worn it, replying, "Oh, nothing. Just a little something I bought for myself."

"For yourself?" he asked.

"Sure," I nonchalantly replied. "Judy said it would make me feel good."

"I like the way she thinks," he growled, pulling me close enough that I could feel every inch of his interest, "I think it would make us both feel good." Planting a kiss on the small of my neck, his hands slid slowly down my torso, tugging at the waistband of my pajamas. I felt a mixture of desire and unease, my body waking up with his touch and recalling the last time I'd worn the lingerie in question. I couldn't ever wear it for Charlie.

"There's a cute shop called Bett's Boutique in town. It's owned by a friend of mine. Maybe we can stop in, and we can choose something together," I suggested. "As long as it's not red."

"What's wrong with this one?" he pointed. "And what's wrong with red? You've always liked red," he insisted.

"That one's just for me," I explained. "You can choose one for me to wear *especially for you*. It'll be fun. And I think I'm just over red these days," I declared, my innuendo lost on him. Maybe he'd never seen that fire engine red number after all. Good.

"We've never shopped for lingerie together before. Can't hurt to spice things up a little," he pulled me close.

"Great, after brunch then," I decided. Breaking away from my husband, I returned the set to its place in the wardrobe. "I've really got to get ready. I can't be late."

"Right. How could I forget about brunch?" he replied, a hint of sarcasm in his tone.

"Because you wanted to," I muttered under my breath, my back to him.

Grabbing my shoulders, Charlie spun me around to face him. "Please don't go, Charlotte," he pleaded, his eyes searching mine for some understanding. "Don't go to Broadway. At least not yet. Not right now."

"Why? Give me one good reason why I should stay," I challenged him.

"Because you're everything to me. I love us. And I don't know if we can survive you leaving right now," his voice cracked. "I've felt you pulling away from me for a long time and I didn't know how to get you back. I've watched you slipping further and further with each passing day. You stopped showing any interest in me and I didn't know how to make you happy anymore. Every inch you put between us felt like a mile. You were so focused on starting our family and making our home. I thought you wanted to be at home with the girls. When you got the offer to come out here, I was terrified that I'd already lost you. I can't lose you. I love you. I love us. I love our little family. I just want to make you happy. Wherever and whatever that means. Please just let me."

Swallowing the lump in my throat, I felt tears begin to roll down my cheeks. "What took you so long?" I asked, wishing he'd only said it sooner.

* * *

Walking into the Rockland Grille, I stood up a little taller, tuned in to my posture. This was it and first impressions were everything. After the hostess pointed me in the direction of Mr. Dean's table, I took out my compact, quickly checking my reflection. Adjusting my strand of pearls so the clasp landed at the back of my neck, I rolled the pearls between my fingers for a moment sending a quick wish to Dad that they'd bring me luck. Satisfied, I made my way over to a table by the window where Bobby waited with two other people.

"Lottie, I'm so glad you could join us," Bobby welcomed me. "Allow me to introduce my friends. This is the great playwright Dillon James," he nodded to the man on his right. Taking his hand, I firmly shook a greeting. "And this," he turned his gaze to the woman on his left, "is Layla Gardner, choreographer extraordinaire. Dillon, Layla, this is Charlotte Abbott."

Shaking hands with Layla, I said to them, "I'm honored to meet you both. This is truly my pleasure."

"The pleasure is all ours," Mr. James began. "We absolutely loved the show. I had no doubt it would be great with this guy at the helm," he nodded in Bobby's direction. "But I have to say you, my dear, have star quality. You really stole the show."

"Thank you," I said, taken aback by his immediate praise.

"I have to agree. Your performance was spectacular, flawless form," Layla added.

"Wow, I don't know what to say," I replied.

"Say you'll come to New York," Layla suggested, cutting right to the chase, hands clasped on the table before her.

"Lottie, may I call you that?" Dillon asked.

"You sure can, that's what my friends call me."

"Fabulous, I can see that we'll be fast friends. If I do say so myself, I've written a smash hit," he began, fanning his fingers to pantomime a marquee overhead, "Springtime in Suburbia. It's a commentary on life in the suburbs. The picture-perfect images you see versus the gritty reality of what goes on behind closed doors. I know it sounds grim the way I've just described it, but it's actually a quite campy musical. A comedy if you will."

"It sounds very interesting," I said. "Pretty on the nose if you ask me."

"That's what I was going for. Bobby here tells me that you came here as a suburban housewife and mother yourself, so I'm sure you can relate."

"I certainly can," I laughed.

"I think that perspective could really add something special to the show," he said. "And Layla here is a master of communicating a story through dance. I'm confident that she'll be able to convey the message beautifully while also keeping the audience entertained."

"I have it all right here," Layla jumped in, tapping her temple. "Just get me a rehearsal space and I'm ready to go."

"I have to say this sounds perfect for you Lottie," Bobby piped up. "I can't think of a better fit."

"That's right. Intensive rehearsals, I'm talking twelve-hour days, and a Broadway run with two or three shows per day," Dillon explained. "It's a pretty rigorous schedule. Think you're up for it?"

Looking around at the expectant faces around the table, I kept my composure, pausing for a moment before replying, "I can't thank you enough for thinking of me. It is the greatest compliment I've ever received. But I have to give my regrets."

"Charlotte, you're sure?" Bobby implored.

"I am," I asserted. "I've realized that I've been holding on tight to a childhood dream that no longer fits my reality. It just doesn't work. I'm content to stay in Rockland surrounded by friends and family, to launch my studio with my best friend, to create a life. I found all I never wanted here, and it's a perfect fit."

"You're sure?" Dillon asked, perplexed.

"I'm sure," I smiled.

"In that case, maybe I'll run the script by you. I want to have a pulse on real suburban housewives," he said.

"Happy to help," I obliged. "I actually have a suggestion if you're open to hearing it."

"Shoot," Dillon replied.

"There's another dancer that I'd recommend for the part. She's young and chomping at the bit. Her talent is off the charts. And she was made for Broadway."

"Bianca?" Bobby guessed.

"You've got it," I said.

"Actually, Charlotte's right," Bobby agreed. "I've always thought she'd be a big name someday. She's had a rough go of it, but just recently really got her act together and has stepped up. I have no doubt that she'd be a great fit."

"Bianca," Layla wracked her brain, "the solo!"

"That's her," I confirmed.

"She *was* fabulous," Dillon stated, pondering the idea. "I was originally thinking brunette for this part, but I can make it work with a blonde. She does have a star quality. She commanded attention during that solo."

"She always delivers in that department," I laughed.

"Bobby, can you set up a meeting?" Layla asked.

"Sure can," he promised.

"Wonderful," Dillon exclaimed, clapping his hands together. "I have to say I admire your gumption and I appreciate you being so candid, Lottie. Not many people would turn down Broadway. With a strong conviction like yours, I'm sure your studio will be a smashing success. Keep an eye out for future Broadway stars for me."

"That I can do," I said, confident in my decision.

"Now that we've gotten that out of the way," Dillon continued, "let's brunch!"

* * *

Stepping out of the restaurant and onto the sidewalk, I took a deep breath of the brisk winter air. Invigorated, I looked up at the sky in gratitude. I had done it. I had finally forged my own path. Giving up Broadway didn't feel like a loss after all; everything I needed was right here.

I was listening to my heart instead of reaching for old dreams that no longer served me. Bianca was just starting out with a promising career ahead of her. Broadway was her future, not mine. My dream was to create a full life here in Rockland, to finally find my way home.

Reaching the Inn, I heard a familiar birdsong. Looking up, I caught sight of the same little bluebird hopping along the branches of a tree overhead. As I watched him, flurries began to fall. Shaking his tiny body to remove the snowflakes, a small blue feather drifted down, landing at my feet. Bending down to pick it up, I held it between my thumb and index fingers. Smiling as I admired the bright blue hue, I lifted the feather skyward in reverence, whispering, "I made it, Dad. I'm home."

About the Author

Courtney Coty grew up in New England, studying graphic design at Northeastern University and working in design and education before writing her debut novel. She lives in Connecticut with her husband, two sons, and two dogs. When she's not hiding the Xbox controllers, you can find her binge-watching Netflix with a hot cup of tea or brainstorming ideas for her next book.

You can connect with me on:

https://linktr.ee/courtneycotyauthor

Made in the USA
Middletown, DE
28 April 2023